WITCH ME LUCK
A WICKED WITCHES OF THE MIDWEST MYSTERY
BOOK SIX

AMANDA M. LEE

WINCHESTERSHAW PUBLICATIONS

Copyright © 2015 by Amanda M. Lee

All rights reserved.

No part of this book may be reproduced in any form or by any electronic or mechanical means, including information storage and retrieval systems, without written permission from the author, except for the use of brief quotations in a book review.

❦ Created with Vellum

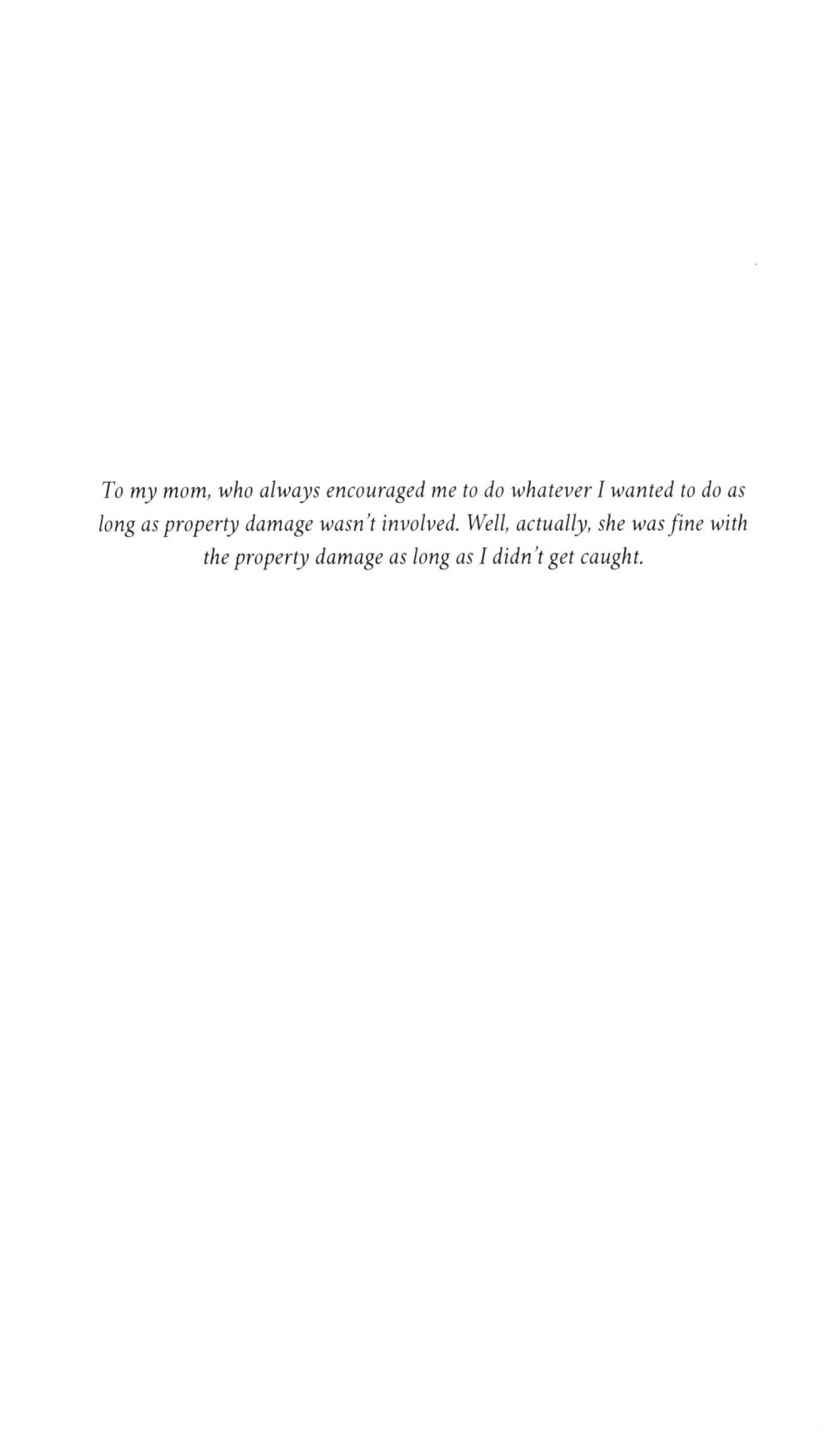

To my mom, who always encouraged me to do whatever I wanted to do as long as property damage wasn't involved. Well, actually, she was fine with the property damage as long as I didn't get caught.

PROLOGUE

"What do you think? I think I look like a princess." Lila Stevens pivoted in front of the full-length mirror, showing off the pink prom monstrosity so her boyfriend, Nick Spencer, could get a better look.

"It looks like a bottle of that crap my mom used to give me when I had a stomach ache as a kid," Nick replied, nonplussed.

Lila made a face. "It does not."

"Yes, it does," Nick said. "It's just really ... bright."

"It's supposed to be bright," Lila said. "I want to stand out. It's my senior prom, after all. We both know I'm going to be named queen. I have to look good when I'm crowned."

"Well, you'll definitely stand out," Nick said. "So ... um ... mission accomplished."

"That's all you have to say?" Lila narrowed her green eyes and pushed her dark hair from her face. "Don't you want to tell me how beautiful I look?"

Nick pressed his lips together and shifted uncomfortably. "Sure. You look beautiful."

"That's not very convincing."

"I don't know what you want me to say," Nick said. "It's a dress.

You're wearing it. It makes noise when you walk. I'm not a fashion critic."

"Oh, whatever," Lila said, turning back to the mirror. "I think I look like an angel." Lila decided to acknowledge she wasn't the only customer in the store. "What do you think, Bay?"

I was hiding behind a rack of dresses further back in the store, hoping Lila wouldn't catch sight of me. I guess I should have picked a better spot to hunker down. Lila had made it her mission to torture me for as long as I could remember. If I had any idea she was going to be in the store today, I would have delayed my visit. Since my mother was on me to buy a prom dress, though, I hoped to sneak into Rosalie's Dress Boutique, make a purchase that didn't stand out, and escape without anyone noticing.

It didn't appear that was in the cards.

"You look nice," I said, averting my gaze.

"Oh, now, don't be jealous," Lila said. "Tell me what you really think."

I really thought she looked ridiculous. I'd seen three-year-olds with access to the Disney princess clothing racks without parental supervision with better fashion sense. I wisely kept that to myself.

"I think it's pretty." I purposely moved to another rack, my eyes trained on the bevy of dresses. None of them were my particular style, but if I didn't come home with something my mother was going to pick one – and no one wanted that. I'd end up looking like a reject from the disco era.

"Pretty?" Lila arched a perfectly waxed eyebrow. "I look like a princess."

Funny, that was just what I'd been thinking. In my world, that wasn't a compliment, though. "You definitely look like a princess."

Lila shot a smug smile in Nick's direction. "See. Even a loser like Bay Winchester knows beauty when she sees it."

I bit the inside of my lower lip and pulled a blue dress from the rack and held it out in front of me. It was simple, and pretty. The lines were basic, and it definitely wasn't something that screamed "look at me." It was perfect.

"That's nice," Nick said, studying the dress. "It matches your eyes."

"Thank you," I mumbled.

Lila made a face, her gaze bouncing between Nick and me. "Sure, if you like something like that," she said. "Of course, Bay doesn't want to stand out. She's happy being plain. Right, Bay?"

I ignored her.

"Don't listen to her," Nick said, leaning against the wall and gazing at the dress in my hand. "At least you'll be able to sit down and relax. Lila is going to need a whole other person to carry the back of that dress around. It's stupid."

"Don't talk to her," Lila said.

"Why not?"

"Because I said so," Lila said. "You know I don't like her. She's weird. Her whole family is weird. Do you want people to think you're weird because you're talking to her?"

"I don't really care what people think," Nick said. "In three months, I'm out of here. I don't see why you're so worried about what people think anyway. It's not like it matters. Besides, you talked to her first."

Lila scowled. "I'm popular for a reason," she said. "It's because I don't engage with people like ... her. You should keep that in mind. If you hang around with losers, then you become a loser. You have a bright future in front of you, even if you're barely going to graduate. At least you have a football scholarship. Bay doesn't have anything in front of her. She'll be living with her mother, aunts and cousins for the rest of her life."

Lila laughed hollowly. "In fact, she's such a loser, she'll probably add thirty cats to the mix by the time she hits thirty."

I rolled my tongue over my teeth, a biting retort on the tip of my tongue. I never got a chance to utter it, though, because the bell over the front door of the shop jangled, causing the three of us to shift our attention to the front of the shop. My heart sank when I saw my cousin, Thistle, standing there.

Her hair, which she'd recently chopped off in an attempt to drive her mother insane, was a vibrant green hue. Her eyes flashed when she caught sight of Lila.

"Oh, speaking of losers," Lila drawled. "Nice hair, Thistle. Are you auditioning to be a leprechaun for the summer parade?"

"Nice dress, Lila," Thistle replied, unruffled. "Are you auditioning to be Prince Charming's guttersnipe third wife?"

Lila wrinkled her nose. "You are so ... obnoxious."

"I'll take that as a compliment coming from you," Thistle said, moving toward me. "Did you find a dress?"

"How did you even know I was here?" I asked, mortified. It was one thing for Lila to verbally abuse me in private. It was quite another for her to do it in front of my family.

"I heard our moms talking," Thistle said. "If you don't come back with a dress, you're not going to like the one your mom has picked out for you, by the way. It has sequins."

I pinched the bridge of my nose to ward off the building headache. "Great."

"That one is much nicer," Thistle said. "Why don't you try it on?"

I glanced at Lila, unsure. "Not right now. Let's leave and come back later."

"Come on, Bay," Thistle said. "You can't let her get you down. I know she's an evil witch, but she's just a person. She doesn't have any power over you."

That was easy for Thistle to say. Lila was mean to her, but she didn't seek her out. Whenever Lila needed a pick-me-up, she did it by doing something horrible to me. I had no idea why she got her power from picking on others, but she did. "Let's just leave."

Thistle shook her head. "No. Go try the dress on."

"But ... ."

"Try it on," Thistle pressed. She scorched Lila with a hateful look. "She won't say a thing to you. Isn't that right, Lila?"

"I have no interest in even being in the same room with her," Lila said. "Trust me."

"Of course you don't," Thistle said. "She's not a football player, and you haven't had two bottles of cheap wine to blame for being easy."

Lila furrowed her brow. "I don't know what that means."

"It means you're a slut," Thistle shot back. She pushed me toward the dressing room. "Try that on. I'll be right here."

"I am not a slut," Lila said. "You stop telling people that."

"That's probably your problem," Thistle mused. "If you were getting any, you wouldn't be so mean and nasty all of the time. You just can't help yourself."

Nick snickered, causing Lila to cuff him. "That is not funny!"

"Ow!"

Lila jumped down from the raised step in front of the mirror and stalked across the store. "I've had just about enough of you losers," she said. "I can't even stand to look at you."

"Then turn around," Thistle said. "You're not going to like what happens if you don't."

Lila was haughty. "Oh, and what's that?"

"What always happens when you go after Bay?" Thistle challenged.

"I win, and she looks like an idiot."

"And then I beat the crap out of you," Thistle reminded her. "My new hair is making me feel like the Hulk. I'd be careful if I were you."

"Oh, you're so full of yourself," Lila sniffed. "If Bay doesn't want to be picked on, she should probably stop being such a loser. I mean … who walks around talking to themselves all the time? A loser, that's who."

"Shut your mouth," Thistle hissed.

I put my hand on Thistle's arm to still her. "She's not worth it," I said. "Let's just go. We can come back later."

"Oh, we're not coming back later," Thistle said. "Now, go try that dress on. I'll handle the bubblegum princess."

"This dress is made by a very important designer!" Lila stamped her foot on the floor angrily. "It was specially ordered just for me."

"Since when is Bubble Yum a dress designer?" Thistle asked.

Lila lashed out, her hand heading for Thistle's face. Thistle was too quick, though, and dodged her easily. Since the circumference of Lila's dress was so large, as she leaned forward, she couldn't maintain her balance and tumbled forward.

"Omigod! I can't believe you did that," Lila screeched. She tried to push herself up from the floor, but couldn't find her footing amidst the yards of pink taffeta and chiffon. "Help me!" She held out her hand to Thistle, but my cousin batted it away.

"Help yourself," Thistle said.

"Nick, help me," Lila pleaded.

Nick sighed as he moved around her. His hands rummaged through the mountains of fabric as he searched for something to grab on to.

"Oomph," Lila said. "That hurts."

"Well, I can't find your waist," Nick said. "It's like trying to wrestle a pig."

"I am not fat!"

"I didn't say you were fat," Nick said. "I just said … stop moving around so much."

"Get me off this floor right now," Lila demanded. "There are probably germs … and bugs … and Winchester cooties all over the place."

"Oh, we don't have cooties," Thistle said, watching the tableau play out in front of her with a wide smile. "I heard you have herpes, though, so you should really be wishing for something as cool as cooties."

"You shut your filthy mouth," Lila said. "You and your weird cousin should just get out of here. No one wants you here. Everyone in this town hates you. You were losers as kids, and you're still losers."

"We're not the ones on the floor flailing about like a beached whale," Thistle said.

"Stop looking at me." Lila was beside herself. "Just … go away. This is all your fault."

"You tried to hit me," Thistle reminded her. "You missed and you fell over. If I didn't know better, I'd say you were drunk, and that's exactly what I'm going to tell your mother when I see her next time."

"Thistle," I warned. "Don't make this worse."

"Yes, Thistle," Lila said, her teeth grinding as Nick struggled to pull her to a standing position. "If you make this worse, I'm going to make sure Bay has the worst prom ever. It will be the stuff of nightmares."

"Don't you threaten her," Thistle said.

"Then walk away," Lila said. "It's going to be better for everyone if you just walk away."

"I've got you," Nick said, triumphant. He straightened, and the unmistakable sound of ripping fabric filled the store.

"What was that?" Lila's eyes were wide. "What was that?"

"I'm sure it was nothing," Nick said. "I ... it was nothing." He was intently studying Lila's backside, and no one believed him.

"Oh, if you've ruined this dress ... I'll ruin you."

Lila shuffled back to the mirrors and climbed up on the step, twirling to see the back of her dress. From our position, Thistle and I could already see the damage Nick's foot had done.

When Lila caught sight of the gaping hole in the back of the dress, her face was murderous. "It's ruined!"

"I think it looks better," Thistle said. "With your butt hanging out like that, no one will be looking at your ugly face."

"You're both going to pay for this," Lila said. "You have no idea what I'm going to do to you. You're going to wish I'd never been born."

I often speak before I think, which is a family trait, and this was no exception. "I think the whole town wishes you hadn't been born."

Thistle snorted. "You've got that right. Come on, Bay. Let's see how that dress looks on you. I think our work here is done."

"You're going to pay for this," Lila warned one more time. "You have no idea what I'm going to do to you. I'm going to make the rest of your lives hell. Just you wait."

ONE

"I don't want to do this," I complained, leaning back in my desk chair and fixing The Whistler's resident ghost, Edith, with a hard look. "This is the worst thing that's ever happened to me."

Edith was used to my theatrics, so she wasn't exactly driven to fits of histrionics over my pronouncement. "Something tells me you'll live."

"You don't know that," I said. "You're a ghost. You have no idea how harsh the real world is these days."

"Oh, I understand about the real world," Edith said. "I watch a lot of television."

Since dying at her desk in the newspaper office decades before, Edith didn't have a lot to do. She didn't like leaving the place she felt safest, so television was her new best friend. Unfortunately, she went through phases. She liked shows like *Mad Men* because they reminded her of better times (better in her mind, at least). When she took the time to watch something else, like *The Walking Dead*, she was convinced the world was coming to an end. The day I tried to explain *Game of Thrones* to her was one of the worst of my entire life – and that's saying something since I've been haunted by a vengeful poltergeist and stalked by crazy murderers so many times I've lost count.

"Television is not the real world," I reminded her. "Television is fantasy. It's an escape."

"You're only saying that because you refuse to believe the zombie apocalypse is coming," Edith said. "I happen to know it's on the horizon. It's only a matter of time. I saw Frank Dorchester buying an ad the other day, and he had a wound on his neck. He's going to turn into a zombie any day now."

I rolled my eyes. "You're a ghost. You can't be turned into a zombie. You know that, right?"

Edith pursed her lips. "I'm aware of my current situation. I don't need to be reminded of it every time I turn around."

"I'm sorry." Edith is a lot of work. There's a reason I toil away on my newspaper duties from home three days a week. Most days she's too much of a distraction for me to maintain focus in the office.

Edith considered my apology for a moment, and then appeared to shake off her melancholy. "Well, it's neither here nor there. What's wrong with you?"

"Haven't you heard? It's Hemlock Cove's fifteenth anniversary."

"So?"

"So they're having a weeklong celebration to mark it," I replied.

"I'm still not seeing the problem."

I tried again. "The town is going to be full of people who don't live here."

"Isn't that good for a tourist town?"

I sighed. Edith had a point. Since Hemlock Cove magically rebranded itself into a tourist destination, the economy had picked up. That was the whole point of the rebranding, after all. The manufacturing base died decades ago, and the town needed a way to survive. Since it was located in northern Lower Michigan, there weren't a lot of options. Setting the town up as a magical destination – witches and hauntings serving as kitschy vacation getaways – had been a stroke of genius. My own family benefited. Of course, we were real witches pretending to be fake witches, but that was another problem entirely.

"It is good," I admitted. "The inn is booked for the whole week. We're usually booked to capacity on the weekends this time of year, but midweek is kind of dead. That's not going to be a problem this week."

"So, tell me what's really wrong," Edith prodded.

"Everyone is coming back to town."

"Define everyone."

"Everyone who used to live here," I said, frustrated. "Everyone who graduated and moved away. Everyone I went to high school with."

"It's a big reunion," Edith said. "That's what people do when they have a reunion."

"Yes, but I don't want to see the people I went to high school with," I said. "I hate them. They hate me. I have no interest in catching up, or listening to how great their lives are. I just don't want to do it."

"Do you think they have better lives than you?" Edith asked pointedly.

"No."

"Are you unhappy with your life?"

"Of course not."

"Last time I checked, you were editor of a newspaper and had an attractive man to spend time with," Edith said.

I hate it when Edith makes sense. Bringing my FBI agent boyfriend Landon Michaels into the mix was hitting below the belt. There was nothing to complain about where he was concerned. "I'm happy with my life," I said. "I just ... I wasn't happy back then. I don't want to feel like I did when I was in high school. Not again."

Edith clucked sympathetically. "Were you unpopular?"

That was an understatement. All through elementary school I was known as the weird girl who talked to her imaginary friend. Since no one could know I was actually talking to ghosts – that's one of my witchy abilities – I always had to hide what I did. By middle school, rumors about my family were swirling. People were both fascinated with, and terrified of, the Winchester witches. And my crotchety Aunt Tillie was only part of the fascination. It was a hard cross to bear, and instead of dealing with it head-on I opted to try to fade into the background.

Five years in an urban population after college gave me some self-confidence – more than I ever had when I hid from everything and everyone during my teenage years. I was just afraid my newfound self-assuredness would fall to the wayside the second I was with my former classmates. I was nervous, and my anxiety was giving me a stomachache ... or an ulcer. I wasn't ruling out an ulcer.

"I was definitely unpopular," I said.

"Were you bullied?"

"What do you know about bullying?"

"It's a hot-button topic on all of the morning shows," Edith said, her eyes serious. "Bullies are horrible people. They're worse than people who kick puppies."

I wasn't sure whether that was true, but her sentiment was heartfelt, so I graced her with a small smile. "I'm sure I'll be fine."

"Is Landon coming to spend the week with you?"

"He'll be here for the weekend," I said. "He's trying to finish up a case today, but if he doesn't he won't be here until the weekend."

"Well, that's too bad," Edith said. "If all those horrible wenches who were mean to you in high school saw him, they'd know how successful you are."

"I'm successful without Landon," I said. "He's a bonus."

"A handsome bonus."

"A handsome bonus," I conceded. Talk of Landon was making me whimsical and scattered, so I forced thoughts of him out of my mind. "We're doing a big spread for the newspaper this week. We're publishing a reunion edition tomorrow, and that's already done and sent to the printer. The weekend edition is going to be double the normal size, though. It's going to be a lot of work."

"Do you have to do all of the work?"

I shook my head. "No. I'll write a few articles, but we have two freelance writers and a couple of photographers working the events, too."

"That's good," Edith said. "That way you'll be able to enjoy some of the festivities."

"Yeah, I can't wait."

"That sounded like sarcasm," Edith chided. "Don't you at least want to try to have a good time?"

"I plan on having a good time."

"Then why are you pouting in here? They're setting up the town square for the festival right now. Shouldn't you be ... I don't know ... covering that?"

"How is decorating the town a story?" I asked.

"You don't know. Some people like that stuff."

Boring people. "I think I'm safe missing it," I said. "Besides, I have a few other things to take care of."

"Like?"

"Like I have to ... schedule things for next week."

Edith knew I was lying. "It's a weekly newspaper."

"I know."

"You usually have one article and fifteen ads."

"I know."

"What are you scheduling for next week?" Edith pressed.

"Um ... ."

"An interview with me."

I jolted when I heard the voice at my office door, lifting my head and focusing on Sam Cornell. His dark hair was pushed back from his face, and his smile was amiable and a little tense as he regarded me. In addition to opening a new business in Hemlock Cove, and admitting he'd first come to town as a way to get close to my family, Sam was dating my cousin, Clove. Our relationship was a work in progress. Part of me wanted to believe Sam was a good guy, mostly because Clove seemed to really like him. The other part of me couldn't help but be suspicious of him, though.

"Sam."

"Hello, Bay," he said, walking into the office. "Hello, Edith."

Edith's eyes widened. Since Sam's lineage ran to another line of witches, he boasted certain abilities. He wasn't magically strong like we were, but he wasn't bereft of magical sight. Apparently Edith had missed that newsy tidbit.

"He's fine," I said, trying to calm Edith. "He knows about ghosts."

"Is he a witch, too?" Edith asked. "Is he a male witch?"

"He's … complicated," I said. I turned my attention to Sam. "What's up?"

Since Sam and Clove started dating he'd been making an effort to get along with the rest of my family. Landon was still suspicious of him, and Aunt Tillie was convinced he was hiding a demonic tail in his jeans, but I couldn't decide how I really felt about him. I didn't trust him, but I didn't think he was out to hurt us either. He was an enigma.

"I came to check in with you," Sam said. "I know you're busy this week, but the renovations on the Dandridge are done. I was hoping you would still be willing to do a story on it."

The Dandridge was a former lighthouse that had fallen into disarray. After his initial attempt to get to know me through the newspaper, Sam opted to partner with state officials and purchase the lighthouse so he could set it up as a haunted attraction. He'd done a lot of work on the property, and Clove helped him every step of the way. Since news in Hemlock Cove is limited during a normal week, covering the refurbishment of the Dandridge would be an easy article.

"I'll definitely do a story on it," I said. "It shouldn't take too long. I can come out one afternoon, you can show me around, we can get some photos, and it should be a quick afternoon.

"This week is all about the anniversary celebration," I continued. "We can still find time to get together if you want. Like I said, it won't take long."

"That sounds good," Sam said. "Just give me a call. Clove has my number."

"I'm sure I'll see you around," I said. "It's a celebration, after all. I'm sure Clove will drag you all over town."

"She seems excited," Sam said. "You, on the other hand, look like you'd rather cover another murder than the reunion celebration."

That was an apt observation, which made me feel terrible. "I just don't have the happiest memories of the people I went to high school with. It wasn't as bad for Clove. People liked her."

"What about Thistle?"

"Thistle really didn't pay any attention to the kids in high school," I said. "She didn't care what they did, and they left her alone because she was so ... ."

"Mean?" Sam asked.

"I was going to say persnickety."

Sam held up his hand and laughed. "I didn't mean anything by it."

"It's fine," I said, waving off his apology. "She was mean. She admits she was mean. It worked out well for me, though, because I was too shy to be mean."

"You're not shy now," Sam said. "I wouldn't worry about what a bunch of idiot high-schoolers thought about you a decade ago. You're successful now. You have nothing to be ashamed of."

"I'm not ashamed," I said. "I'm just ... nervous."

"I'm sure it will be fine," Sam said. "And, if it's not, you still have Thistle to be mean to all of them if the mood strikes. And, if that doesn't work, Aunt Tillie is always handy with a curse. I'm sure she'll be itching to mete out some ... justice."

He was right. Well, things were looking up on that front.

TWO

I left The Whistler at noon and headed toward Thistle and Clove's magic shop, Hypnotic, with lunch on my mind. While my cousins hadn't questioned my feelings about the upcoming reunion, I knew they were aware of my trepidation.

Clove was sympathetic to my plight. Thistle was irritated. She didn't understand my fear, and she most certainly wouldn't coddle me when it came down to it. In situations like this, Clove was the cousin I wanted to be around. Thistle was still the one I wanted on my side during a fight. She punches like a man, and she pulls hair like a beauty queen contestant on steroids.

Hemlock Cove is a small town, and the main drag basically consists of two streets. The newspaper and library anchor one end of town, Hypnotic and a string of kitschy stores anchor the other. Everything else is wooded land and bed and breakfasts.

When I was younger, I hated living in the middle of nowhere. As an adult, I relish it. I like the feeling of wide-open places and familiar spaces. While I'd been itching to get away from Hemlock Cove as a young adult, I can't picture ever leaving now. Not again. This was home, and Edith was right: I am happy here.

I hopped up on the sidewalk in front of Hypnotic, my shoulders feeling lighter for the first time in days. I'd been dreading the reunion since I heard about it weeks before. As it drew closer, though, my dread grew until it was so big I couldn't think about anything else. I knew that was counterproductive, and I was determined to rise above it.

That is until I saw ... her ... standing in front of Hypnotic.

I pulled up short as Lila Stevens' green eyes met mine in the reflection of the store's front window. She turned slowly, a wide smile on her face. She looked like a black widow, and I was certain I was the fly from which she was about to suck the juices.

"Bay Winchester," Lila said, tilting her head to the side so her long, dark hair fell past her shoulders. "It's been a long time. You look ... interesting."

Interesting? That had to be an insult. It was insulting, right? It was a simple statement, yet it was filled with something I couldn't immediately identify. "Lila. You look well."

"It's so good to see you," Lila said, her enthusiasm feigned and forced. "It's just a real ... joy."

"You, too." I didn't bother to try to fake an emotion. Disgust isn't easy to hide, and I didn't have the energy to do it right now. I kept my voice flat as I regarded her.

"I'd heard that you moved down to Detroit after college," Lila said. "I see that didn't last."

"I didn't like the city," I replied. "I like the country better. When I got the opportunity to take over The Whistler, it seemed like a natural fit. I was happy to come home."

"Yes, I heard you're the editor there now," Lila said, waving her manicured hand for emphasis. "That has to be such a letdown. I mean, you got to cover actual stories in the city. What are you covering here? Festivals and advertorials. It's so sad. You must be depressed. Are you depressed? You look depressed. That would probably explain your outfit."

If I ever thought a decade could erase my hatred of Lila, I was mistaken. In fact, two minutes with her only served as a reminder of how awful she really was. "Actually, I'm perfectly happy at The

Whistler," I said. "While some weeks are boring, others are exciting. We've even had some murders over the past few months. I've been pretty busy."

That was nothing to brag about, but Lila always brought out the worst in me. It was as though my mouth had a mind of its own.

"I've heard," Lila said. "My mother keeps me informed on all of the Hemlock Cove gossip. She's just beside herself with the sudden increase in violence. She's afraid she's going to be murdered in her bed. She's terrified. It seems all of the recent troubles are tied to you and your family, though. You must be really upset about that."

"It hasn't been tied to my family," I argued. "It hasn't had anything to do with my family."

"Wasn't Clove's father dating a woman who was smuggling children to be used as sex slaves?"

I frowned. "That's not Uncle Warren's fault," I said. "He had no idea what she was doing."

"And wasn't there a guest at The Overlook who tried to kill all of you because he was looking for something hidden in your basement?"

"Again, that didn't have anything to do with my family," I said. "His grandparents hid something in our basement. We didn't even know what was going on. We can't control what our guests do."

Lila ignored my explanation. "And didn't you discover a dead body in the corn maze last year? Some people were conducting some sort of satanic ritual, and you were right in the middle of that, too."

"We weren't in the middle of it," I argued. "We just ... ." How was I supposed to explain our actions? It's not as though I could tell Lila that a ghost led me to two murderers. "I think it's better if we just agree to disagree."

"Oh, what fun would that be?" Lila asked, her voice positively steeped in sarcasm. "I much prefer watching you squirm."

So much for things remaining pleasant – or at least tolerable – between us. "Well, I think you're going to be disappointed," I said. "I have no intention of performing like a trained monkey for your enjoyment."

"Oh, don't be so bitter," Lila said. "You always were a pouty mouse.

You just need to suck it up. We're adults now. There's no reason to act like a child."

"Then why are you acting like a teenager?"

"I'm not," Lila said. "You're reading far too much into our conversation. It's like you want me to be the bad guy, so you turn me into the villain in your fantasies. It's a little sad, really."

Narcissist, party of one, your table is ready. "I'm not reading anything into our conversation," I said. "Why don't we just agree to stay away from each other during the festivities this week? I think that would be better for both of us."

"It's a small town, Bay," Lila said. "Avoiding each other seems like a lot of work, and since I have a high-profile job, and this is my vacation, I have no intention of working this week."

"Well, then I'll do the work," I said. "Just ... stay away from me." I pushed past her and moved toward Hypnotic. The door opened before I could enter, though, and Thistle stepped out. Her gaze was trained on Lila, and the look on her face made my heart sink. Now Lila was the prey and Thistle was the wild animal hunting her.

"Well, well, well," Thistle said. "Why is the dogcatcher never around when there's a mangy stray on the loose?"

Lila squared her shoulders and turned to Thistle, smirking when she caught sight of her bright pink hair. "I ... well ... I see some things never change. Your hair is ... there are no words."

"I think the word you're looking for is awesome," Thistle said. "You probably don't know what that means, because every time you look at your reflection you think you're looking into a funhouse mirror, but this is what awesome looks like."

"Still nasty, I see," Lila said, brushing some invisible lint from the front of her peasant blouse. "You should try to grow up, Thistle. The only thing that belongs in a funhouse is your hair, well, and your entire family."

"I'll tell Aunt Tillie you said so," Thistle said, bristling. "I'm sure she'll be thrilled to hear you're back in town."

Lila's face drained of color. Aunt Tillie's reputation was well earned, especially where Lila was concerned. Every time she tortured me as a child, and especially as a teenager, something awful happened to her. A few times, it was random karma. Most of the time, though, it was Aunt Tillie, seeking revenge. She hadn't been overly fond of us as teenagers – mostly because we kept stealing pot and wine from her secret stash – but she was loyal to a fault. It was one thing for her to mess with us. It was quite another for someone else to do the same.

"And how is your Aunt Tillie?" Lila asked. "Mother says she should be locked up in a home because she's senile. Apparently she's really slipping. That must be horrible for you to deal with."

I made a face. "There's nothing wrong with Aunt Tillie."

Thistle cleared her throat.

"There's nothing more wrong with Aunt Tillie than normal," I clarified. "She certainly isn't senile."

"Mother says she poisoned all of the women at the senior center several years ago because she thought they were cheating at cards," Lila pressed.

"Your mother says a lot," Thistle said, refusing to refute the argument. Aunt Tillie maintained she'd been falsely accused in the great Senior Center Poisoning of 2009, but we all had our doubts. I wasn't living in Hemlock Cove at the time, so I couldn't comment. "I'll make sure Aunt Tillie knows your family has been maligning her. I'm sure that will make her … happy."

Lila arched an eyebrow. "Happy?"

"She loves it when she has someone to focus on," Thistle said.

The truth was we loved it, too. That meant that she wasn't focusing her evil attention on us. Lila's return to Hemlock Cove might actually be good news for us on that front.

Lila swallowed hard. "Well … I'm glad to be of service."

"Oh, you have no idea how happy we are for you to be of service," Thistle said. "We absolutely love it. You can service our Aunt Tillie as much as you want for the next week."

Lila shifted uncomfortably. "I'm not sure what that means."

"You will," Thistle said, grabbing my arm and dragging me toward the door of her store. "You definitely will. I'd duck and cover if I were you."

"I'm not afraid of your crazy aunt," Lila shot back. When she glanced over her shoulder to see whether anyone was listening, I fought the mad urge to laugh. "I'm not afraid of her at all."

"That's good," Thistle said. "Aunt Tillie loves a challenge. She pulls out all of the stops when she's around nonbelievers. You have a good day, Lila. I wouldn't worry about Aunt Tillie gearing up for war until tomorrow. She needs time to plan, after all. Have a nice night."

"You just … don't tell her," Lila said, her voice dropping. "Don't tell her. I was just joking."

"Oh, it's too late for that," Thistle said. "I have to tell her. It's a family thing. We can't lie to each other."

Even when we want to, I added silently.

"I was just joking," Lila said. "You know I was joking, right?"

Thistle shook her head.

"Bay?" Lila asked, hopeful.

"I can't lie to my family," I said. "It's not fair. I have to show Aunt Tillie some loyalty." Yes. I'm enjoying this way too much.

"Well, fine," Lila said. "I'm not afraid of her anyway. You two are just … horrible people. You've always been horrible people. You always will be horrible people. I don't know why I thought the years would bless you with some maturity."

"Me either," Thistle said, shoving me into Hypnotic forcefully. "Maturity is highly overrated. We're happy being immature. We get it from Aunt Tillie. Now you have a nice night … and stay away from my cousin. You're going to regret it if you don't."

THREE

"Why didn't you throw her through the window?" Thistle asked once she closed the door and Lila was safely out of earshot. "I would have gladly paid to have the glass replaced."

"What's going on?" Clove asked, looking up from her spot behind the counter. Her face was awash with curiosity and confusion. "Aunt Tillie hasn't followed through on her promise to burn the town square down if the bakery doesn't bring back chocolate éclairs, has she?"

"No," Thistle said. "And I'm on her side where those éclairs are concerned. They were awesome. I have no idea why Mrs. Gunderson stopped selling them."

"She said she couldn't get the dough anymore," I said. "Apparently she ordered it frozen." That had been a personal affront to all of the kitchen witches in my family when they found out. You don't buy dough. In our house, you make everything from scratch. That didn't stop any of us from salivating after those éclairs, though.

"So, why are you two fighting?" Clove asked.

"We're not fighting," I replied.

"Yet," Thistle clarified. "We're not fighting yet. If you don't get it together and tell Lila Stevens where to stick it, we're going to have a huge fight. I'm going to make you eat a whole garden of dirt."

I made a face. Even though we were adults, a few holdovers from our childhood continued to thrive. Wrestling each other down – sometimes in broad daylight – was one of them. Lila might have a point about the maturity thing.

"Lila Stevens is here?" Clove wrinkled her nose. "Please tell me she looks hideous."

"She looks fine," I said. "She didn't have a horrible, disfiguring disease like we all hoped for when we were teenagers."

"We could still make that happen," Thistle said, wagging her finger in my face. "It doesn't have to be a permanent disease. We could give her leprosy for just a week."

"Oh, that sounds fun," Clove said, her face brightening. "Maybe her nose will fall off. All that money her mother spent on that nose job when she was fourteen would fly right out the window then."

"I like that idea," Thistle said, satisfied with herself. "Can we find a spell for that?"

"We're not giving her leprosy," I said. "Not for a week. Not for a day."

"Fine," Thistle said. "How about we give her a beard? She's got a square jaw. She would look like she's transitioning. That could be a lot of fun."

I pursed my lips. That suggestion wasn't as destructive. "Not yet," I said. "Let's just see if she stays away from us, shall we? We don't have to go after her if she leaves us alone."

"She's not going to leave us alone," Thistle said. "It's not in her nature. She likes to attack others. That's how she gets her power. She's like those wraith things in Harry Potter … what are they called?"

"Dementors," Clove supplied helpfully.

"Yeah, she's like a Dementor," Thistle said. "Instead of sucking life force out, though, she feeds on pain and misery."

"She really is evil," Clove said. "Did she say anything to you, Bay?"

"She was just being herself," I said. "It's not a big deal."

"It is a big deal," Thistle said. "She's mean to you. She purposely goes after you. I'm not going to put up with it, and neither are you. If she starts anything … even once … I'm going to make all of her hair fall out."

"She'll just buy a wig," Clove said. "We should make her boobs shrink. That's the only reason she gets attention."

"Oh, she'll stuff them," Thistle said. "We have to think of something truly awful."

"I thought you were going to tell Aunt Tillie what she said?" I asked. "That's pretty awful. Aunt Tillie is going to torture her for an entire week straight."

"Oh, I'm telling Aunt Tillie," Thistle said. "Lila deserves some extended Aunt Tillie time. I want to do something to her, though. I want to … hey, do you know what we should do to her?"

I was almost afraid to ask. "What?"

"We should make her … you know … incontinent for the week."

I tilted my head to the side, considering. "That's really mean."

"Incontinent? Does that mean she's not good at her job?" Clove asked. "Who cares if she's good at her job?"

"Not incompetent," Thistle said. "Incontinent. It means she can't control her bladder."

"Or her bowels," I added.

"Oh, so she would make whoopsy in her pants? That's awesome." Clove was usually the one who balked at our revenge fantasies. For her to take part in them was a definite personality shift. I think Sam was starting to have a negative influence on her sweet nature.

"Who says 'whoopsy?'" Thistle asked.

"You know what I mean," Clove said. "I think it's a great idea. She'll have to wear those adult diapers all week."

"And none of her pants will fit," Thistle said. "This is a great idea. I'm glad I thought of it."

"I think we should just leave her to Aunt Tillie," I said.

"Why?" Thistle asked.

"Because I don't want to be the kind of person who does something like this because Lila used to be mean to me in high school," I said. "Shouldn't I be above all of this?"

"Have you met the other members of our family? We're never going to be above this," Thistle said. "It's genetically impossible. Anyway, I don't ever want to be above this. Lila Stevens is a blight on humanity. You need to either join our team, or get out of the way. That woman is going down."

"But ... ."

Thistle cut me off. "No. I'm not going to just let you sit around and be tortured by that horrible menace. It's not going to happen."

"Fine," I said, resigned. "I don't want to be a part of it, though. Do what you want. I just want to make it through the next week without looking like a complete and total idiot."

Thistle's face was unreadable when she glanced back at me. "That's what we want, too. Trust us."

AFTER A TENSE LUNCH during which Thistle and Clove continued to brainstorm over hamburgers and fries, I left Hypnotic and headed back to The Whistler.

Part of me was thrilled my cousins were loyal enough to plot revenge on my behalf. The other part was embarrassed they had to. I had no idea why Lila made me so crazy. It was as though every ounce of courage I owned fled whenever she was in front of me. It was like magic – a really ugly magic that only mean girls could utilize.

I hated her. My mother told me never to use the "h-word" in conjunction with another person, but I couldn't help myself. I truly hated Lila. I hated who she was, and I hated what she represented. She was one of those awful individuals with absolutely no redeeming qualities.

I was halfway back to the newspaper office when a figure detached from the shadows beneath the hardware store awning and stepped into my path. I involuntarily took a step back when Lila's wretched face swam into view.

"Oh, really? Can't you just leave me alone?"

Lila ignored my outburst. "I want to talk to you."

"Well, I don't want to talk to you," I said. "In fact, the last thing in this world I want to do is talk to you. Can't you just understand that and leave me alone?"

"I don't care what you want," Lila said. "I've never cared what you want."

"Well, I don't care what you want either," I said. "So, just ... ." I waved my hands in front of me.

"What are you doing?" Lila asked, staring at my hands. "Is that some sort of secret signal so your family knows to come and pounce?"

"It's the signal to go away," I replied. "That's what I want you to do. I want you to go away."

"Well, I want to talk to you," Lila said.

"Why?"

"Can't two old friends catch up?" Lila was playing a game. I just couldn't figure out which one.

"We were never friends, and I don't want to catch up," I said. "Besides, I have to get back to the paper. I have work to do. Unlike you, I'm not on vacation this week."

"I want to talk to you first," Lila said, holding her hand out to stop me from leaving. "Believe it or not, I don't want to fight with you."

I didn't believe her. "What do you want?"

"I just want to make sure that you're aware I didn't mean to say anything bad about your Aunt Tillie," Lila said. "I was really only repeating what my mother told me, so if your aunt is angry, she should plot revenge against my mother."

It shouldn't have surprised me that Lila was willing to throw her own mother to Aunt Tillie, but I was still taken aback. "Seriously? You've been hanging around for an hour just to make sure I don't tell Aunt Tillie you were talking badly about her?"

"No. Of course not."

"Your secret is safe with me, Lila," I said. "I have no intention of telling Aunt Tillie what you said."

Lila looked relieved. "Really?"

"Really," I said. "Of course, Thistle is dying to tell her, so that's a whole other problem for you to deal with."

"Oh, can't you stop Thistle?"

"No," I said. "If you want to stop Thistle, you're going to have to beg her. She likes chocolate éclairs. If you can find one of those, you're golden."

"I am not begging Thistle for anything," Lila sneered. "That's just … beneath me."

"Well, then deal with Aunt Tillie's wrath," I said. "I don't care what you do." Actually, that wasn't true. I kind of wanted to see what Aunt Tillie would do to Lila with a whole week to plot against her.

"You're going to tell your Aunt Tillie that Thistle is lying," Lila said.

"No, I'm not."

"Yes, you are," Lila said. "I am not going to spend an entire week hiding from that woman. It's not fair."

"I'm not telling Aunt Tillie anything," I said, moving around Lila. "Fight your own battles."

Lila grabbed my arm, digging her fingernails into the soft flesh inside of my elbow. "If you don't talk to your Aunt Tillie, I'm going to make this week miserable for you."

I jerked my arm away from her. "If you don't stay away from me, I'm going to let both Thistle and Aunt Tillie off their leashes," I countered. "Trust me, you do not want that."

"I can make your life a lot more uncomfortable than you can make my life," Lila said.

"Do you want to place money on that?"

"Just … keep your crazy aunt away from me," Lila said. "I am not going to … ."

The rest of her sentence was cut short by two loud bangs, and then the sound of people screaming. Lila dropped to her knees quickly, covering her ears in the process. I didn't have the same fight-or-flight response. I was more interested in finding out where the noise came from.

I scanned the storefronts, my eyes landing on the steps to the bank. My head told me not to cross the street. My curiosity got the better of me, as it always does. I broke into a run, instinct pushing me forward. Something was clanging in the back of my brain. Someone was in trouble. From the sound of the screams, a whole lot of people were in trouble. When I hit the top of the steps, the bank door flew open and a dark figure barreled through it. I pulled up short, confusion flitting through my brain. I didn't have a chance to grasp what was going on, though, because the figure was heading in my direction – fast.

The figure knocked me off balance as it pushed past me, and I careened toward the pavement before I could collect myself. I did register the gun in the figure's hand, and the black mask over its face.

Then I hit the ground. Hard.

Despite the pain coursing through the hand I'd extended to break my fall, I forced my body to turn so I could watch the figure flee around the corner. That's when the screams in the bank amplified, and everything in Hemlock Cove tilted on its side. Again.

FOUR

The paramedic disinfecting the scrape on my hand an hour later was trying to be gentle, but I couldn't stop cringing every time he rubbed the antiseptic against my raw skin.

"I'm sorry," he said.

"It's fine." There was no way I was going to complain about an injured hand, especially given what happened inside of the bank. It had taken me a few minutes to ascertain what was going on, but once I made my way inside, things had become clear.

The dark figure had been a robber. Unfortunately, instead of firing a warning shot into the ceiling, he'd shot errantly into the crowd as he tried to make his escape. One of the clerks, a young woman named Amy Madison, was shot in the chest. She'd been transported to an area hospital, and everyone was waiting on word of her prognosis. I didn't know her well, but what I did know was enough to pray for her recovery.

"Are you all right?" Chief Terry asked, moving to my side and placing a hand on my shoulder. "He didn't hurt you, did he?"

"I'm fine," I said. "He just knocked me down."

"Just for the record, when you hear gunshots in a bank, you're supposed to run the other way," he said. "You don't run inside."

"I know," I said, rubbing my forehead. "I didn't think. There's no need to yell at me."

"I'm not going to yell at you," Chief Terry said. He'd been Hemlock Cove's top cop for more than a decade, and he was used to the Winchester women popping up in investigations. He was much calmer than he used to be.

I was still suspicious. "You're not?"

Chief Terry pointed to a spot over my left shoulder. "I'm going to leave the yelling to him."

Somehow I knew whom he was pointing at even before I turned. When my gaze fell on Landon, his eyes keenly scanning the scene, my heart rolled. I was excited to see him. He'd been stuck in Traverse City working for the past three days, and our only contact had been via dirty text messages. As happy as I was to see him, I was not looking forward to the lecture I was sure would follow our happy reunion.

When Landon caught sight of me, he made a beeline in my direction. He ducked under the police tape and flashed his badge to the paramedic before moving to my side. "Are you okay?"

"I'm fine," I said, lifting my hand for his inspection. "I just got knocked over."

Landon cupped my hand and studied the wound. "Is this the only thing that got hurt?"

I nodded.

"Well, I guess it could be worse," he said, leaning over and giving me a quick kiss. "I guess you can add 'surviving a bank robbery' to your list of exploits now."

"I wasn't inside for the robbery," I said.

Landon knit his eyebrows together. "Then how did you get hurt?"

I realized – too late, of course – that I'd made a mistake. Now I was going to have to tell him the truth about my actions in front of a crowd. He was going to go ballistic. "Well ... ."

"I can't wait to hear how you explain this," Chief Terry said.

I made a face. "You see ... ."

"Just tell me what you did," Landon said. "It's going to be a lot worse if you drag it out."

"I didn't technically do anything," I said.

"She was across the street when the clerk was shot," Chief Terry said. "She ran toward the bank."

Landon's face was grim. "I see."

"She got knocked over when the robber ran out of the bank," Chief Terry said. "She's lucky the guy was trying to get away and didn't have time to focus on her."

"Thank you for your help," I said, pressing my lips together tightly as I shot Chief Terry a dark look. The man had spent the better part of my life fighting for me and taking my side, making me feel my ideas were important and my opinion mattered. At times like this, though, I often wished he wasn't so involved. "I'm so glad you told Landon before I could."

"At the rate you were going, it would've been Christmas before you got it out," Chief Terry replied. "I was just helping you along."

That's not how it felt. I risked a glance at Landon. "Are you going to yell at me?"

"Do you want me to yell at you?"

"Not particularly."

"Then I'm not going to yell at you," Landon said.

There had to be a catch. He was never this easygoing when I was involved in trouble. "Why?"

"Because I think you already know that what you did was stupid," Landon said. "Yelling at you isn't going to make that any clearer. So, I'm not going to yell."

"See, you say you're not going to yell, but you look like you really want to yell," I said. "You have that pinched look you get right before you go after Aunt Tillie's wine."

"I don't have a pinched look," Landon shot back.

I pointed at his forehead. "You really do."

"Don't push me right now, Bay. I'm trying really hard to control my temper. If you push me, I'm going to lose it, and we're both going to regret it."

I lowered my finger. "I'm sorry."

"Oh, how can you stay mad at her when she makes that face?"

Chief Terry asked, grabbing my chin and tipping my head up. "She looks so cute and miserable. She's like a puppy."

Landon rolled his eyes. "That must be why I want to swat her with a rolled-up newspaper."

"Just let it go," Chief Terry said. "She's got enough problems."

"What problems?" Landon asked, curious.

"Criminy, and here comes one of them now," Chief Terry said, turning swiftly. "I do not want to talk to that viper, so … I'm going to question some more people who were in the bank. Whatever she wants, it's up to you to deal with her."

Landon shifted his head to study the woman heading in our direction. "Who is that?"

"The worst person ever," I grumbled.

"Do you want to be more specific?"

"Um, excuse me, are you a police officer?" Lila asked, sidling up to Landon with a pretty smile.

"I'm with the FBI," Landon said.

If Lila was posturing before, she positively preened now. A police officer might be fun to flirt with, but a handsome FBI agent was a catch. "Wow," Lila said, her voice breathy. "That's impressive. Do you have an office around here?"

I made a sound in the back of my throat, something akin to a growl, and then forced my attention from Lila. If I looked at her for too long, I was going to claw her eyes out. I knew exactly what she was doing, and I already didn't like it.

"I work out of the office in Traverse City," Landon said. "Do you need help with something?"

"Well, one of the other police officers said I had to stay close because I was a witness to the terrible tragedy that occurred here earlier today," Lila said. "I was just wondering how long I would have to stay."

"I'm not sure yet," Landon said. "I'll get a uniform to take your statement as soon as possible."

"I'd much rather give you my … statement," Lila said, touching his wrist lightly. "You're a professional, after all."

"Every law enforcement official present here today is a professional," Landon said. "I'm sure I can get someone to take your statement in the next few minutes. Then you can be on your way, ma'am."

"Oh, call me Lila. Ma'am makes me turn around and look for my mother."

"Sure. Lila." Landon turned back to me. "Are you sure you're okay?"

"I'm fine."

"We're going to talk about this later," he said. "I mean talk, not yell."

"I can't wait."

"You can talk to me later," Lila offered helpfully. "I'm staying at the Dragonfly Inn."

Well, that was just a punch in the gut. The Dragonfly was the inn my father and uncles opened a few weeks before. That meant, if I wanted to see my father this week I was going to have to risk seeing Lila, too. "What?"

"No one is talking to you, Bay," Lila said. "Just sit there and look … however it is you usually look."

Landon shifted his gaze between Lila and me, confused. "Is something going on here?"

"She's the Devil," I said.

"Oh, don't listen to her," Lila said, rubbing her hand along Landon's forearm. I wanted to rip her arm off and beat her to death with it. "She's always been jealous of me. It goes back to high school."

Landon's face was unreadable. "I see."

"I was popular," Lila continued. "Bay was … well … Bay was special. She had imaginary friends."

Understanding washed across Landon's face. He was well aware of my witchy abilities, and he was also aware of the trouble I'd had in school thanks to them. "Well, I guess it's good for her that I happen to like people with imaginary friends." He shot me a small wink, immediately making me feel better.

Lila shifted. "What?"

"I had an imaginary friend growing up, too," Landon said. "His name was Gordon, and he was a magic goat."

I knew he was making it up, but the idea was so surreal I couldn't help but smile.

"Well, Bay's imaginary friend hung around until she was in high school," Lila said. "She was a total loser."

"My imaginary friend still hangs around," Landon said. "Am I a loser, too?"

"Of course not," Lila said. "You're too cute to be a loser."

Landon kept his face placid, but I could tell Lila's machinations were starting to wear on him. "Ma'am, if you just have a seat over there I'll have a uniform come and get your statement in a few minutes."

"Why are you taking her statement and not mine?" Lila asked, her lower lip jutting out. "She's a nobody."

"First, I'm not taking her statement," Landon said. "It's already been taken. Second, I'm not taking any statements. I'm here to help the police with their investigation. I'm not in charge."

"I'd still rather give my statement to you," Lila said. "Perhaps we could do it over dinner? I was on the sidewalk when the bank robber ran out of the building. I could have pertinent information for your investigation."

"You dropped to the ground and covered your face," I said. "You didn't see anything. You were too busy whimpering like a little ... ."

"You should have dropped to the ground and covered your face," Landon snapped.

Lila shot me a triumphant look. "So, how about that dinner?"

"I already have plans for dinner," Landon said.

"Oh, now, come on," Lila prodded. "I'm sure dinner with me will be much more stimulating than whatever else you've got planned."

"I seriously doubt that," Landon said, refusing to play Lila's game. He extended his hand to me. "Come on, Bay. I'm starving, and you and I need to have a talk."

I sheepishly placed my uninjured hand in his and let him tug me to my feet. "We're just going to talk, right? You said there won't be any yelling, and I'm holding you to that."

"Please, we're having dinner with your family," Landon said.

"There's going to be yelling. I just plan on holding off until I see Aunt Tillie."

"She hasn't done anything to you yet," I protested.

"She will," Landon said.

"How do you know that?"

"Because she always does." Landon turned back to the paramedic. "There's nothing wrong with her hand other than the obvious, right?"

The paramedic shook his head. "Her wrist might be a little sore because she landed on it, but it's not broken and she didn't sprain it. She should be fine."

"Good," Landon said, slipping his arm around my waist. "I have plans for her tonight, and she can't be hobbled."

Lila's face was a mask of anger and resentment as she glared at us. "What is going on here?"

"I'm sure someone will take your statement directly," Landon said. "Bay is done here, though. We're going to dinner at the inn, and then we're going to bed early because I haven't seen her in three days and I've missed her. I have no idea what you're doing."

Landon linked his fingers with mine and dragged me from the bank steps. I could feel Lila's eyes on my back as we walked down the sidewalk. Once we were out of her earshot, I couldn't contain myself. "I know you're mad at me, but that was the nicest thing anyone has ever done for me."

Landon shook his head, annoyed. "I don't like her."

"Join the club."

"I'm still angry with you."

"I know," I said, sighing.

Landon leaned over and gave me a quick kiss. "I wouldn't worry about me being angry," he said. "It probably won't last very long."

"Just until you see Aunt Tillie," I said.

He smirked. "Just until we're alone and you're naked. I really did miss you."

I was a member of that club too.

FIVE

"I have to ask, did you recognize the guy who ran into you outside of the bank?"

Landon was mostly quiet, contemplative, during the drive to The Overlook. He didn't appear angry, but he wasn't overly friendly either.

I shook my head. "It happened really fast."

"When you heard the gunshots, what did you think they were?" Landon's gaze was focused on the winding driveway, but there was an edge to his voice.

"I didn't really have time to process it," I said. "In my head, I think I knew what it was. I just … nothing like that has ever happened here before. Well, Mel Dixon once tried to rob the bank, but he did it with a water pistol filled with scented doe urine. I just … I didn't think."

Landon's jaw clenched as he parked. "That's what I figured." He killed the engine, exhaled heavily, and then turned to me. "I don't want to fight."

"We're going to, though, aren't we?"

"No. It's just … every time I think you're starting to get it and think things out, you do something like this."

"I didn't mean … ."

"You never mean to do it," Landon said. "Your intentions are always good. Well, they're always good in situations like this. Sometimes I wonder what you're thinking when you're dealing with your family, but that's a whole other issue – and one that's entertaining, so I let it go. This is important, though.

"You need to think before you do stuff like this," he continued. "You need to think about what would happen to the people who would still be here if you died. You need to think about me occasionally."

I faltered, surprised by his admission. "I ... ."

"Just think about it, Bay," Landon said, pushing the door of the Explorer open and hopping out. "You have a lot of people who would miss you."

I sat in the Explorer a full minute after the door shut. When I finally regained my faculties and glanced through the windshield, I found Landon waiting for me. Once I joined him in front of the Explorer, I searched for the words to somehow make this better. "I really am sorry."

"I know you are," Landon said, grabbing my hand. "Just ... think. That's all I ask. Now, come on. If this parking lot is any indication, we're going to be dealing with a full house tonight, and that means Aunt Tillie is going to put on a show."

"Are you sure you want to deal with this?" I asked. "We could go back to the guesthouse and order a pizza or something."

"Pizza? Your mother is one of the best cooks in the state. I don't want pizza."

"Okay," I said. "Just ... we're okay, right?"

Landon leaned over and gave me a soft kiss. "We're fine. I'm sure I'll have nightmares about you being killed by a bank robber tonight, but you'll just have to distract me when I wake up in a cold sweat."

"How do you want me to distract you?"

"I find that nudity and bacon are always good ways to start."

I pursed my lips, fighting the urge to laugh, but finally giving in. "I'll give it some thought."

"Thought? Woman, you should know you're getting bacon-scented perfume for Christmas this year."

"Oh, well, that sounds ... nice."

Landon grinned. "Don't worry. I'll get you an outfit to match."

"OH, GOOD, YOU'RE HERE."

My mother was aflutter behind the big desk in the lobby of The Overlook. Her face was flushed with excitement, but she also looked overwhelmed. When my mother and aunts opted to renovate the old family homestead and turn it into a bed and breakfast, I'd initially doubted they could pull it off. While they were all master cooks, and fussy enough to keep the inn clean, they weren't exactly known for their organizational skills.

To my surprise, they pulled it off, and The Overlook was the most successful inn in the area. That didn't mean my mother and aunts lacked the propensity to freak out when the mood struck. My mother appeared to be in the mood.

"What's wrong?"

"We're completely booked," Mom said.

"I thought that was a good thing."

"It is. We've just got a lot going on. It's good you're here. Someone needs to ... rein in your aunt."

I narrowed my eyes. "Which one?"

"Which one do you think?"

Aunt Tillie. Crap. "What did she do now?"

"She's just being ... a pain in the-you-know-what."

"Ass?" Landon asked, raising an eyebrow.

"Don't be a smart mouth," Mom warned. "I can only take so much this week. We have a lot going on, and you adding your special blend of sarcasm to the mix won't help."

"Where is Aunt Tillie?" I asked, patting Landon's arm. He seemed surprised by my mother's admonishment. She usually doted on him, thinking he was her only chance of marrying me off. He wasn't used to being on the end of her ire stick.

"She's in the kitchen," Mom said. "She's overseeing dinner preparations."

Since Aunt Tillie hadn't bothered to cook anything that wasn't related to her wine business since the first President Bush was in office, I knew that had to be a special torture for my aunts. "I'll go and … distract her."

"Good," Mom said. "Since Annie and Belinda are out of town until next week, your aunt seems bored."

Belinda and Annie Martin were a recent addition to our small family. Eight-year-old Annie stumbled upon Thistle and Aunt Tillie after a car accident, and after a close brush with death – and Annie's father – Belinda recovered from the injuries she sustained in the accident. She worked at The Overlook full time now, but she still had some belongings to claim from Minnesota, and that's where the duo had traveled for the week. It was a bad time to go, but Belinda's former landlord was threatening to throw everything out, so they had little choice.

"Aunt Tillie's really taken a shine to Annie," I said.

"It's funny, she never liked you, Clove and Thistle when you were kids, but she absolutely adores Annie."

"Maybe she's mellowing," Landon suggested.

"Oh, you're cute," Mom said, patting his cheek. "She'll never mellow."

"She won't," I agreed. "Evil only gets stronger with age."

Landon rolled his eyes. "Come on, Trouble. Let's see what your aunt is up to now. I hate to say it, but I've missed her a little these past few days."

Mom furrowed her brow. "That's not funny."

"It wasn't a joke."

Mom blinked rapidly, surprise at his admission rolling off of her. "Well, that's just … ."

"Don't worry," I said, grabbing Landon's hand and tugging him into the inner sanctum of the bed and breakfast. "It won't last long. He's feeling all fuzzy and nostalgic now, but five minutes with Aunt Tillie will cure him of that."

"Oh, I kind of like him when he's a softy."

"I'm never a softy," Landon challenged. "I'm hard."

I shot him a dubious look. "Do you want to rephrase that?"

Landon realized what he said, but it wasn't in his nature to back down. "No." He lowered his voice. "I'll show you how hard of a man I am later."

"I heard that," Mom called to our retreating backs. "You're a disgusting man."

"That's what you get for eavesdropping."

We found Marnie and Twila buzzing about the kitchen a few minutes later, and instead of resting in her recliner in the corner Aunt Tillie perched on a stool, watching them work. A few months before, we'd removed her old recliner because it smelled – and there was a possibility an errant scorpion was living in it – and she'd been a bear until we bought her a new one. The fact that she was ignoring the chair now was significant – and worrisome.

"What's going on?" I asked.

"We're cooking a big dinner," Twila said, her hands busy ornately icing a cake.

"We're offering three big desserts because it's the first night everyone is here," Marnie added, placing a pie on a trivet to cool.

"I'm supervising," Aunt Tillie said, nonplussed.

"I heard."

I've always thought Aunt Tillie resembles a hobbit. She's short, not quite five feet tall, and her face is round. The look she flashed me now gave her an evil quality that was more "deranged Sith lord" than "Shire-loving hobbit."

"What did your mother say about me?" she growled, more than asked.

"She said you were supervising," I said.

"Oh, you're such a bad liar," Aunt Tillie said. "I know she said something about me. What was it?"

"She didn't say anything about you," I protested.

"She said you were enthusiastic," Landon said, studying Marnie's pie. "What is this? It smells good."

"Blackberry."

"Well, I know what I'm having," Landon said.

"You have to eat your dinner first," Twila said. "You can't have dessert until you eat dinner."

"And we've gone all out," Marnie said. "We have a pork roast and a beef roast, we have a full array of summer vegetables, and we have three summer salads, including that cucumber and dill one you love so much, Bay."

"Oh, yay!" I'm surprised I'm not as wide as the kitchen the way my family cooks.

"I'm having two desserts tonight," Landon said, winking in my direction.

"You have such a fresh mouth," Aunt Tillie said.

"Oh, he's just happy to see Bay," Twila said. "He's been away for days. He's a man in love."

Landon froze at Twila's words. My aunt was teasing, but that was a phrase neither of us had uttered. Not yet, at least. Instead of addressing the elephant in the room, Landon changed course.

"So, did you hear what Bay did today?"

He had a funny way of showing his affection. Instead of dealing with what Twila said, he'd decided to offer me up. "I ran into Lila Stevens," I interjected smoothly.

All three of my aunts made identical faces, causing Landon to smirk. "I see you all like this Lila as much as Bay does."

"We haven't seen her in years," Marnie said carefully. "She was a ... troublesome child."

"She had issues," Twila agreed.

"She was a little ... ."

"Don't finish that sentence," Marnie warned, waving a finger in Aunt Tillie's face. "She had a few personality defects."

"And most of those defects were pointed at Bay," Aunt Tillie supplied.

Landon studied me for a moment as I shifted uncomfortably. "Yeah, I pretty much figured that out." He decided to change the subject again. "Do you need help taking this out to the table?"

"No," Twila said. "It's not that we don't trust you to carry the food out, but ... ."

"We don't trust you," Marnie said. "We'll take the food out. You two go and get settled, maybe have a drink or something. Dinner will be on the table in about twenty minutes."

"Mom told me to ... ." I glanced at Aunt Tillie, unsure how to proceed.

"What did your mother tell you to do?" Aunt Tillie asked.

"She told me to make sure everything was okay in here and then do exactly what you suggested we do," I said.

Landon snickered, but he followed me out of the kitchen. Once we were safely on the other side of the door, he dropped a quick kiss on my cheek. "Coward," he whispered into my ear, causing a shiver to run up my spine.

"She wasn't doing anything," I protested.

"I'm sure your aunts would beg to differ."

"I ... do you want a drink or not?"

"Oh, I want a drink," Landon said. "I have a feeling this is going to be a long night."

"What makes you say that?"

"Just a feeling," Landon said.

"I think you're wrong," I said. "I think everything is going to be fine."

Landon smiled. "I love that you still seem like a little kid sometimes. You have this earnest quality that sneaks in from out of the blue. It's ... refreshing."

"Are you saying this is one of those times?"

"I'm saying that tonight has all the makings of a disaster written all over it," Landon said. "Come on. Let's get some alcohol in you. I bet you're going to need it."

SIX

"Did we miss anything?" Thistle and Marcus let themselves into the library where Landon and I were hiding out. They'd been together almost a year now, and his calm demeanor was welcome when Thistle worked herself into a snit. Since seeing Lila this afternoon charged her revenge batteries, Marcus' presence could only help.

"We've been in here," I said.

"Oh, come on," Thistle said. "What good are you if you can't fill me full of awesome gossip? I heard you ran toward gunshots this afternoon, by the way. Good job."

I shifted my gaze to Landon briefly. He merely raised his eyebrows. "I didn't tell her."

"It's all over town," Thistle said. "Lila has been telling everyone she tried to run into danger to save everyone, but you got in her way."

I scowled. "I hate her."

Landon reached over and rubbed the back of my neck. "You need to relax. Don't let her get to you. She's just a … ."

"Filthy, lying, disgusting, whorish … ."

"Thank you, Thistle," Landon said, rolling his eyes in her direction. "Maybe you should get a drink. You seem … testy."

"Lila Stevens makes me testy," Thistle said.

"From the sound of it, she makes your whole family testy."

"That's because she's evil incarnate," Thistle replied.

"I thought Aunt Tillie was evil incarnate," Landon said.

"She's a different kind of evil," Thistle explained, deadly serious. "Lila is the kind of evil that tries to suck your soul. She feeds on you. She tries to make you weaker so she can swoop in and peck your eyes out while you only have the strength to sit there and let her."

"Nice visual," Landon deadpanned.

"Aunt Tillie is the kind of evil that wants to get her own way no matter what," Thistle said. "Lila wants that, too, but they go about it in different ways. Aunt Tillie wants to crush her enemies. She doesn't want to feed off of them. She doesn't need their strength. She has more than enough of her own."

Landon snickered. "You have a way with words," he said. "Some people might even consider you paranoid."

"Just because I'm paranoid doesn't mean they're not out to get me," Thistle said.

Marcus sat down on the sofa next to Landon. "She's been this way since I picked her up from the store an hour ago. She's got some interesting revenge plans for Lila."

"I heard them this afternoon," I said.

"Oh, we came up with more after you left," Thistle said. "How would you feel about giving her a month-long visit from the period fairy?"

Landon made a face. "Gross."

"How could you even tell? She already acts like she has constant PMS," I pointed out.

"That's true," Thistle said, tilting her head to the side. "I still think incontinence in the way to go."

Landon rolled his eyes again. "Why don't you just send Aunt Tillie after her?"

"That was my suggestion," I said. "Thistle wants to do both."

"You have no idea the things she did to Bay when we were growing up," Thistle said. "I'm not just letting it go, so don't even suggest it."

Landon shrugged. "Do what you want," he said. "I spent five minutes with her this afternoon and I already dislike her."

"You can help me plan," Thistle said.

"I can't wait."

We all glanced up when Twila poked her head into the library. "What are you doing in here? You know dinner is served at seven on the dot. It's three minutes past the hour."

"Sorry," Thistle mumbled.

Twila studied her daughter's vibrant pink hair for a moment. Thistle had switched it over from blue the day before. "That color is much better with your complexion," she said. "It doesn't wash you out like the blue does."

"I'm glad you approve," Thistle said, faux sweetness dripping from her tongue. Twila's hair was from the Ronald McDonald hair care line, so casting aspersions on her daughter's hair choices was akin to tossing gasoline on the low flame that already was Thistle.

"It makes you look ... friendlier," Twila said. "With your attitude, that can only help. Now, get your butts to the table. Everyone else is already there."

Thistle scrunched her face up as she watched her mother go. "She does that on purpose."

"What?" Landon asked.

"She compliments my hair so I'll be forced to change it."

"I don't think that's what she was doing," Marcus said.

"That's exactly what she was doing," Thistle said. "I should know. I do the same thing to Clove."

"See, evil is genetic," I teased.

WE FOUND the table busy in the dining room. Landon and I settled at the near end next to Aunt Tillie, and Thistle and Marcus made their way to the far end. Once seated, and after receiving a scathing look from my mother for our tardiness, I took the opportunity to scan the table.

Most of the faces belonged to people I didn't recognize. Sure, somewhere in Hemlock Cove's illustrious past these people had been a part of the everyday comings and goings, but I didn't know them. It was the face at the very end of the table that jumped out, though. That one I did recognize.

"Nick Spencer." The name was out of my mouth before I realized it.

"Bay Winchester." Nick hadn't changed much since high school. His brown hair was a little longer, and he was dressed in a mock turtleneck and simple blue jeans. His brown eyes flashed when they landed on me, and his smile was as charming as ever.

"Oh, that's right, you two graduated together," Mom said, her gaze bouncing between Nick and me.

"We did," Nick said. "You look ... good."

My cheeks were burning. "Um ... well ... thanks."

Landon tilted his head so he could give Nick his full attention. "You went to high school with Bay?"

Nick nodded. "And Clove and Thistle, too, but we were ahead of them. We graduated together."

"Were you friends?"

"Sure," Nick said.

"You weren't friends," Thistle said, startling when Clove elbowed her in the stomach. "Why did you do that?"

"Because we're supposed to be having a nice dinner," Mom said, her voice tight.

"Well, he's the one lying," Thistle said. "Blame him. He wasn't friends with Bay. He dated Lila. He was mean to her – just like his girlfriend."

"I wasn't mean to her," Nick argued. "I was just ... you have no idea how hard it was to date Lila."

"Then you should have dated someone else," Thistle suggested. "I think a garden slug would have been a step up."

"Thistle," Marcus warned.

"What?" She was incensed.

"Shut up and eat your dinner," Mom ordered.

"You shut up," Thistle grumbled.

"Listen, I'm really sorry if I did anything in high school that upset you," Nick said. "That's what happens in high school. You do stupid things. If it's any consolation, seeing how you turned out, I wish I'd dated you."

"Oh, well, that's possibly ... flattering," I said.

Landon cleared his throat. "Well, your stupidity is my gain."

"Oh, are you two dating?" Nick asked, unruffled.

"We are," Landon said, reaching for the platter of roast in the middle of the table.

"For how long?"

"Long enough that you don't have to concern yourself with it," Landon said.

I shot him a look. "What are you doing?"

"I'm eating dinner," he said. "And I'm having a discussion with your former ... classmate."

Then why did it feel like he was marking his territory? "Okay." There was no way I was picking an argument with him now.

"Don't worry about it," Aunt Tillie said, directing her attention to Landon. "Nick doesn't have enough personality to entice Bay. He never did. You're safe."

"Thanks," Landon said dryly.

"I have personality," Nick said. "It's just ... high school is hard. I wanted to fit in. That's why I dated Lila. It's not like I liked her. Although ... I hear she's still hot."

"Of course you didn't like her," Aunt Tillie said. "That would make you an idiot."

"Aunt Tillie!" Marnie glared at her. "You need to eat your dinner and be quiet. Our guests don't want to hear your ... opinions."

"That's not true," a woman at the center of the table said. "That's why we picked your inn. We were told you have dinner theater every night."

Landon snorted. "That's a nice way of putting it."

"We do like our dinner theater," I said. "I just didn't think we were going to put on a show quite this soon."

"Speaking of dinner theater, I heard Bay tried to stop a bank robbery today," Aunt Tillie said.

I froze in my chair. I fought the urge to look in my mother's direction, knowing exactly the expression I would find there.

"What?" Mom's voice can echo on a normal day. When she kicks it up a notch, it's terrifying.

"I did not try to stop a bank robbery," I said carefully. "I was just trying to ... see what was going on."

"Did you know this, Landon?"

"I was made aware of the situation," he replied, keeping his eyes on his plate.

"Wow. Hemlock Cove had a bank robbery? That's out there," Nick said. "Nothing that exciting ever happened when I lived here."

"That's because you're a milquetoast," Aunt Tillie said.

"Aunt Tillie," Twila warned. "You leave him alone."

"What's a milquetoast?" Nick asked, confused. "Is it something really bad?"

"It means you're boring," Thistle said, reaching for a bottle of wine. "Don't worry about it. I'm pretty sure you already knew you were boring. It shouldn't come as some big shock to you."

"Thistle!"

"Oh, what? Aunt Tillie started it," Thistle said.

"You're on my list, missy," Aunt Tillie said, extending a gnarled finger in Thistle's direction.

"I've been on your list for weeks," Thistle pointed out.

"That should give you a hint of just how much of a pain you've been the past few weeks," Aunt Tillie said. "I wouldn't push it."

"Don't you push it either," Mom admonished her. "We gave you very clear instructions about how you were supposed to act this week."

"They must be caught in my spam filter," Aunt Tillie said. "Well, I never got the list, so I can't be expected to abide by rules I haven't been made aware of. Bummer."

"Spam filter?" Clove wrinkled her nose. "Since when do you use email?"

"I'll have you know, I'm very computer savvy," Aunt Tillie said. "I could be a hacker if I wanted to."

"When did you even get a computer?" Clove asked. "I thought you were banned from the Internet after you ordered all of those bugs ... I mean things ... when the Dragonfly was under construction?"

"I'm an adult," Aunt Tillie said. "You can't ban me from anything. Shut your mouth and eat your dinner. You're going to be on my list, too, if you're not careful."

"What did I do?" Clove protested. "It was an honest question."

"Where did you get a computer?" Mom asked, turning to face Aunt Tillie. "We lock ours up now so you can't get on it. You can't buy one in town, so where did you get it?"

"Don't worry about it," Aunt Tillie said. "Now, someone hand me some pork roast. I love a good baked pig."

Mom made a face. "I am worried about it. Where did you get a computer?"

I shrank in my chair, something that didn't escape Landon's attention. "Did you give her the computer?"

"I ... ."

Five sets of eyes swiveled to me.

"How could you possibly give her a computer?" Thistle asked. "You know what a menace she is when she has a credit card and unlimited access to military surplus stores."

"I ... you have to understand ... ."

"I issued very specific rules," Mom said. "Your great-aunt is not allowed on the Internet. You know why."

"Porn?" Nick asked, clearly enjoying the conversation.

"That's not funny," Mom said.

Nick sobered. "Sorry. I thought it was part of the show."

"Move over, Thistle," Aunt Tillie said. "Nick the Quick there just joined you at the top of my list."

"What happens to people on the list?" A man asked, intrigued.

"Horrible things," Marcus muttered.

"Karma," Aunt Tillie corrected.

"You can't distract me," Mom said. "Did Bay give you a computer?"

"I have no idea what you're talking about," Aunt Tillie said. "Is someone here going to feed me? I think my blood sugar is crashing."

Landon reached to the middle of the table and stabbed a slice of the pork roast so he could deposit it on her plate. "Happy?"

"I need potatoes, too."

"Bay, did you give your aunt a computer?"

I sighed. "She said she wanted to play euchre on it," I said. "I loaded a few card games on my old laptop. I needed a new one. Since she can't go to the senior center these days, I thought it might keep her busy."

"Why can't she go to the senior center?" Nick asked.

"Because she poisoned all the people there when she thought they were cheating," Thistle said.

"I allegedly poisoned people," Aunt Tillie said. "Allegedly." She looked to Landon and sent him her best "I'm innocent" look. "I'm really persecuted in this town."

"I'm sure," Landon said. "What harm can she really do on the computer?"

Marnie rolled her eyes. "You've met her. She can do harm with a cotton ball if you give her enough time."

"Oh, you're on my list, too," Aunt Tillie said, getting to her feet. "In fact, you're all on my list. Every single one of you." She moved toward the kitchen. "I'm so upset I can't even eat. I hope you're all happy. Upsetting an old woman like this, you should all be locked up." She flounced through the kitchen door. "I'll know if you talk about me when I'm gone," she called from the other room. "And you'll be sorry!"

"Yay!" A middle-aged woman at the middle of the table broke into applause. "This dinner theater really is amazing. I'm so glad we came to stay here. If this is the first night, what's going to happen the rest of the week?"

That was a very good – and terrifying – question.

SEVEN

"Well, that was fun," Landon said, linking his fingers with mine as we moved along the back pathway that led from the inn to the guesthouse I shared with my cousins.

"You told me it was going to be awful," I said.

"I did. Even I didn't expect that, though. I thought they were going to jump all over you because of the bank robbery. That's what I was hoping for."

"You were hoping my mother would yell at me?"

"If your mother yells at you then I'm not the villain," Landon said. "As much as I enjoy playing around with your family, I don't want to be the villain where you're concerned. That never works out for me."

"When have I ever treated you like a villain?"

"I seem to remember you thinking I was a crazy drug dealer."

"You were undercover as a drug dealer at the time," I reminded him. "How was that my fault?"

"I think you should believe I have an honest face," Landon teased, leaning down so he could give me a lingering kiss. "I just want you safe, Bay. I figured if your mother yelled at you, you'd be more likely to listen."

"I didn't mean ... ."

"I know," Landon said, taking a step away from me. "I don't want to fight. We've been apart for days. Can we please not fight?"

"I'm not trying to fight," I said, jutting my lower lip into a pout. "You're trying to fight."

"Am I on your list?" Landon's blue eyes danced with amusement.

"You're at the top of my list," I said, reaching over to tug on his hair.

"Good," Landon said. He gave me another kiss. "Tell me about this Nick guy."

"Yeah, what was up with that?"

"Up with what?"

"You were all … growly … with him."

"I wasn't growly," Landon said. "I was having a perfectly nice conversation with him."

I waited.

"One in which he was aware that you were already taken," Landon conceded.

I couldn't hide my smile. "It's nice that I'm already taken."

Landon pursed his lips. "You growled like a bear when Lila started hitting on me this afternoon."

"I did no such thing."

"You did, too," Landon said, laughing. "You actually growled. I thought it was kind of cute."

"Well, that's because she kept touching you," I sniffed. "Nick didn't get close enough to touch me. Lila was … petting you. She was stroking you like you were a cat and she wanted you to curl up in her lap and take a nap."

"I'm pretty sure napping wasn't what she had in mind."

I scorched him with a look.

"I wouldn't worry about Lila," Landon said. "She's a little too obvious. I like my women to be mean to me for weeks before they fall under my spell."

"I was not mean to you."

"You kept accusing me of stalking you."

"That's because you kept showing up," I said.

"I only followed you because you were acting all ... squirrelly. I had no idea what you were doing, but I knew it couldn't be good. And, look, I was right."

"Who solved that case?"

"Me."

I stuck my tongue out at him. "You couldn't have solved that case without me."

"You got me shot."

I faltered. "I ... ."

"That was a rotten thing to say," Landon said, instantly contrite. "I didn't mean that. I thought we were joking."

"It's fine."

"It's not fine," Landon said. "I know you're sensitive where that's concerned ... especially after my mother blamed you."

A few weeks earlier, Landon's family visited the inn for an extended stay. When Landon's mother found out he'd been hurt in the line of duty, partially because of my presence at a crime scene, she hadn't taken the information well. We'd moved past the issue, but it still hurt to think about it.

"It's really fine," I said, slipping my hand back into his. "We don't have to dwell on it."

"Good," Landon said. "Tell me about the things Lila used to do to you when you were a kid."

This night just keeps getting better and better. "I don't see why that's important."

"I want to know," Landon said softly. "You seem really upset about it. It's been ... what ... ten years? It must have been pretty bad."

"I don't know that it was worse than anything other kids go through," I said, averting my gaze from his probing stare and focusing on the moon. "It was just years and years of ... stuff."

"I think Chief Terry told me a little bit about her," Landon said. "Several months ago, we were having a discussion, and he told me that a lot of kids were mean to you because you were different. They thought you were talking to yourself when you were really talking to ghosts."

"I know," I said. "I was eavesdropping on your conversation."

"Tell me, Bay," Landon prodded. "You might feel better if you let it out."

I sighed, running a hand through my hair as I tried to compose myself. "It was just a lot of little things," I said. "She called me names. She put gum in my hair. She picked on my clothes."

"Was there something wrong with your clothes? Your mother doesn't seem the type to dress you in rags."

"No. But they weren't designer clothes like Lila's mother bought for her. She always thought she was better than us."

"That's on her, Bay," Landon said. "That's not on you. That's the type of person she is. What else?"

"I ... I don't know," I said, frustrated. "In high school she'd always make a point of spreading rumors about me."

"Like?"

"Like I was a lesbian, or I had a crush on the janitor, or ... you know ... just stupid stuff," I said. "It seems stupid to think about it now, but it was horrible then."

"Just for the record, if you want to be a lesbian, I'm all for it – as long as I'm invited to watch," Landon said.

I stuck my tongue out.

"I know it's hard to forget those things," Landon said, turning serious. "Look how well you turned out, though."

"You spent half the afternoon telling me I was an idiot."

"I didn't say you were an idiot," Landon countered. "I said I wanted you to think before you ran into danger. There's a difference."

"I guess."

Landon grabbed my shoulders and forced me to face him. "Bay, I ... am very attached to you," he said. "I don't want to think about something happening to you. I happen to like how you turned out. Please don't let bad memories hurt you. They're in the past. Let them go."

"You're good for my self-esteem," I said, finally meeting his gaze.

"You're good for my ... everything," Landon said, pulling me in for a hug. "Now, come on. Let's see what kind of revenge Thistle is cooking up. I'm mildly curious to see how far off the rails she runs this week."

"**WHAT** IF WE gave her lockjaw for the week?" Thistle suggested.

She was holding court in the middle of our living room, a chocolate martini in hand.

"I think I'm behind," Sam said, shifting on the chair he shared with Clove. "Why do we hate this Lila person?"

Sam wisely opted to avoid dinner, so he'd spent the past half hour catching up on all of the gossip and shenanigans he missed.

"She's evil incarnate," Marcus and Landon answered in unison. They had memorized the family line on Lila.

"Ah, I see," Sam said. "Carry on."

"What do you think about lockjaw?" Thistle asked.

"It wouldn't stop us from having to see her face," Clove said.

"So, wait, you hate her, too?" Sam asked, rubbing Clove's shoulders. "I thought only Bay and Thistle hated her."

"Of course I hate her," Clove said. "She was mean to Bay."

"Was she mean to you?"

"Not like she was to Bay," Clove said.

"Was she mean to you, Thistle?" Sam asked.

"She was afraid of me," Thistle said, puffing her chest out proudly. "I rained fired and brimstone down on her every chance I got."

"Not literal fire, right?" Landon asked. "Because that would be a felony."

"Don't rain on my parade," Thistle ordered.

"Sorry. I didn't mean to rain." Landon reached over and grabbed my hand, focusing on my palm lines as he traced his fingers over them. "Have you guys considered simply ignoring her?"

"What?" Thistle's eyebrows nearly flew off her forehead.

"I think that's a good idea," Marcus said. "If you ignore her, it will hurt more than giving her negative attention."

Thistle swiveled, hands on hips, and fixed her boyfriend with a hard look. "Are you a girl?"

Marcus was taken aback. "No."

"Then you don't know how girls think," Thistle said. "You can't simply ignore her. If there was a flash flood, would you ignore that?"

"No."

"If your house was on fire, would you ignore that?"

"No."

"If you got Chlamydia, would you ignore that?"

Marcus was flustered. "No."

"And that's exactly why we can't ignore Lila," Thistle said. "By the way, who would you get Chlamydia from?"

Marcus' face flushed. "How did this conversation get away from me?"

"Have another beer," Landon suggested. "If you're drunk enough, none of this will matter."

"I think we should let Aunt Tillie deal with her," I said. "By the way, did you tell Aunt Tillie that Lila was talking smack about her?"

Thistle frowned. "No. I forgot. Don't worry, I'll tell her at breakfast tomorrow. I figure that will be enough to dislodge all of us from her list. Lila can have the whole thing to herself."

"Nick can stay there, too," Landon said.

"Who is Nick?" Sam asked.

"Some guy Bay went to high school with," Marcus explained. "I knew him from a baseball league when I was here for summers. He was telling Bay how good she looked tonight and Landon … well … he didn't take it well."

"I took it fine," Landon said.

"You were one second away from turning into King Kong and thumping your chest as you tossed him off the Empire State Building," Thistle scoffed. "Give me a break."

"I was just having a conversation with him," Landon said. "It's not my fault he doesn't understand boundaries."

"What boundaries?" Clove asked. "All he said was that he wished he'd dated Bay instead of Lila in high school."

"He also pointed out she was hot," Landon said.

"How is that bad?" Thistle asked. "It's always nice to hear you're hot. Don't you think Bay is hot?"

"Of course I think she's hot," Landon said. "I can, though. She's ... mine."

"Yours?" Thistle narrowed her eyes. "Are you suggesting Bay is your property?"

"Yeah, that's exactly what I was saying," Landon deadpanned. He glanced over at me. "That's our cue to go to bed."

"Wait! I'm not done planning," Thistle said.

"Well, we're done," Landon said. "I'm tired, and I haven't seen my ... witch ... in days. I want to go to bed."

"You only want to fornicate like bunnies in spring," Thistle said.

"Guilty as charged," Landon said. He got to his feet and extended his hand in my direction. "Come on, growly, let's go to bed. I've just about had my fill of your family for one evening."

Thistle made a face as we shuffled toward the bedroom.

"Good night," I said to everyone.

"Hey, Landon?"

Landon turned back to Thistle, weary. "Yes?"

"You're at the top of my list now," she said.

"Well, I guess I'm a popular guy today," he said, smiling down at me. "Come on, Bay. I have a list of my own I want to get to, and we don't need an audience.

"Everyone have a ... good night," he said. "And don't you dare wake us up too early tomorrow. Bay is going to need her rest."

EIGHT

"I'm surprised you're so relaxed this morning," I said, eyeing Landon as we let ourselves in through the back door of The Overlook. The family quarters had a separate entrance at the back of the building. It was only accessible through the kitchen, which none of the guests ever braved.

"Why do you say that?"

"We were up late," I reminded him.

"Yes, but when I slept, it was hard," Landon said.

"So ... no bad dreams?"

Landon tugged on a strand of my hair. "No bad dreams," he said. "However, you're going to give me indigestion if you don't let this go. I'm not angry. I am, however, going to lock you in the guesthouse if you ever do anything like that again."

"You're going to lock me in the guesthouse?"

"I'm going to chain you to the bed," Landon said. "Don't worry. I'll keep you hydrated and reward you when you're good."

"You're sick."

"Hey, when I daydream, that's what I think about," Landon said, pulling up short when he caught sight of Aunt Tillie sitting on the sofa. She was watching a morning chat show, and she seemed intent on whatever was playing out on the screen.

"What are you doing?" I asked.

"I'm watching these idiots discuss global warming," Aunt Tillie said. "What does it look like I'm doing?"

Landon looked her up and down. "Is there a reason you're dressed in camouflage?"

"I'm preparing for war."

"With who?"

"The enemy." Aunt Tillie refused to look at Landon, and I could tell it was driving him crazy.

"Who is the enemy?"

"Terrorists."

Landon sighed, pinching the bridge of his nose. "Do you think there are terrorists in Hemlock Cove?"

"It depends on how you define the word 'terrorist.'"

"How do you define it?"

"People who tick me off."

Landon glanced at me. "She's your aunt. Do something with her." He let go of my hand and started moving toward the kitchen. "And whatever she's up to ... it had better be legal."

Once he was gone, I fixed my gaze on Aunt Tillie. "What are you really doing?"

"Driving your mother nuts."

That was generally a short trip. "Why are you doing that?"

"They're trying to confiscate my computer."

"Are you doing anything on it you shouldn't be doing?"

"Are you the computer police?"

I scowled. "Just try to behave," I said. "This is an important week for them. You know that. When a lot of these people left town, the inn wasn't up and running. They've turned it into a success. They're proud. Can't you give them just this week?"

Aunt Tillie tilted her head to the side, considering. "No."

I swallowed my laugh. "What if I give you something else to focus on?"

"Like what?"

"Lila Stevens."

Aunt Tillie narrowed her eyes. "What did she do?"

I told her about our conversation the day before. When I was done, Aunt Tillie was already on her feet. "I'll be a ticked-off witch."

Sometimes she's spot on.

"I can't believe she said that about me," Aunt Tillie said. "I'm going to ... ." She mimed some form of overt violence that I didn't quite recognize.

"How about you just do something that keeps her away from me for the rest of the week?" I suggested.

"Oh, don't you worry about Lila Stevens," Aunt Tillie said. "When I'm done with her, she's going to wish she'd never been born."

That was good enough for me. For now.

"WHAT WERE you two talking about in there?" Landon asked, pouring me a glass of tomato juice as I settled in the open chair next to him. The table was full again, and the guests were talking amongst themselves excitedly.

"What's going on with them?" I asked, inclining my head.

"They're waiting for Aunt Tillie's grand entrance," Landon said. "They think breakfast is going to be a show, too."

"Huh."

"See, I don't like your tone," Landon said. "What were you two talking about?"

"I gave her a task so she can keep busy and out of my mother's hair."

"What task?"

"It doesn't matter."

Landon cleared his throat. "Is this going to come back and bite me?"

"No."

"Fine. Did you find out why she's wearing camouflage?"

"She's just trying to irritate my mom."

Landon barked out a coarse laugh. "I wondered if it was something like that." He glanced around the table. "Why aren't Thistle and Clove here?"

"Would you come if you didn't have to?"

"How did I have to come?"

"If you wanted food before you left for work for the day, you had to come here," I said. "We're even out of cereal."

"You're so domestic," Landon said, kissing the tip of my nose. "You're like one of those women in the cleaning commercials."

"You're funny."

"I'm fine with coming here for breakfast," Landon said. "I'll have a long day, and I already had a long night because you're so frisky all of the time. I can use the fuel."

"I am not frisky."

Landon meowed like a perky cat.

"What was that?" Mom asked, walking out of the kitchen with a pan of French toast in her hand.

"I was just … that smells good," Landon said, straightening in his chair. He was overly affectionate this morning, and I had a feeling it had something to do with the time we'd spent apart. The thought warmed me.

"Were you two talking about something you shouldn't be talking about at the breakfast table?" Mom asked.

"Oh, good, the show is starting," one of the women said.

"There's no show at breakfast," Mom said firmly. "We're just … having a discussion. Which reminds me, we haven't finished the discussion from last night. You didn't think I forgot that little tidbit about you trying to stop a bank robbery, did you?"

I shot Landon a hopeful look. "Mom … ."

"We've already talked about it," Landon said. "She knows she made a mistake. I don't think there's any reason to harp on it."

He really was in a good mood this morning.

Mom eyed him for a few seconds. "You two look all … sparkly … this morning. Why is that?"

"Why do you think?" Aunt Tillie asked, breezing into the room.

I fought the urge to laugh when I realized she'd added the combat helmet to her ensemble.

"Why are you wearing that?" Mom asked, her eyes widening. "Why in the world are you wearing that?"

"Oh, is war coming?" One of the men farther down the table was smiling at Aunt Tillie.

"You have no idea," Aunt Tillie said. "The good news for everyone is that my list has been wiped clean for the week – except for one name."

"I'm almost afraid to ask," Mom sighed. "Who are you focusing your considerable efforts on?"

"It had better be Lila Stevens," Thistle said, pushing through the kitchen door and joining the breakfast crowd. Clove was close behind.

"I didn't think you were coming down for breakfast," I said.

"I could smell the French toast from the guesthouse," Thistle said. "Plus, I want to spend a little time with Aunt Tillie before I have to go into the store today."

"Why?" Twila asked, suspicious.

"Can't I just want to spend time with my aunt?" Thistle asked.

"Not unless you've had a lobotomy," Mom said. "You two fight like … well, I can't think of a good analogy because it's just that bad … so I don't believe you're going to join forces for anything good."

"We've joined forces before," Thistle protested.

"And when has that ever worked out?"

"Each and every time," Aunt Tillie said. "You leave that girl alone. Don't pick on her."

Mom's mouth dropped open. "What?"

"Just let it go," Landon said. "You're ruining my happy morning."

"Stop smiling like that," Mom instructed. "I know you're thinking something dirty."

"Oh, you have no idea," Landon said. "Someone pass the French toast."

"That smells amazing," Nick said, walking into the room and smiling at everyone in turn. "Ladies, I can't tell you what a great night of sleep I had. It was the best night of sleep I've had in years. You're all miracle workers."

"Well, thank you for the nice compliment," Marnie said, pleased. "Are you ready for some breakfast?"

Nick had always been charming, but a decade of life experience had allowed him to up his game. It was pretty impressive. Still, there was something about his little act that bothered me.

"I'd love some breakfast," Nick said. Instead of moving to the end of the table and sitting where he had the night before he pulled out the open chair next to me and settled between me and another guest. "Good morning, Bay."

"Good morning," I murmured, risking a look at Landon out of the corner of my eye. His face was unreadable, and he seemed fixated on his huge pile of French toast.

"I see you're here again," Nick said, smiling at Landon. "Do you live here with Bay?"

"Sometimes," Landon said, his answer taking me by surprise. "I work out of Traverse City, but I'm here as often as I can be."

"Oh, so do you have to drive back over to Traverse today?" Nick asked. I couldn't decide whether he was genuinely interested or was trying to get on Landon's good side.

"I'm in town for the week," Landon said.

I turned my attention back to him, surprised. "You are? You didn't tell me that. I thought you came to town because of the bank robbery yesterday."

"I finished up my case in the afternoon, so I was coming here anyway," Landon said. "I volunteered for the bank robbery case so I'd have a reason to stay here with you all week."

Oh, that was kind of sweet.

"Case? Are you a police officer?" Nick asked.

"I'm with the FBI."

"Oh." Nick straightened in his chair. "That's ... wow. That sounds like a neat job."

"Yeah, Landon, you're neat," Thistle said, forking a huge chunk of

French toast into her mouth, a thin thread of syrup clinging to her chin.

"I think you're neat," I said, patting his knee.

Landon smirked. "That's what's written on my business cards."

"You have business cards?"

Landon arched an eyebrow. "How do you think people call me with tips?"

"I want one."

"I'll give you a stack of them later," he said. "You can write dirty suggestions on them and then give them to me when you want me to make them happen."

My mother, who had been checking to make sure everyone at the table was set before sitting down, cuffed him on the back of the head. "That will be just about enough of that."

"Sorry," Landon mumbled around a mouthful of food.

"Nice," Aunt Tillie said. "Classy."

Landon swallowed. "You're wearing a combat helmet."

"I'm ready for combat."

Landon rolled his eyes and then shifted his attention to me. "Are you going to be at the newspaper office all day?"

"Probably not," I said. "I have to check in on a few of the events downtown."

"Events?"

"There's a pie-baking contest," I explained.

"Well, that sounds … fun," Landon said, smirking. "Do you want to meet up for lunch?"

"I thought you had to work on the bank robbery?"

"I do. That doesn't mean I don't have time for lunch – especially if I get to spend some quality time with you."

"I'm sure I can make time for lunch," I said.

"Good. I'll pick up food and bring it to you. I'll text you when I'm coming."

"Okay."

"Oh, you're so domestic," Thistle said, purposely needling me. "It's like watching a 1950s sitcom."

"Leave them alone," Aunt Tillie instructed. "I think they're cute."

"Since when?" Mom asked.

"Since I found out Lila was back in town and her mission was to make Bay's life miserable," Aunt Tillie said.

Next to me, Nick stiffened. "Lila is back in town? How does she look?"

"She is back in town," I said. "She looks hideous."

"Well, that's disappointing. I heard she held up pretty well."

"I think the whole town thinks that's disappointing," Aunt Tillie said. "I wouldn't worry about her. I'll take care of Lila."

"What is that supposed to mean?" Mom asked.

"Don't worry about it," Aunt Tillie said. "Focus on your breakfast and … I don't know … do some dishes or something."

Mom's eyes flashed. "Excuse me?"

"She wants you to mind your own business," Thistle said.

"I'm liking you today," Aunt Tillie said, smiling at Thistle. When Thistle returned the smile, my heart dropped. It was as if the Joker and Penguin were joining up to destroy Gotham. This couldn't be good. I didn't get a chance to comment on the new development, though, because the sound of someone clearing his throat at the dining room door caught everyone's attention.

Chief Terry stood there, his eyes serious as he studied the room.

"Oh, Terry, you're here," Mom said, getting to her feet. "I wasn't sure you were coming. Do you want breakfast? You can sit next to me."

"There's no room next to you," Marnie said. "He can sit next to me."

My mother and aunts have been vying to be the center of Chief Terry's world for as long as I can remember. He seems to like the attention, and goes out of his way not to show one of them more favor than the other. I had no idea what would happen if he ever gave in and actually tried to date one of them. I think a black hole would open up in our kitchen and swallow us whole.

"I would love breakfast," Chief Terry said. "I don't have time, though. Actually, I came here to see if Landon would make a trip out to the Dandridge with me."

"Sure," Landon said, getting to his feet. "Why are we going out to the Dandridge?"

Chief Terry was pale, and his eyes were dark. "We got an anonymous call this morning," he said. "Someone gave us a lead on the robber from yesterday."

"And you think he's out at the Dandridge?" Clove asked, alarmed. "Does that mean Sam is in danger?"

"No, Clove," Chief Terry said carefully. "That means Sam is the suspect."

NINE

"What?" Clove's dark eyes were wide as she shakily got to her feet. "Are you joking? You think Sam is a bank robber?"

"Clove, we don't know anything yet," Chief Terry said. "Don't fly off the handle. I just want Landon to go question him with me."

Clove threw her napkin down on the table. "You're going after Sam because you've always hated him," she said. "Admit it!"

"Clove, you know that's not true," Chief Terry said.

"Of course it's true," Clove said. "Sam wasn't even in town yesterday."

I stirred. "Yes, he was."

Clove furrowed her brow. "No, he wasn't. He said he was hanging out at the Dandridge all day."

I glanced at Landon, unsure.

"What do you know?" Landon asked gently.

"He stopped in the newspaper office right before lunch," I said. "He wanted to talk about writing an article on the Dandridge next week."

"How long was he in the office?" Chief Terry asked.

"Not long," I replied. "Ten minutes tops."

"Where did he go afterward?"

"I'm not sure," I said. "I was under the impression he was going back home. He didn't say either way, though."

"What did you do?" Chief Terry asked.

"I walked down to Hypnotic."

"Why didn't you tell me you saw him?" Clove challenged. "Why are you bringing this up only now?"

Was she accusing me of making this up? "I honestly forgot," I said. "I got distracted by Lila and all the revenge talk. I didn't think it was a big deal."

"So, that was before the bank robbery," Landon said, rubbing his chin. "How long were you in Hypnotic?"

"About forty-five minutes."

"That gives him the opportunity," Chief Terry said.

"There were a lot of people downtown yesterday," Clove protested.

"Clove, I'm not saying he's guilty," Chief Terry said. "I just want to talk to him."

Clove was so angry her hands shook as she gripped them in front of her. "You've been looking for a reason to turn on him," she said, her eyes filling with tears. "You've finally got it."

She stormed toward the kitchen door.

"I hope you're happy."

YOU DIDN'T HAVE to come with us," Landon said, shifting his head so he could study me in the back seat of Chief Terry's Land Rover. "I'm sure Clove will have calmed down by the time we get out there."

"I'm not sure that's true," I said. "Did you see her face?"

"She was upset," Landon said. "I don't see how she can blame you."

"Well, she does," I said, staring out the window and focusing on the winding country road that led to the Dandridge. "You heard her. She thinks I made up seeing Sam at the newspaper office yesterday."

"I don't think she was saying that, Bay," Chief Terry said. "I think she was just hoping there was a misunderstanding. She can't possibly think you would make up a story because you dislike Sam."

"I don't dislike Sam," I said. "I ... ." Was that the truth? Did I like

Sam? Did I hate him? I wanted to like him because Clove liked him. Still, Sam's arrival in our lives had been mired in subterfuge and lies. I couldn't help but be leery.

"What are you thinking?" Landon asked.

"I'm trying to decide whether I dislike Sam."

"I know the feeling," Landon said. "I want to dislike the guy, but I can't help but feel he really cares about Clove. I hope he hasn't snowed us, because if he's guilty I think Clove is going to be in for a world of hurt."

"Whether he's guilty or not, just the suspicion is hurting Clove," I said.

When Chief Terry pulled into the gravel parking lot adjacent to the Dandridge, I wasn't surprised to see Clove's car already there. It was parked at an angle, as though she couldn't bother to spare the time to pull in completely.

"You don't think they ran, do you?" Chief Terry asked, worried.

"No matter how upset she is, Clove wouldn't just pick up and leave," I said.

"And if Sam is innocent, he has no reason to run," Landon said. He hopped out of the Land Rover and opened my door. We stood next to each other as he grabbed my hand and leaned in. "It's going to be okay. Clove is just upset," he said softly.

"I hope so," I said. "I can't ... she's always going through crap with men. It's as if she has abysmal taste, and yet she was the one who was always desperate to find someone."

Landon ran his hand down the back of my hair, smoothing it. "Clove is tougher than she looks."

"Is she?"

Landon shrugged helplessly. "In your family, she has to be. Come on. Let's get this over with."

Sam opened the door before Chief Terry could knock, and his face was a mask of anger and concern when he met my gaze. "I suppose you're here to ask whether I'm a bank robber."

"We need to ask a few questions," Chief Terry said. "Can we come in?"

Sam's eyes were still on me. "Are you here in an official capacity?"

"I'm here because of Clove," I said.

"Do you think I'm a bank robber and Chief Terry and your boyfriend are going to drag me away in cuffs?"

I honestly had no idea. "I think Clove is upset, and I'm here to help her."

Sam pushed the door open and ushered us inside. "Well, come on in."

The Dandridge looked drastically different than it had weeks before. The walls were painted, and the furniture was new, and the stained-glass windows leading up the spire to the lighthouse were truly breathtaking. I could see why Clove was spending so much time here.

"He's innocent," Clove screeched when she caught sight of us.

"Sit down, Clove," Landon instructed. "You're going to pass out if your face gets any redder. We're not here to arrest Sam. We only want to ask him some questions."

"It's all right, Clove," Sam said, sending her a reassuring smile. "Sit down. I'm not a bank robber, so everything is going to be fine."

"Of course you're not a bank robber," Clove said, throwing herself on Sam's couch dramatically. "Don't be ridiculous."

Sam shot Landon and Chief Terry an apologetic look. "She's been a little worked up since she got here."

"And how long ago was that?" Landon asked.

"About ten minutes."

That was plenty of time to run, I told myself. If he was guilty, he would have run.

"How many speeding laws did you break to get here that quickly, Clove?" Landon asked.

"Oh, arrest me," Clove said, holding her wrists out. "I'm obviously a threat to the community."

Landon rubbed the heel of his hand against his forehead. "Why don't we start with some simple questions, okay?"

Sam nodded as he sat down next to Clove. He drew her hand into his and waited. I realized he was trying to reassure her even though he was the one being questioned.

"Were you in town yesterday?" Chief Terry asked.

"I think you already know the answer to that," Sam said, jutting his chin in my direction. "Hasn't Bay already told you that I was in the newspaper office?"

"She has," Chief Terry conceded. "I need to hear it from you, though."

"I was in town for about forty-five minutes," Sam said. "I left here a little before noon and went straight to the newspaper office. I figured Bay would be having lunch with Clove and Thistle at Hypnotic, and I didn't want to miss her."

"What did you do after that?"

"I went to the hardware store because I needed some brackets to put up a shelf."

"Do you have a receipt?"

Sam paused. "I should have," he said. "There's a bag on the kitchen counter. It should be in there. I haven't taken anything out of it yet."

Landon started moving through the room. "This way?"

Sam nodded.

"I'll be back in a second."

Chief Terry kept his eyes trained on Sam. "Did you do anything else in town?"

"Like rob a bank?" Clove spat.

My heart rolled painfully. She was hanging on by a thread.

"No," Sam said. "I got the brackets and came back here. I did some gardening after that, and no I don't have a witness. Then I had a quick dinner here and spent the night at the guesthouse with all of them. I came back here first thing this morning."

Chief Terry glanced at me for confirmation, and I nodded.

"Why do you believe her?" Clove asked. "Why not ask me?"

"Because he's afraid you're going to fly off the handle and scratch his eyes out," Sam said. "It's okay. Just … breathe."

Landon returned from the kitchen with a slip of paper in his hand.

"Does it have a timestamp?" Chief Terry asked.

"Yeah," Landon said. "It says 12:25 p.m."

"That doesn't exactly clear him," Chief Terry said. "The robbery happened right before one."

"I know," Landon said. "We can't take the word of an anonymous caller, though. We don't have any evidence."

"Then why are you here?"

"To ask questions," Landon said. "We're not here to accuse anyone."

"Whatever," Clove mumbled.

"Believe it or not, Clove, I'm hoping we can clear Sam and I'm hoping we can do it quickly," Landon said. "I don't want you to be miserable, and I certainly don't want Bay to be miserable. As long as you're upset, she's going to be upset."

"She's not upset," Clove said. "She's been looking for a reason to turn on Sam since she met him."

"That's not fair, Clove," I said. "You know very well I have a reason to be … wary … where Sam is concerned."

"He apologized for lying when he first came to town," Clove said. "You know why he did it. He only wanted to get to know us before telling us the truth."

"He still lied," I said.

"Oh, like you've never lied," Clove said.

I pressed my lips together and pushed a strand of my hair behind my ear, trying to calm myself. "I don't know what you want me to say."

"I want you to say that you believe him," Clove said.

I met her challenging gaze. "I want to believe him."

"Let's try to stay on topic," Landon said. "Sam, do you own a gun?"

Sam shook his head.

"Not even a hunting rifle?"

"No."

"A handgun?"

"He already answered that!" Clove's eyes practically glowed.

"Let's try something," Chief Terry said, trying to head off a potential showdown. "Sam, stand up."

"Why?"

"Just do it."

Sam did as instructed.

"Now, Bay, you were up close and personal with the robber," Chief Terry said. "Was he the same size as Sam?"

I realized what he was doing. I took a step forward and studied Sam carefully. "I don't know," I said finally. "It all happened so fast, and he was coming at me."

"Move toward her," Chief Terry said.

Sam took two quick steps in my direction and then ceased his forward momentum before he got too close.

"I think Sam is smaller," I said. "Not by a lot, but by about two inches. He looks thinner, too."

"How sure are you?" Landon asked.

That was a very good question. "Fifty percent."

"Those aren't great odds, Bay," Landon said. "You're saying the robber may or may not be the same size as Sam."

"What do you want from me? I'm doing the best I can."

Landon held up his hand. "I'm not saying you're not," he said. "I just … I need you to really think about this."

"I am."

"Okay," Landon said. "Give it some thought."

Chief Terry's phone chimed with an incoming call, and he pulled it from his pocket and moved to a spot behind the couch to take it. While he was busy, Landon focused on Sam.

"We're not going to arrest you," Landon said. "We have no evidence. I need you to figure out whether anyone would try to point the finger at you for some reason."

"I haven't been in town long enough to make enemies," Sam said.

"What about out of town?"

Sam shrugged. "I'll think about it."

"Do that," Landon said. "Also, I have to say this – and I'm sorry – it would be better if you didn't leave town."

"I have no intention of leaving," Sam said.

"Good."

Chief Terry put his phone back in his pocket. His face was grave when he rejoined us. "This just got worse," he said.

"Who was that?"

"The hospital. Amy Madison succumbed to her injuries this morning. She never regained consciousness."

My hand flew to my mouth. "Oh, no."

"So, this just went from a robbery to a murder," Landon said. "Great."

I could think of another word for it.

TEN

"I heard there was some excitement yesterday."

I'd forgotten to shut my office door when I got to The Whistler about a half hour before. I didn't realize the owner, Brian Kelly, was in the building. That was a mistake I was going to regret.

"The bank robbery? Yeah."

"How are we going to deal with that given all of the town anniversary celebrations?"

Brian didn't often care about the daily operations of The Whistler. He handled the advertising, and he cared about making money, but he'd opted to ignore the content in recent months.

"I don't know," I replied honestly. "We can't ignore it."

"Well, just write up a brief and put it on page two," Brian said. "It's a bank robbery. It would barely be news in the city."

He obviously hadn't heard the new development. "The teller who was shot, Amy Madison, she died this morning."

Brian's eyes widened. "How do you know that?"

That was a touchy subject, and I wasn't sure how much to tell Brian. I've never trusted him, and the only reason I bothered to show him any respect was because I'd adored his late grandfather, William. When William died, he'd left a stipulation in his will that whoever took over day-to-day operations of the newspaper had to keep me on as editor. Brian didn't like it, mostly because he wanted to sell the newspaper and that was out of the question, but he'd taken to letting me do pretty much whatever I wanted.

"Chief Terry told me this morning," I said finally.

"Oh, was he at the inn for breakfast?"

Brian rented a room at The Overlook for months following his relocation to Hemlock Cove. A few weeks ago, he'd purchased a house on the outskirts of town. Having him out of my family's hair was a relief.

"He came out during breakfast," I said. That wasn't technically a lie. I was just leaving Sam's part of my morning out of the discussion. Brian was responsible for initially bringing Sam to town. They'd been friendly with one another, but I had no idea whether that friendship continued. I figured it was Sam's job to tell Brian the truth if he wanted him to know.

"Well, that changes things," Brian said. "Do what you think is best. Maybe we can put the anniversary celebration above the fold, and put the murder below. That way it will still be on the front page."

That didn't seem very respectful to Amy. "We have a few days before we have to decide on anything," I said. "Maybe we'll be lucky and this will be solved quickly."

"That would be nice," Brian said. "Okay, well, I trust you have it all under control. I have to go down to the pie-baking contest."

I glanced up at him, surprised. "Really?"

"I'm one of the celebrity judges," Brian said, winking. "I have to be there for all the early rounds, so it's going to be an all-day extravaganza."

"Well, have fun," I said. "You should know my mother is entering a pie. Twila and Marnie are, too. It's supposed to be extremely competitive."

"That sounds fun," Brian said. "What about Aunt Tillie? She's not entering a pie, is she?"

Brian was terrified of my persnickety aunt – and for good reason. She'd threatened to curse him so many times I'd lost count. "Aunt

Tillie doesn't bake. Besides, I think she's spending the day with Thistle."

Brian arched an eyebrow. "Why? Is the world coming to an end?"

That was an apt question. "I think they're just ... brewing up some trouble."

"Well, that's terrifying," Brian said. "I'll see you later."

Once he was gone, Edith popped into view. "He just talks, and talks, and talks."

I hadn't seen Brian in almost a week, so I found that statement funny. "What's up with you?" I asked. "You haven't seen any new ghosts around, have you?"

"I've been here," Edith said. "You know I don't like leaving unless I absolutely have to. Why? Who died?"

"One of the tellers at the bank was shot during a robbery yesterday," I said. "She died this morning."

"That's terrible," Edith said. "You know, in my day, things like that just didn't happen."

I made a face. "Aren't you convinced someone poisoned your meal and that's why you're dead?"

"I think your Aunt Tillie did it," Edith said. "There's a difference."

Despite the rumors about Aunt Tillie, I had a hard time believing she would poison Edith. Curse her? Sure. Poison her? Probably not. Edith wasn't enough of a concern in Aunt Tillie's life to warrant poisoning. "Well, we'll just have to agree to disagree on that one. I need you to keep your eyes open, though. If you see a new ghost, I need to hear about it."

"Do you think the teller is going to come back?"

"Her name is Amy Madison," I said. "I think there's a good chance she'll show up. Her death was quick and traumatizing. I have no way of knowing for sure, but I have a feeling we'll be seeing her again."

"Okay," Edith said, shrugging. "I'll be on the lookout. I actually plan on venturing out a little more than usual over the next few days."

"Why?"

"A lot of people are back in town," Edith said. "I might know some of them. I want to see how badly they've aged."

Well, that figured. "Okay. Have fun."

AFTER ABOUT TWO hours alone with my laptop, I decided to see what was happening downtown. When I left the newspaper offices, I wasn't surprised to see the town square brimming with people. The festival was still undergoing final touches, but most of the visitors seemed happy to mill about and catch up with one another.

I waved at a few friendly faces and made my way to the red tent where the pie contest was in full swing. The judges, Brian among them, sat at a rectangular table at the center of the tent. I knew Chief Terry was supposed to be one of the judges, but I wasn't surprised to see his chair filled by the librarian, Phyllis Bristow, instead.

"This is exciting, isn't it?" Mom said, appearing at my side and grabbing my elbow. "They've already made the first cut. It's down to five pies."

"I'm assuming yours is one of them," I said.

"Of course it is."

Despite Mom's enthusiasm, I had trouble garnering the energy to get excited about pies given Clove's current angst. "Have you seen Clove?"

Mom sobered, but only marginally. "Not since she stormed out this morning. I thought she was with you."

"She was out at the Dandridge when we got there," I said.

"Was Sam arrested?"

"No. They don't have any evidence. He was just warned to stay in town."

"Do you think he's guilty?"

"I have no idea," I said. "I want to believe he's innocent, because if he's not Clove is going to be devastated. I just don't know."

"I understand why you're suspicious about Sam," Mom said. "The truth is, though, other than his initial lie, he's been forthcoming with us. He hasn't done anything that would make us think that he's out to get us."

"He still lied."

"And we lie every day," Mom said. "We don't volunteer who we are or what we can do to people unless we trust them. You seem to forget, Sam didn't know he could trust us then any more than we know we can trust him now.

"Sooner or later, you just have to decide whether you're going to trust someone," she continued. "So, the question is: Do you trust him?"

"I don't know."

"Until you do, nothing is going to be settled," Mom said. "You have to understand that Clove trusts him."

"Clove should trust me, too," I shot back. "She should know I wouldn't make something up just to mess with Sam."

"She doesn't think you made anything up," Mom said. "She's searching for a way to vindicate Sam. Don't take everything so personally."

"I'm not taking things personally."

"Oh, please," Mom said, waving off my argument. "You've always taken things personally. It's in your nature. You can't help yourself. You're very sensitive sometimes."

"I am not sensitive."

"That's not necessarily a bad thing," Mom said. "Although, in this case, I do think it's a bad thing. You've always worried what other people think about you. Can't you just let that go?"

"Clove isn't just my cousin, she's one of my best friends," I said. "How do I let that go?"

"It's not just Clove, though. You've also gotten yourself worked up because Lila Stevens is back in town. Don't think I don't know what Aunt Tillie and Thistle are conspiring about. They're going to do something horrible, and they're going to do it because they don't think you'll stand up for yourself."

The conversation was getting uncomfortable. "I stand up for myself."

"You do now," Mom agreed. "You didn't as a child, though, and I'm worried that you're going to regress because of Lila. I hope you don't."

"I'm not going to regress."

"Good," Mom said, patting my arm. "Make sure you don't. Now, I need to go make sure your aunts aren't trying to sway the judges."

"Did they make the final five pies, too?"

"Of course they did," Mom said. "They're excellent bakers. They're just not as good as I am."

"Well, good luck," I said. "I'm sure you'll win."

"I'm sure I will, too."

Mom disappeared into the crowd, leaving me alone with my thoughts. Part of me hoped she'd win. She was my mother, after all. The other part of me hoped no one from my family would win, because if one of them was named victor the other two were going to be impossible to deal with.

After watching the tasting for a few moments, I let my eyes wander. That's when I found an ethereal form loitering in front of the bank. Her blonde hair was cropped short above her shoulders, and her brown eyes were busily scanning the crowd. She gestured toward people a few times. I couldn't hear her voice, but I had a feeling I knew what was happening. Amy Madison might have died, but her soul was lingering – and it was confused.

I subtly escaped from the shadow of the tent and walked toward the bank. Even though I was excited to see the teller, I didn't want to draw attention to myself, so I forced my pace to remain even. Thankfully for me, the bulk of the town's attention – visitors and residents alike – was focused inside the tent. I could hear some squawking, and without turning around I knew Marnie and Mom were going at each other. I recognized their voices, even if I couldn't make out the words.

When I got to Amy, her face was awash with misery.

"Hi," I said, keeping my voice low.

Amy's eyes widened when she realized I was talking to her. "You can see me?"

I nodded.

"How? Aren't I dead?"

"You died this morning," I said. "I can just … see things sometimes."

"People always said there was something different about you," Amy said. "I guess they were right."

"In some ways," I said. "In other ways, they have no idea what they're talking about."

"Well, I guess it doesn't matter now," Amy said. "I'm dead. It's not like I can tell anyone except you that you can talk to ghosts."

I forced a small smile for her benefit. "I suppose."

"What happens to me now?" Amy asked. "Am I stuck here forever?"

"It depends," I said. "You have a choice in the matter. If you want to stay, you can stay. If you want to go, you have to make the choice to let go."

"Does everyone who dies become a ghost?"

"No. In the grand scheme of things, the number of people who stay behind is generally pretty small."

"Why am I here?"

"I'm guessing you're here until they find whoever killed you," I said. I glanced over my shoulder to make certain we weren't drawing attention and then continued. "What do you remember about the robbery?"

"Not much," Amy said, shrugging. "It happened really fast. I was talking to Mrs. Donahue about her free calendar. She claimed she never got it this year, but I knew she did. She just likes to hoard them. I have no idea why. It's summer, for crying out loud. I have no idea why she would need one now.

"Anyway, someone came in through the front door," she continued. "He had a gun in his hand, and he was wearing all black, including one of those knit masks."

"You're sure it was a man, though?"

"I am. You can just tell. He had broad shoulders and a narrow waist. He had no hips, and he was wearing those big, clunky combat boots. No woman would ever wear those."

She had a point. "Did you recognize his voice?"

"I ... I don't know. I was afraid of the gun. It just sounded like a voice. I don't think I recognized it."

"Okay," I said, briefly considering my options. "If you want to move this along, you might consider going to all of the anniversary events and listening to people as they talk. You might be able to identify who killed you."

"I guess," Amy said. "A fair doesn't sound like much fun if you can't eat elephant ears or ride the roller-coaster."

"I know," I said, sympathy rolling over me. "I just ... there's not much else for you to do."

"I guess," Amy said. "There's no time like the present to start, right? I'll go now."

"Come out to the inn and find me if you discover anything," I said.

Amy merely nodded in response. When I turned my attention back to the fair, I was stunned to find Lila standing two feet behind me. Her green eyes were wide – and vicious – and she looked as though she had just won the lottery.

"Oh, this is priceless," she said.

ELEVEN

"Lila," I said, squaring my shoulders. "Why are you here? I thought you liked to be the center of attention. Shouldn't you be sharing your ... pie ... with the rest of the town?"

"Oh, don't do that," Lila said. "Don't try to distract me. I know what I just heard."

"They say dogs can hear things other people can't," I said, giving in to my snarky side. My mother was right. Cowering in front of Lila wasn't going to get me anywhere. She was going to go after me no matter what. Hiding wasn't going to stop that.

"You were talking to yourself again," Lila crowed. "You still do that. You still hang out with your imaginary friends. That is just so ... pathetic."

"Plenty of people talk to themselves," I said.

"You're not even going to deny it?"

I didn't see the point. "No. I was just running through a list of things to do today."

"No, you were telling your imaginary friend to come out to the inn to see you," Lila said. "I heard you. I can't wait to tell your FBI boyfriend about it, by the way. I know he was standing up for you yesterday, but that's only because he has no idea what kind of loser you really are."

"Stay away from Landon," I warned.

"Are you afraid of a little competition?"

"You're not my competition," I said. "You're not anything to me."

"Then why do you look so worried?"

Did I look worried? Probably. I wasn't worried about Lila going after Landon, though. Well, mostly. My life was full of enough worries to make Lila a distant concern. "You know what, Lila? I think you should do whatever it is you want to do. If you want to tell Landon what you heard, go right ahead. I'm sure he's at the police station with Chief Terry right now."

"How do you know?"

"Because Chief Terry came to the inn to get him this morning," I said. "The teller from the bank died. They're now working on a murder, not just a bank robbery. That makes their job more difficult."

"Landon is staying at your inn for the anniversary celebration? That's interesting."

"He's not staying at the inn," I said smugly. "He stays at the guesthouse with me."

Lila pursed her lips. "Do you really expect me to believe that?"

"I don't care what you believe," I said. "It's the truth. If you want to go after him, knock yourself out. You're not his type. Trust me."

"Because you're his type?"

"Because I trust him," I said, realizing I believed the words. Landon initially walked away when he found out what we were, but since he returned, he'd accepted every one of the strange things he'd witnessed. There was nothing Lila could do to entice him. "So go and get him," I said. "Just don't come crying to me when it blows up in your face."

"You're boastful, but I don't think you're truthful," Lila said. "I'm going to call your bluff."

I watched as she smoothed her hair and started down the street. When I saw Chief Terry and Landon standing in the parking lot next to the police station a block down, I realized she was heading in their direction. I couldn't stop myself from following her.

Landon and Chief Terry were entrenched in a serious conversation as Lila approached.

"Well, there you are," Lila said, smiling broadly at Landon. "I wondered where you'd been hiding yourself."

Landon shifted uncomfortably. "Ms. Stevens."

"I told you to call me Lila."

"Is there anything you need, Ms. Stevens?" Landon asked. His gaze was focused on Lila, and I didn't think he knew I was trailing her.

"I just wanted to see you," Lila cooed. "Our brief encounter yesterday only whetted my appetite. I thought maybe we could get some lunch. I mean, it's not every day you get to meet a real, live FBI agent. Especially one as ... charming ... as you."

"I already have lunch plans," Landon said, turning his attention back to Chief Terry.

Lila faltered. "But ... ." She clearly wasn't used to being turned down. "I'll pay."

Landon was nonplussed. "I'm good. Thanks." He finally shifted his gaze, and when his eyes landed on me they were hard to read. "Here comes my lunch date now."

Lila glanced over her shoulder, scowling when she saw me standing a few feet away. "Oh, good grief! You've got to be kidding me. You're going to lunch with her? You know she's a freak, right?"

"I guess it's good I like my women freaky," Landon said. "Do you want to eat with us, Terry? We still have a few things to discuss, and I'd rather not work late tonight if I can help it."

"Um ... sure," Chief Terry said.

Landon dodged around Lila, his gaze focused on me. "Are you hungry, Bay?"

"Sure."

I wasn't sure what was happening, but whatever it was, Lila didn't like it. "You realize she was just standing in front of the bank talking to herself, right?"

Landon stilled. "So? I talk to myself all the time."

"She was telling her imaginary friend to come and visit her at the inn," Lila said. "You don't find that ... odd?"

"No," Landon said. "I like it." He held his hand out to me. "Come on. You didn't get to finish your breakfast this morning. I'll buy you a big lunch."

I took his hand wordlessly.

"W-what is going on here?" Lila asked, her gaze bouncing between Landon and me. "I just told you that your friend there is talking to herself in public. I invited you to lunch. I even offered to pay. You're still taking her to lunch?"

Landon refused to turn around as he dragged me across the street. "Yup."

"**DO YOU** want to tell me what all of that was about?" Landon asked once we were settled at the diner ten minutes later.

"She's evil."

"Other than that."

"Amy Madison was in front of the bank," I said. "I talked to her for a few minutes, and Lila overheard the end of the conversation. She was practically salivating, she was so excited to tell you."

"Yeah, I figured that out myself," Landon said, leaning back in his chair and playing with the straw wrapper in front of him. "Why was Lila inviting me to lunch?"

"Because she wants you," I said.

"Did she tell you that?"

"Yes."

Landon glanced at Chief Terry. "What do you think about Lila?"

"I think Bay is right," he replied. "I think she's evil. She's always been a menace."

"See, the problem is, I don't think she really wants me," Landon said. "I just think she wants to beat Bay. What else happened?"

"I just told you."

"There has to be something I'm missing," Landon said. "I know I was never a teenage girl, but it can't be normal to hold a grudge for this long."

"I don't know what you want me to say," I said. "She's always hated me."

"Just because you were different?"

"In a small town, that's enough," Chief Terry said, trying to help me. "There aren't a lot of people to begin with, and you either fit in or you get pecked to death by the other chickens."

"She's just so ... overt," Landon said. "There's something off about her."

"I told you, she's ... ."

"Evil. I got it." Landon reached over and cupped my hand. "You know you don't have anything to worry about, right?"

"That's what I told her."

"But then you followed her," Landon said.

"I ... ." Well, crap. How do I explain that? "I just wanted to see what she would do."

Landon studied me for a moment. "She's not going to do anything," he said. "I won't let her. Don't get all ... worked up."

"I'm not worked up."

"You look worked up."

"Well, I'm not."

"You do look a little worked up," Chief Terry said. "Lila Stevens is not worth your time or your worry. You were always ten times the kid she was."

"I think you're just saying that because you like to flirt with my mother and aunts," I teased.

Chief Terry's face was serious. "I'm saying that because you were always a good kid," he said. "You rarely caused problems, and you were always eager to help. Lila was an entitled brat as a kid, and her mother didn't do her any favors by letting her grow into an entitled adult."

"That's nice. Thank you."

"Like it or not, I think having Aunt Tillie in your house was good for you guys as kids," Chief Terry said. "You were never allowed to get too big for your britches."

Actually, Aunt Tillie often cursed us by making our pants too small to wear. That saying really had no basis in our household, but I let it go. "I know I should ignore Lila," I said. "Everyone keeps telling me that, but it's as though she always seeks me out. It's impossible to ignore her."

"Then take her down," Landon said.

My eyebrows flew up. "What?"

"You have two people in your life who are chomping at the bit to go after her," Landon said. "Why don't you let them? In fact, why don't you join them?"

"Don't you think that's a little immature?"

"I think it's massively immature," Landon said. "I also think that's the only thing Lila is going to respond to. She's going to keep going after you as long as you let her. So stop letting her."

I swiveled to Chief Terry. "Is that what you think, too?"

"I think you've put up with enough," Chief Terry said. "You're not the same scared girl you were back then. You're not terrified all the time. You're not hiding. You have your family. You have Aunt Tillie. Heck, you have the long-haired FBI agent. They're all willing to back you up. You should let them."

"There is nothing wrong with my hair," Landon said, running his fingers through his black locks. "I have to keep it long in case I get an undercover assignment."

That was always his excuse, but I think he liked his hair long. "Your hair is beautiful. Don't ever cut it."

"See," Landon said, tilting his chin obstinately in Chief Terry's direction. "She knows quality when she sees it."

Chief Terry snorted. "You two are cute. If you had told me a year ago I would be in favor of this relationship I would have called you a filthy liar. Now, though, I have to say you two seem like a good match. He even knows when to let Aunt Tillie off her leash."

"I'm not sure I want to do that," I said. "I need to give it some thought."

"Do what you want," Landon said. "We're behind you. I just don't want to sit here and watch you be miserable. Things are going to be tough enough over the next few days if we can't find a way to clear Sam. You shouldn't let Lila make things worse. This is your town, too. Put your foot down."

His words warmed me. "I'll give it some thought."

"Do that," Landon said. "I don't want this Lila thing to get away from us. The more you let her push you around, the more desperate she's going to get where I'm concerned. She doesn't want me because of me, she wants me because of you. You're the one who is going to have to handle it."

"What is she going to have to handle?"

I froze when I heard the voice, turning quickly to find my father standing behind me. "Dad! What are you doing here?"

"Looking for you, actually," he said. "I checked the newspaper office and it was empty. You weren't at the pie contest. The secretary at the police station said she thought you were here. She was right."

Chief Terry shifted uncomfortably next to me. Since my father left Hemlock Cove when I was a child, returning only recently to open his own inn with Clove and Thistle's fathers, there was an unspoken rivalry between the two men. Chief Terry filled in when my father wasn't there, and Dad didn't appreciate his constant presence in my life now.

"Did you need something?" I asked.

"I wanted to invite you to dinner tonight," Dad said. "We're having a big feast. I'm sure you'll be busy at The Overlook with your mother this week, but I didn't think one meal would be cause for concern." He glanced at Landon. "Since you're in town, you're obviously invited, too."

"Thanks for the invitation," Landon said. "It's up to Bay, though."

Dad focused on me. "What do you say? Can you wrangle up your cousins for a nice dinner? We'd kind of like to show you off to our guests."

I felt trapped. "Sure. I think we can work something out."

Unfortunately, I had a feeling that "something" was going to be a big fight between the women in my family.

TWELVE

"This is an absolutely terrible idea," Thistle said, leaning forward in the back seat of Landon's Explorer so she could pinch me. "Terrible!"

"He trapped me," I said, jerking my arm away. "He approached me in public. What else was I supposed to do?"

"Tell him no."

"Oh, please, you wouldn't have told your father no."

"Yes, I would."

"You're lying."

"I'm going to beat the crap out of you later," Thistle said, studying the front of the Dragonfly Inn as Landon parked. "This is just so … stupid."

Since their return to town, our fathers had made several attempts to spend time with us. Most of those attempts involved food. I think they were under the misguided notion that we wouldn't embarrass ourselves in front of other people. They obviously didn't know us.

"It's one meal," I said. "What could possibly go wrong?"

"Oh, great, you just jinxed us," Thistle said. "Now we're going to go down with the ship."

"What ship?"

AMANDA M. LEE

Thistle narrowed her eyes. "Don't you think the people on the Titanic thought it was just one boat ride?"

She was clearly losing her mind. I met Marcus' steady gaze. "It's your job to make sure she doesn't do anything ... bad."

"Oh, sure, task me with the impossible," Marcus grumbled.

"What did you just say?"

"I said that you're the light of my life," Marcus said. "Let's just get this over with." He pushed open the back door and hopped out, pulling Thistle after him. "Please try not to make a scene," he said before giving her a quick kiss.

"I don't make scenes."

"Of course not," I said. "You would never make a scene."

"You're dead to me," Thistle snapped.

Landon led the way up the front steps of the Dragonfly. "At least Clove isn't here," he said. "If she were here we'd definitely be dealing with a scene."

"Speaking of Clove, have you seen her today?" I asked Thistle.

"She didn't come to work," Thistle said. "She texted me to say she was busy and I was on my own. When I tried to call her back, the phone went directly to voicemail. I think she's sending us a message."

"I think the message is that she hates us," I said, rubbing my forehead.

Landon slipped an arm around my waist. "She doesn't hate you. She's just upset."

"She hates me."

"You're having a rough week," Landon said, smiling down at me. "First your high school nemesis comes back and fawns all over me because I'm so hot, and now Clove hates you because you can't exonerate Sam. You really are a terrible person."

I scowled at him. "You're not helping."

"I know." He gave me a soft kiss. "Let's get this over with. I'd rather sit through ten dinners with Aunt Tillie and her combat helmet than one with your father."

"That's because Uncle Jack thinks you've always got your hand up Bay's shirt," Thistle teased, referencing an unfortunate hammock incident from a few weeks ago. "I think he wants to cut all your fingers off."

"I forgot about that," Landon said, his face blank. "Wasn't that the same weekend you shared a bed with Aunt Tillie and Marcus?"

Thistle glared at him. "You promised never to bring that up again."

"I did no such thing."

"Bay promised."

"I'm not Bay," Landon said.

I pinched his side. "Do you really want to start a fight now?"

"No," Landon conceded, holding up his hands. "I'd rather put up a united front than split apart. Can we table all fights until we get back to the guesthouse?"

"Fine," Thistle said, pushing in front of him and opening the door. "When we get back home tonight, though, I'm going nuts."

"I can't wait."

The four of us filed into the inn to find the one thing that could break our truce: Sam and Clove.

"Uh-oh," I muttered.

"I think I need a drink," Landon said.

"I DIDN'T KNOW you guys were going to be here," Clove said, her eyes restless as they bounced around the room. "I would have declined the invitation had I known you would be visiting this establishment as well."

Well, that was interesting. Clove had somehow turned into a robot.

"Are you talking like that for a reason?" Thistle asked.

"I have no idea what you mean." Clove's tone was icy, her words clipped.

"She's kind of ... tired," Sam said by way of apology. "I tried to make her take a nap this afternoon, but she was kind of ... ."

"Oh, we know what she was," Thistle said. She shifted uncomfortably. "How are you?"

"I'm fine," Sam said. "I got a lot of gardening done today."

"When he wasn't being questioned by cops for a crime he didn't commit," Clove seethed.

"Knock it off, Clove," Landon warned.

"You knock it off," Clove shot back.

"I'm not doing anything."

"You're being ... you."

"I seriously need a drink," Landon said.

I rubbed his back. He wasn't the only one. "Clove, if you want to talk about this, maybe we should go outside."

"I don't want to talk to you," Clove said. "You're the one who told the police that Sam is a bank robber."

"I did no such thing!"

"I was there. I witnessed it."

"I was there, too," Landon said. "She didn't do anything of the sort. Stop attacking Bay because you're upset. She's not your enemy."

"Oh, you always take her side." I had never seen Clove this snide.

"I am taking her side," Landon said. "She's had a long day. She's been worried about you. Why don't you ask Sam whether he thinks Bay said he was the robber."

"I've already told her that's not what she said," Sam said, pinching the bridge of his nose. "She won't listen. She's been all over the place all day. I'm not sure what to do. I was stunned when she came outside and told me we were coming to dinner here."

"How did you even know about the dinner?" I asked. "We left a note for you at the guesthouse, but you haven't been back all day. You're not picking up your phone either."

"I don't live at the guesthouse anymore," Clove said.

"Since when?"

"Since my family turned on me and cast me out."

If I didn't know better, I would think Clove had been into Aunt Tillie's wine stash. "We cast you out?"

"I can't even look at you," Clove said, tilting her chin up and focusing on the chandelier in the middle of the lobby. "It hurts too much. You're officially dead to me."

Apparently I was dead to the better part of my family tonight.

"Oh, good grief," Thistle said. "Have you been watching *Gone With the Wind* or something? You're acting like a crazy person."

"You're crazy."

"You're the craziest."

"All of you shut up right now." We jerked our heads when Uncle Teddy, Thistle's father, poked his head into the room. "We can hear you in the dining room."

"Our voices do carry," Thistle said, nonplussed. "I blame our mothers."

"I blame your mothers, too," Teddy said. "They're obviously the ones who taught you that it's okay to act this way in public."

I shot him a dirty look. "Don't you dare say anything bad about our mothers."

Teddy was taken aback. "I'm sorry. That was uncalled for. I just ... everyone can hear you guys fighting."

"Get used to it," Landon said, tugging on my arm and heading toward the dining room. "It's going to be a long dinner."

"You're done fighting, right?" Teddy asked.

"Of course," Clove sniffed, slipping her hand in Sam's. "We're adults."

Teddy focused on his daughter. "Right?"

"Oh, you're cute," Thistle said. "You know very well we've only begun to fight."

"That's what I was afraid of," Teddy grumbled.

"SO DOES EVERYONE KNOW EVERYONE?" Dad asked, glancing around the large table excitedly. Much like The Overlook, the Dragonfly was packed. Since the Dragonfly had been in operation for only a few weeks, this was a boon for their bottom line.

"I don't think so," one of the women at the middle of the table said.

"Okay, I'll do the honors," Uncle Warren said. He introduced everyone in turn, stopping long enough to give Clove's shoulder a squeeze as he passed. Either he was oblivious to what was going on or he was trying to pretend we hadn't been engaging in a screaming match five minutes earlier.

Once everyone was introduced, I spent the next five minutes trying to ignore the fact that Lila sat directly across the table from Landon and me. I'd forgotten she was staying here – or maybe I had just buried the information – but she seemed happy with the turn of events.

"I heard you guys arguing out there," Lila said, sipping from her glass of wine. "Trouble in paradise?"

"No," Landon said, sliding his arm around the back of my chair. "We're still living in paradise."

Dad frowned. "I didn't realize you were in town this week, Landon. How can you get away with not going to work?"

Dad and Landon had made great strides in their relationship. They were still reliably testy with one another when the opportunity struck.

"I knew the town was having a big festival," Landon said. "I worked sixteen hours a day earlier in the week so I could finish my case on time and spend the rest of the week with Bay."

"Well, that's nice," Dad said.

"Then you guys had a bank robbery that resulted in a murder," Landon said. "I'm working from here right now."

"I hadn't thought about that," Dad said. "Do they have any leads?"

Landon kept his eyes trained on Dad, not offering even a hint that Sam had been questioned. "No."

"Oh, that's not true," Lila said, giggling. "I heard you guys in the lobby. Clove's boyfriend is a suspect. Isn't that right, Clove?"

I scowled. "Leave her alone," I hissed.

"Shut up, Bay," Lila said. "No one is talking to you. How does it feel to date a bank robber, Clove?"

"He is not a bank robber," Clove said.

"No, he's not," Landon agreed. "We have absolutely no evidence to suggest Sam is the robber. You should probably stop eavesdropping on conversations you're not a part of, Ms. Stevens."

"Lila."

Landon ignored her. "We're investigating the case. We don't have any solid leads yet. Sam is not a suspect."

Technically, Sam was a person of interest. I knew Landon was trying to ease the situation by denying he was a suspect, but it was still a minor lie.

"That's not what you people were saying in the lobby," Lila said.

"Drink your wine, Ms. Stevens," Landon snapped.

"Does Hemlock Cove have a lot of robberies?" Eric Vaughn, a middle-aged man introduced by my uncle a few minutes earlier, interrupted.

"No," Landon said. "I believe there has been only one other attempt in the past fifty years, and this was the only one with a real weapon." He reached for a bottle of wine and poured some into his glass and mine.

"And it just figures that the culprit would be dating a Winchester," Lila said.

"Shut your mouth," Thistle exploded.

"Thistle!" Teddy was on his feet. "Don't talk to our guest like that."

"She's not a guest," Thistle said. "She's the Devil."

"I think I'm missing something," Warren said.

"Lila is mortal enemies with your daughter and nieces," Landon said.

"Mortal enemies?"

"Pretty much," Landon said. "Apparently she tortured Bay all through school, and they all hate each other."

"I don't believe that," Dad said. "Lila has been nothing but a delight since checking in. We even had tea together this morning. She was very interested in everything about the inn."

I glared at Lila. "Seriously? You're spending time with my father? You're a piece of work."

"Your father happens to be a delightful man," Lila said. "I was just trying to figure out how you went so wrong when you have half of his genes."

I clenched my hands on my lap.

"I don't know who you're trying to fool, but we all know why you're cozying up to Uncle Jack," Thistle said. "You're doing it because you get off on torturing Bay. You always have." Thistle glared at my father. "The fact that you're letting this ... woman ... manipulate you is very disappointing."

"I'm confused," Dad said, helpless.

"What's confusing?" Clove asked. "Lila has been terrible to Bay for her whole life. Now you're taking Lila's side. I'd say that's pretty much par for the course where you're concerned."

I was surprised Clove was taking up my cause.

"I think you guys are overreacting," Teddy said.

"Of course you do," Thistle said. "You don't really know us."

"That's right," Clove said. "We always overreact."

"We like it," I said.

"I think things are getting out of control," Dad said. "Why doesn't everyone just apologize to each other and let it go?"

"Because that's not the way we do things," Thistle said.

"That's because you're immature," Lila said. "You're still stuck in high school."

I opened my mouth, a hot retort on my lips, but it was cut short by the electricity going out.

"Oh, what now?" Dad asked.

"I think the locusts are coming," Landon said, his hand on my neck. "Everyone duck and cover."

THIRTEEN

"You're sure your circuit breaker is out here?" Landon asked, keeping me close as we skirted the outside of the Dragonfly. "Aren't most circuit breakers located inside?"

"This is an older building," Dad explained. "It would have been really expensive to move the box inside. Instead, we just spent money to encase the box in a special area outside. It was a lot cheaper."

"Great," Landon said.

"It's there," Dad said, pointing.

Landon let go of my hand and moved to the square annex. "Let's just hope the circuits flipped. I'm not an electrician. If something else is wrong, I don't know how to fix it."

"We haven't had any problems," Dad said.

"Maybe Lila sucked all the energy out of the room," I muttered. "She is a vampire."

Landon grinned. "She's evil. I'll be back in a second. Try not to do anything you'll regret."

"What does that mean?"

Landon cast a pointed look in my father's direction. "I'll be back in a second."

Dad watched Landon disappear inside the small room. "He's around quite a bit these days."

"I like it when he's around."

"I can see that. You two seem very ... close."

"Is there something wrong with that?" I asked.

"No," Dad said hurriedly. "I just ... it must be hard on you."

"What?"

"He's with the FBI. His life is probably in danger on a regular basis. How do you deal with that?"

"My life has been in danger more times than his since we met," I said. "He has his own share of worries where I'm concerned. I don't really think about it."

"I guess I hadn't considered that," Dad said, rubbing the back of his neck. "I ... what's the deal with you and Lila?"

"She's the Devil."

"You mentioned that," Dad said, smiling wryly. "Can you be more specific?"

"She just ... ."

The inn's lights flashed on.

"Oh, thank God," Dad said. "It was just the circuit breaker after all."

Apparently he'd forgotten his question. It was just as well. I wasn't in the mood to tell my father how miserable Lila made my childhood. I didn't want to sound bitter, especially when he was still grappling with the fact that he'd been absent for most of my formative years.

Landon joined us. "I'd have an electrician come out and check it just to make sure. Maybe it was just a fluke."

"Thanks," Dad said, extending his hand to Landon.

Landon shook it. "I didn't cure cancer. I just flicked a switch." He slung his arm over my shoulders. "Shall we go in and finish the most uncomfortable dinner ever?"

"The food will be good," Dad said. "I ... I'm sorry about the Lila thing. I don't know what to do about it."

"You could kick her out," I suggested.

Dad faltered. "I'm not sure that would be good for business."

"It would be good for family loyalty," Landon said, leading me toward the inn.

"I...."

"It's fine, Dad," I said. "Don't worry about it."

Landon shook his head, but didn't offer further argument. The sound of rustling in a nearby bush caught his attention as we passed and he stilled to study the area.

"What are you looking at?"

"I heard a noise."

"It's probably just an animal," Dad said. "Don't worry about it. Let's eat."

"I ... just a second," Landon said, resigned. He moved over to the bushes and looked down, his face a mask of mirth and ire when he glanced back up. "You're right. It was an animal."

"Raccoon?" Dad asked.

"I'm thinking more like a ... mole."

I watched as Landon reached down and dragged a struggling Aunt Tillie from her hiding spot. Dad's face fell when he saw her, while I felt inexplicably bolstered by her presence.

For her part, Aunt Tillie didn't look disturbed by her capture. Her face was bright as she regarded all of us. "So what's for dinner? I'm starving."

"YOU'VE GOT to be kidding me," Thistle said, her face splitting into a wide grin when she caught sight of Aunt Tillie. "She cut the power?"

"I did no such thing," Aunt Tillie said. "I was searching for ... mushrooms."

"Mushrooms?" Warren said, his face flushed. "You were looking for mushrooms?"

"What? That's a thing," Aunt Tillie said. "I need them for a special recipe I'm brewing."

"And you were looking for them at night?" Teddy asked. "Does anyone else think that sounds ... suspicious?" He looked to Landon for support.

Landon shrugged. "I happen to love mushrooms." He settled back in his chair. "Why don't you sit next to me, Aunt Tillie. I think everyone would be more ... comfortable ... if you were close to me."

"She can have my chair," Lila offered. "Or she can take your chair and sit next to Bay and you can sit by me." Lila patted the open chair next to her for emphasis.

"I'd rather sit next to Aunt Tillie," Landon said.

Lila's face fell. "Well ... fine."

"Hello, Lila," Aunt Tillie said, hoisting herself up in her chair and resting her elbows on the table as she stared at my nemesis from across the table. "I see the years have been hard on you."

"What are you talking about?" Lila asked. "I look exactly the same as I did when I was in high school."

"Well, that's true," Aunt Tillie said. "You looked like an ugly ferret then, too."

Lila narrowed her eyes. "You've always hated me."

"I'm sure that's not true," Dad said, nervous. "Tillie is just ... feisty."

"No, it's true," Aunt Tillie said, unruffled. "I have always hated her. She's earned it."

"She has," Thistle agreed.

Aunt Tillie shifted her gaze to Clove. "How are you, missy? I haven't seen you since this morning."

"I'm fine."

"You don't look fine."

"Well, I am."

"You'll feel better by the end of dinner," Aunt Tillie said. "I promise."

Landon narrowed his eyes suspiciously. "What's happening at the end of dinner?"

Aunt Tillie smiled. "Dessert."

"Are we sure she's not the one who turned out the lights?" Warren asked.

"Of course I didn't," Aunt Tillie said. "Why would I do that?"

"Then what were you doing here?" Warren asked.

"I told you, I was looking for mushrooms."

"You can't find mushrooms at night."

"That shows what you know," Aunt Tillie said. "I can always find mushrooms whenever I look. I'm gifted."

"You're ... something," Lila said.

Aunt Tillie turned her attention back to Lila. "I'm surprised you came back to town."

"Why?"

"Because everyone here hates you," Aunt Tillie said.

"Everyone here hates you, too," Lila said. "I don't see you leaving."

"They don't hate me. They live in fear. I encourage it."

Dad swallowed hard. "Tillie, are you sure you want to join us for dinner? I'm sure that Winnie is worried about you."

"On the contrary, I'll bet Mom is perfectly happy to serve a meal without having to worry about Aunt Tillie," I said.

Dad rubbed his forehead. "Of course."

"You're not kicking me out, are you?" Aunt Tillie asked, her eyes wide with faux innocence.

"Of course he's not," Landon said. "That would be bad for business."

The jab was pointed, and Dad didn't miss the meaning behind Landon's words.

"You're always welcome here, Tillie," Dad said. "You're ... family."

The rest of the guests turned back to their meals, but the pall over the table was palpable. Finally, Lila could take the silence no longer. "So, Tillie, I heard you poisoned all the women at the senior center because they ticked you off."

"First, I didn't poison anyone," Aunt Tillie said. "That's a vicious lie." She glanced at Landon. "I'm being framed."

"I'm not on duty," Landon said dryly. "I don't really care."

"They weren't ticking me off," Aunt Tillie said. "They were cheating. I can't stand a cheat."

"How are you not in jail?" Lila asked.

"I'm highly motivated. How are you still single? With a personality like yours, I would think some recent parolee would snap you up."

Lila frowned. "I'll have you know, I'm a very successful person. I don't need a man to complete me."

"You're a terrible liar," Aunt Tillie said. "You've been sitting there trying to flirt with Landon since we came in. You even unbuttoned your shirt a little to try to give him a good look down it. If you're going to be that desperate, you should just whip it off. The boy isn't good with subtlety."

I risked a glance at Landon, expecting to find his face red – with embarrassment or anger. Instead, he was smiling at the interplay. Instinctively, I slipped my hand in his. He didn't look up, but he rubbed his thumb over the bridge of my knuckles.

Lila blushed. "I did nothing of the sort. I was just … hot."

"Hot for something,," Aunt Tillie said. "While we're at the same table, though, I heard that you think I'm mentally incompetent."

Lila shot me a withering look. "I think someone is filling your head with lies."

"That's possible," Aunt Tillie said. "I am mentally incompetent, after all. My mind jumps all over the place. It's like a spider."

"A spider?"

"A spider," Aunt Tillie confirmed. "Kind of like the one in your hair right now."

Lila's hand flew to her hair and she rubbed it recklessly. "Where is it? Get it out!"

Dad leaned over, confused. "There's no spider."

"What is she doing?" Landon whispered.

"I have no idea."

"Oh, you think you're so funny," Lila said, her hair disheveled when she finally lifted her head and faced off with Aunt Tillie. "Is that the best you've got? I remember you as much meaner."

"I'm still mean," Aunt Tillie said. "Just ask these three."

"She's evil," Thistle confirmed. "It's what keeps her young."

"She should try moisturizer," Lila said. "It might hide some of those wrinkles making her face sag like that."

Uh-oh. Those were fighting words if I ever heard them. I leaned forward so I could study Aunt Tillie's face.

"Do you know what your problem is, Lila?" Aunt Tillie asked, her voice even.

"I'm sure you're about to tell me."

"You never grew up," Aunt Tillie said. "You're still stuck in some time warp where you're important and everyone else isn't. Someday ... someday soon ... you're going to realize you're only important in your own mind."

"Have you ever realized that?" Lila challenged.

"Oh, don't worry, I'm important in your mind, too," Aunt Tillie said. "You've built me up. You've given me power. You've ... elevated me."

"Seriously, where is she going with this?" Landon was mesmerized by the conversation. "She appears calm, and she's just sitting there. Even I know she's doing something, though."

"Your guess is as good as mine," I said. "I ... it's like she's weaving a spell."

"Is she?"

"Not that I can see."

"I don't give one fig about you," Lila said. "You're not even a blip on my radar."

Aunt Tillie smiled. "Something tells me that's going to change."

"Something tells me you're crazier than my mother gives you credit for," Lila said.

Aunt Tillie smiled. "Crazy is a state of mind," she said. "When it happens to you, you'll know it."

Aunt Tillie shifted in her chair and smiled at everyone else at the table. "Where is this fabulous dinner I've been hearing about? I'm starving."

"It's coming out," Dad said. "I hope you like Italian. We have three different dishes ... and homemade bread."

"I hate Italian."

I ran my tongue over my teeth. "You like pasta," I said. "You can find something to eat."

"I don't like Italian," Aunt Tillie said, crossing her arms over her chest. "It gives me heartburn."

"Is there something else we can make you?" Dad asked, gritting his teeth as he worked to maintain his temper.

"I'm glad you asked," Aunt Tillie said. "I want pot roast."

"We can't just whip up a pot roast," Dad said.

"Well, then I'm done here," Aunt Tillie said, jumping to her feet. She moved around the table, pausing behind Lila. She leaned close, whispering something in her ear. Whatever it was, it caused Lila to blanch. "Girls, I'll see you for breakfast tomorrow morning."

With those words, Aunt Tillie flounced out of the room.

"What was that?" The guests were stunned.

"She's just ... colorful," Dad said.

I shifted my eyes to Landon. "Did you see what she did right before she left?"

"She threatened Lila," Landon said. "From the look on Lila's face, I'm guessing it was a pretty bad threat."

"She also stole some of her hair from the back of the chair," I whispered.

"Why would she want her hair?"

I arched an eyebrow.

"Oh," Landon said, exhaling heavily. "I guess this means it's officially on."

"You've got that right ... and I want to play the game."

Landon kissed my temple. "I knew that was coming before we found Aunt Tillie in the bushes. Let's eat quickly, shall we? I don't want to spend one more second in this inn than I have to."

"What do you want to do when we're done here?"

Landon smiled, his grin devilish. "I guess you'll just have to wait to find out."

FOURTEEN

"What do you think Aunt Tillie was doing?" Clove asked.

We were back at the guesthouse, and despite Clove's warning to the contrary, she was indeed still living with us. I was surprised she opted to return home given Sam's situation, though. To no one's surprise, he'd decided to return to the Dandridge rather than face an uncomfortable evening with the rest of us.

"She stole some hair," I said.

"She did?" Thistle's eyes lit up. "I didn't see that."

"You probably couldn't from where you were seated," I said.

"Was it when she whispered to her before she left?" Clove asked.

"Yes."

"What was she doing outside?" Thistle asked.

"Hiding in the bushes."

"How did you find her?"

"Landon heard her when we went to the circuit breaker box," I said.

Landon sat in the chair at the edge of the living room, and I was cuddled on his lap with my legs hanging over the arm. He'd been rubbing the back of my neck thoughtfully for the past five minutes. "I think she wanted me to hear her," he said finally.

"What makes you say that?" Marcus asked.

"She's not a novice," Landon said. "If she doesn't want to be caught, she doesn't get caught."

"We've caught her plenty of times," I said.

"Usually by accident," Landon reminded me. "She's the one who threw the circuit breaker. We all know that. The question is: Why? If she wanted to create havoc, she has hundreds of different ways at her disposal. She can conjure havoc with her bare fingers."

"She wanted someone to come out of the house," I said. "She had no idea it would be us, but she had a good idea it would be someone who would recognize her."

"Exactly," Landon said. "Her plan was to get invited into that inn, and she wanted people to be suspicious about the lights so they wouldn't focus on what else she was doing."

"Do you think she went to the inn just to get Lila's hair?" I asked.

"Did she know Lila was staying there?" Thistle asked. "I didn't."

"Lila told me she was, but then the robbery happened and I forgot," I said. "I didn't tell her."

"So what was she doing at the Dragonfly?" Clove asked.

"She was probably plotting something against our fathers," I said. "She's still obsessed with their inn. Maybe taking Lila's hair was an opportunity she couldn't pass up."

"What would she do with Lila's hair?" Landon asked.

"She's probably making a poppet," I said.

"What's a poppet?"

"You'd probably call it a voodoo doll," Thistle explained. "Once she makes it, she can cast as many curses on it as she wants."

"How is that different from what she usually does?"

"She usually builds one spell and then curses us all with it for a set amount of time," I replied. "This would allow her to cast a spell, let it last for five minutes, and then cast another."

"So she would be like a witch on steroids where Lila is concerned,"

Landon mused. "That might be fun. That also might explain why she was trying to get into her head tonight. That was creepy, by the way."

"Are you really okay with that?" I asked. "Doesn't it bother you that she's going to be doing some truly awful things to Lila?"

"As long as she doesn't kill her, I'm fine with it," Landon said. "I think it will be cathartic for you, and a growing experience for Lila."

"I think we're corrupting you," I said.

"It's a good thing I like being corrupted then," Landon said, tickling my ribs. He sobered when he turned his attention to Clove. "Are you feeling any better?"

"I'm fine," Clove said. "I ... I'm sorry I flew off the handle earlier. It's just ... I know he's innocent."

"We all want him to be innocent, Clove," I said. "You know he could have spent the night here if he wanted to, right?"

"I told him that. He said he needed a little time alone. I think I overwhelmed him today."

"I think he expended a lot of energy pretending everything was okay for your benefit," I said. "If it's any consolation, I liked the way he was with you today. He was more worried about you than he was about himself."

"I agree," Landon said. "We don't have any evidence that directly points to him, Clove. All we have is an anonymous phone call. That could be someone trying to point the finger at Sam to shift suspicion from the real culprit."

"Can't you trace the phone call?" Clove asked.

"We're trying," Landon said. "It was from a disposable cell. We can only trace those if someone paid with a credit card. It takes time."

"And until then Sam is on the hot seat," Clove said.

"We're doing the best we can," Landon said. "You have to have faith. Can you do that?"

"I don't have a choice, do I? I just hope he doesn't shut me out while we're wading through this ... crap."

"You don't have a choice," I said. "You have to be there for him and let him talk to you when he's ready."

"I wish it was that easy," Clove said, her face miserable. "I feel like everything is about to topple around me."

"I'M STARVING," Landon said, pulling my chair out at the breakfast table at The Overlook the next morning. "No offense to your father, but that meal last night was not very good."

"You're just used to the best," Mom said, tousling his hair affectionately. "I hope that means you won't be going to dinner there again."

"You know I can't promise that, Mom," I said. "By the way, you didn't tell me who won the pie contest."

Mom made a face. "There was ... tie."

"Were you part of the tie?"

"Yes."

"Who did you tie with?"

Twila and Marnie picked that moment to sweep in from the kitchen, both wearing blue ribbons on their blouses. I guess that answered that question.

"Was there perhaps a three-way tie?" I asked.

"There was," Mom said grimly. "I think the judges rigged the contest."

"Oh, she's just bitter," Marnie said. "She's been telling people she's the best baker in the county for years. Now she's just one of three people who can make that claim."

"Oh, I'm still the best baker," Mom said. "You two got ribbons only because the other judges felt sorry for you."

"Yay, the show is starting." One of the couples from upstairs, Marshall and Carrie Sloane, were happily seated at the table and watching everyone expectantly. "I think they should give out Emmys for small-town theater."

"That would be fun," Landon said, sipping from his glass of orange juice. "I think this whole house could win an award."

"I don't have to take this abuse," Mom said. "You all know I'm the best baker."

"Not according to the judges," Marnie said, fingering her blue ribbon. She was practically singing she was so giddy.

"That's it. We're having another contest. We're all going to bake a pie, and the guests are going to vote."

Carrie clapped excitedly. "Oh good. I love judging things."

"Don't I know it," Marshall grumbled.

Landon bit the inside of his cheek to keep from laughing.

"You're going to be a judge, too, Landon," Mom said. "And Terry."

"Oh, no way," Marnie said. "You'll bully him into voting for you."

"I am not going to be a judge," Landon said. "I like all your cooking equally."

Mom cuffed the back of his head. "You're dating my daughter. You will definitely be voting for me."

"Then Marcus and Sam get to vote, too," Marnie said.

"Fine."

"Great."

"Good."

"There's never a dull moment here," Landon said.

"What did I miss?" Nick asked, stepping into the room.

"Winnie, Marnie and Twila are going to have a pie-baking contest," Carrie said. "We all get to be judges."

"Good. I love pie," Nick said, winking at me as he settled in the seat to my right.

Landon shot him a dirty look. "I'm the head judge."

"You just said you weren't going to be a judge," Mom argued.

"I changed my mind."

"Good," Mom said. "You know quality. That's why you're dating my daughter. You're definitely going to like my pie best."

"Everyone knows I have the best pie in town," Marnie said.

Clove walked into the dining room as her mother uttered the words, but it took her a second to comprehend them. "Is that a euphemism for something?"

"Yes," Marnie said. "My pie is delicious."

Landon snickered, and I pinched his thigh under the table. "Don't," I warned.

"My pie tastes like heavenly whipped cream," Mom said.

Now Nick was giggling. Unfortunately, my mother and aunt had no idea how their words were being taken.

"Mine tastes like … ."

"Stop talking about your pie," Thistle ordered, moving from the kitchen to the dining room with Marcus in tow. "You're going to give everyone a stroke."

"How can anyone have a problem with my pie?" Mom asked.

"Because they're picturing a different kind of pie, you idiots," Thistle said. "Good grief."

"What? Like mincemeat?"

Landon barked out a laugh. "I love breakfasts here."

"Do you eat here a lot?" Nick asked.

"As often as I can," Landon said.

"Are we talking once a week? Twice a week?" Nick's eyes were keen as they studied Landon.

"Every chance I get," Landon said firmly.

"Does Bay cook for you?"

Landon smiled. "Bay has many talents," he said. "Cooking is not one of them."

"Hey, I could cook if I wanted to," I said.

"You never have."

"Fine. I'm going to cook a romantic dinner for us."

"That's really not necessary," Landon said. "You don't need to waste your time doing something like that."

"He really means he's terrified you got your cooking skills from Aunt Tillie," Thistle said. "Don't feel bad. Marcus thinks I can't cook either."

"That's not what I said," Marcus protested. "I said that you don't cook. There's no harm in not being able to cook. You keep saying that I said you couldn't cook, but that's not true."

"I can cook."

"I believe you."

"Do you know what? Bay and I are going to join together and cook you both a big meal," Thistle said. "You're going to be wowed, and then you're going to have to get on your knees and beg us to cook for you again."

"That sounds interesting," Landon said. "When are you going to cook this meal?"

Thistle faltered. "I'm not sure."

I glanced at Clove a second. She looked miserable. "I think we should wait until all three of us can cook together."

Landon followed my gaze. "I think that's a good idea," he said. "Besides, your mothers have planned extensive menus for the whole week. I don't want to miss any of them."

"Me either," Marcus said.

"Fine," Thistle said, crossing her arms over her chest. "Just be aware, I'm going to cook your socks off."

"Just to be clear, the food isn't going to taste like socks, right?" Landon asked.

I slapped his arm playfully. "Why don't you believe we can cook?"

"Because I've seen you burn toast," Landon said.

"That happened once," I protested.

"Only because I unplugged the toaster and you haven't tried to cook since," Landon said.

"Thistle served me cereal with expired milk the other day," Marcus said.

"I did not," Thistle said.

"It was two days past the date on the jug, babe," Marcus said. "It's fine. I'm still alive."

"Those dates are just suggestions," Thistle said. "They don't mean anything."

"Right," Landon said. "They're just suggestions."

Thistle shot him a look. "You're going to cry when I make you dinner."

"Why?" Landon asked, his eyes twinkling. "Is it going to taste that bad?"

"No. I'm just going to hit you that hard."

"You should make him some pie," Mom suggested. "Men love pie."

Landon smiled at me. "Seriously, I love having breakfast here."

FIFTEEN

"What are you doing today?" Landon asked.

We stood in the parking lot in front of The Overlook. After breakfast progressed to near epic proportions of absurdity, I had to tear him away to make sure he made it to work on time.

"The fair opens today," I said. "I'll probably wander around there for a little bit."

"Why don't you wait for me? We can go together this afternoon."

"Won't you be busy with the bank robbery?"

"I don't know," Landon said. "Unless we get some new leads, probably not. I'm not the primary on this. I'm just helping Terry when he needs it. I think I can manage to sneak away this afternoon if you want to spend some time with me. I thought we could even spend some time in that kissing booth you told me about."

I smiled. "I don't think they're having that this time," I said. "The mayor said it sends the wrong message to visitors."

"And what message is that?"

"That we're all horny or something," I said, laughing.

"Well, then I'll build a booth for just you and I to use," Landon teased. He leaned over and gave me a kiss. "How about I come to the newspaper in time for lunch and we eat at the fair?"

"You want to eat carnival food?"

"I love a good elephant ear."

He really is too cute for words sometimes. "I think I can carve out some time for you this afternoon."

"Good," Landon said. "Get all your work done early. I want your undivided attention this afternoon. That means no Thistle. No Clove. No crazy mothers. No disappointed fathers. And definitely no Aunt Tillie."

"Whatever will we do with all that alone time?"

"I have a few ideas." Landon kissed me again. "Be good."

I FELT a momentary twinge of guilt when I parked in front of the Dandridge. I'd known I was going to head straight for the lighthouse when I left The Overlook. I also knew Landon wouldn't be happy with that decision, so I'd purposely avoided telling him.

Sam sat in a chair on the side patio. He seemed surprised to see me. "Aren't I the popular one this week."

I forced a weak smile as I approached him. "I just wanted to see how you were doing."

"I'm fine," Sam said. "You didn't need to come out here."

"I did," I said. "I ... I want to talk to you."

"Is this where you warn me to stay away from Clove?"

The question caught me off guard. "No."

"Then why are you here?"

I settled in the chair next to him and glanced at the surrounding area. There were potted plants on each side of the patio, and someone had planted a blue hydrangea on the far end. That was Clove's favorite plant. "Clove did this."

"We did it together," Sam said. "She picked the hydrangea. She liked the color."

"She always has," I said. "Her mother let her plant as many of them around the house as she wanted when she was a kid."

"I've seen them," Sam said. "They grow quickly, and they're beautiful. They remind me of Clove."

His words were earnest, and they touched me. "You care about her, don't you?"

"I do."

"Then don't shut her out, Sam."

Sam shifted his eyes to me. "I'm not shutting her out. She wanted to go home and make up with you guys. I didn't feel ... comfortable ... being there with you and Landon. It had nothing to do with her."

"I get that," I said. "Just so you know, though, you're welcome at the guesthouse. I know we set up some rules when you and Clove started dating, but we're past them. You're welcome there."

"I needed some time to think."

We sat silently for a few minutes, the only sound coming from the birds chirping in the nearby trees. I came here with a goal, and I hadn't achieved it yet. Part of me thought what I was about to do was a betrayal. The other part of me thought Clove needed it.

"When Clove was little, she had the easiest time fitting in," I said, leaning back in the chair. "Do you know why that is?"

"Because she's sweet," Sam said. "She's tough when she wants to be, but she's also sweet. People like her because she's approachable. No offense to Thistle, but the only people who want to approach her have a death wish ... and you're standoffish."

"I'm not standoffish."

"You are," Sam said. "I knew it from the moment I met you. You don't trust people. I didn't get it then, but I do now. You've been burned by people your whole life because of your gifts. You especially. You couldn't always hide yours, especially when you were a child. That made things hard for you."

"I guess that's true," I said. "I didn't come here to talk about me, though. I came here to talk about Clove. You're right. She's sweet. She's the sweetest one in our family. She was born that way.

"When she was a kid, she'd find every wounded bird and rabbit on the property and nurse them back to health," I continued. "She was broken-hearted when some of them died. She was also thrilled when they survived so she could set them free again. She's always made friends easily. She's always … trusted … easily. She doesn't have a mean bone in her body."

"Are you going to tell me that's a bad thing?" Sam asked.

"Absolutely not," I said. "I wish I was more like her sometimes. We all have our lot in life, though. I'm not telling you this as a warning. I'm trying to make you understand."

"Understand what?"

"I haven't been at my best this week," I said. "The thing is, I had very low self-esteem as a child. People wore me down. I found myself when I was away from Hemlock Cove, though, and I brought back what I learned when I returned.

"Clove is different," I said. "She's never been sure of herself. She makes friends easily, but she's always questioned her worth. That's because she's in a family of loudmouths. Her voice was often drowned out by the rest of us screaming at each other."

"I'm waiting to hear how this applies to me," Sam said.

"Just because she's the quiet one, that doesn't mean she has nothing to say," I said.

"Are you saying I don't listen to her?"

"I think you probably listen to her more than anyone else ever has," I said. "That's why you're a good match for her."

Sam waited.

"I also think you have the propensity to shut her out if you're not careful," I said. "Because Clove is sweet, that doesn't mean she's not tough. You want to protect her, and I'm grateful for that. If you try to protect her too much, though, you'll destroy her."

"I'm not trying to hurt her," Sam said. "I just … I'm an only child. I need time to think sometimes."

"And you're dealing with a lot," I said. "You went to dinner with her last night even though I bet you wanted to be alone."

"The worst dinner ever."

"That doesn't even rank in my top ten," I said, laughing.

"Your family is frightening."

"We are," I agreed. "We're also loyal, and there's not one of us who wouldn't burn this town down to protect Clove."

"What do you want me to do?"

"Give her a chance," I said. "If you need to talk, let her listen. If you need time alone, tell her without hurting her. If you need someone to lean on, she's stronger than she looks. She may be tiny, but she has so much power that it awes me sometimes."

"You're a good cousin to her," Sam said. "You're a good ... sister ... to her."

"People always thought we were sisters when we were growing up, even though we look nothing alike."

Sam rubbed his forehead. "I'm doing the best I can right now," he said. "I would never hurt Clove. Not for anything."

"I believe you." I honestly did. "Don't shut her out. Please."

"I have no intention of shutting her out," Sam said. "In fact, we have a date to go to the fair this afternoon."

"Good," I said. "That will make her happy. Make sure you take her to the House of Mirrors. She loves it. She likes the ones that make her look tall."

"Thanks for the tip." Sam got to his feet. "Thank you for coming here. I appreciate the effort it must have taken you to put aside family loyalty and give me a little insight."

"I don't think that's what I did," I said. "I think I was being very loyal to my family when I told you this. Clove likes you. She believes in you. I want you to understand her."

"I've always understood her," Sam said. "I think I might understand her more than you do sometimes."

That was entirely possible. "Just make her happy, Sam. If we're lucky, this whole thing will be over within a few days. Landon will solve the case – he always does – and we'll be able to go back to our normal dysfunction and let the surreal dysfunction go by the wayside."

Sam smiled. "I'll walk you back to your car."

"You don't have to."

"I think I've been feeling sorry for myself for long enough," Sam said. "I'm going to walk you to your car and then I'm going to go inside and take a shower so I look presentable for Clove this afternoon. I might even cut off a bouquet of hydrangeas for her."

"Chocolate couldn't hurt either," I offered.

"I'll take that under advisement."

Sam and I walked toward the parking lot in amiable silence. During the stroll, a hint of something dark in one of the bushes on the far side of the lighthouse caught my attention. Before I realized what I was doing, I stepped off the paved walkway and headed for the bushes.

"What are you doing?" Sam asked.

"Don't you see that?"

"What?"

"There's something in the bushes," I said.

Sam followed me, squinting. "What is it?"

When we were close enough, I reached for the item and pulled it out. When I held it up, Sam's face drained of color and my heart dropped. It was a knit balaclava, exactly like the one the robber wore when he fled from the bank.

Crap. Instead of helping Clove I'd just tipped this investigation into devastation territory. Why don't I ever ignore my curiosity?

SIXTEEN

"That's not mine," Sam said.

"Okay." I didn't know what else to say. It seemed like an odd spot for a winter mask, but I was in an even odder spot. If the mask did belong to Sam, and he was trying to cover his tracks, I would be an obstacle in keeping his secret. If he was innocent, someone was working overtime to implicate him.

"Seriously, that's not mine," Sam said.

I took a step away from him, hoping my face didn't betray the jolt of fear coursing through me. "I ... believe you."

"No, you don't," Sam said. "You're sitting there wondering whether I'm planning to hurt you. I can see it on your face."

I always was a terrible liar. "Sam ... I need to call Landon. We need to report this."

"If you report this, he's going to arrest me."

"You don't know that."

"We both know that," Sam snapped.

I took another step back, and the motion was enough to still Sam's surging rage. "Are you afraid of me?"

Afraid wasn't the right word. I was definitely uncomfortable, though. "Sam ... just ... calm down. It's going to be all right. Just let me call Landon. He'll figure it out."

"You can't call Landon," Sam said. "He's going to believe I'm guilty."

"I have to call him, Sam," I said, working to keep my voice neutral. "This is evidence. Amy Madison was murdered. He needs all the evidence for his investigation."

"And you need to be in the middle of everything," Sam spat.

"That's not true."

"Oh, shut up," Sam said. "Go ahead. Call him."

I pulled my phone from my pocket, uncertain. "Sam, Landon will do his best to solve this. You have to have faith in him."

"I don't," Sam said. "He's had it out for me since we met. You do what you have to do, though. I'm not going to hurt you, Bay. No matter what you think."

He seemed so earnest I wanted to believe him. I also knew that I had to call Landon. "I'm sorry," I said. I pulled Landon's name up in my contacts. "I really am sorry."

"WHERE WAS THE MASK EXACTLY?" Landon asked, his hands on his narrow hips as he stood in front of the Dandridge.

I pointed to the clump of bushes and watched as Landon and Chief Terry stalked to the spot. Chief Terry had bagged the mask upon arrival, and Landon's questions were short and terse. I could tell he was angry with me, but he was trying to rein it in until we didn't have an audience. That was the only thing I was thankful for at the moment.

"And you didn't see the mask before?" Chief Terry asked Sam.

"No," Sam said. "I didn't notice it until Bay headed in that direction."

"Did you notice it when you walked up from the parking lot?" Chief Terry asked, turning to me.

I racked my brain. "I don't know," I said. "I wasn't paying a lot of attention. I ... Sam was sitting on the patio, and I saw him right away. I headed straight for him. I wasn't looking around."

"And why were you here?" Landon asked. "Didn't you tell me … not two hours ago … that you were spending the morning at the newspaper office?"

"I only wanted to talk to him," I replied carefully. "I … we had some things to discuss where Clove was concerned."

"And what were those things?"

"I don't think now is the time for this conversation, Landon," Chief Terry said. "You two can fight that out later."

"She wanted to make sure I didn't shut Clove out because I was feeling sorry for myself," Sam said. "She was determined to make sure I understood where Clove's head was in all of this. It wasn't anything … nefarious."

Landon's face softened, but his eyes glittered as he studied me. "You could have told me that."

"I didn't want it to be a big thing," I said.

"We'll talk about it later," he said. He took the bag from Chief Terry and looked over the mask. "Is this the mask the robber was wearing?"

"How can I possibly know that? It's a black mask. The robber was wearing a black mask. If it had any identifying marks, I would have told you."

"Don't get snarky," Landon said. "You're in no position to have attitude with me."

I made a face.

"Don't do that either," he ordered. "I don't like it when you make that puppy-dog face."

"I think it's cute," Chief Terry said, patting my shoulder. "That's how you wrapped me around your finger when you were a kid."

"See, this is why she thinks she can get away with murder," Landon said. "You cater to her."

"You cater to her," Chief Terry argued. "That puppy-dog face works better on you than it does on me."

"That's only because she has ways of making me do things that you'd better not be doing with her," Landon said.

Chief Terry cuffed the back of his head. "When I look at her, she's still ten years old. You know that, right?"

"That's not how I look at her."

"I've noticed."

Sam cleared his throat. "As cute as this conversation is, I want to know what this means for me."

"It doesn't mean anything yet," Chief Terry said. "We're going to send it to the state lab and have it tested."

"You're not going to arrest me?" Sam seemed surprised.

"Not yet," Chief Terry said. "If I'm being honest, I'm bothered by the mask showing up here. I'm fairly certain it wasn't here when we questioned you yesterday. I scanned the property when we were here. I think I would've seen it."

"Me, too," Landon said.

"What does that mean?" Sam asked. "Is someone trying to frame me?"

"That's my initial instinct," Landon said. "I'm going to stress for you, though, that I'm not ruling you out as a suspect. But I have trouble believing you'd be stupid enough to put a mask that implicates you in the bushes behind your home."

"Well, I guess that's something," Sam said, rubbing his chin. "I just don't understand. I haven't been here long enough to make enemies with anyone."

"There are a lot of new faces in town," I said. "Well, a lot of new old faces. Maybe someone from out of town robbed the bank and is trying to blame it on the outsider?"

"That's a possibility," Landon said. "We don't have enough information to go on, though. For now, it's just a mask."

"I'll have one of my deputies drive it over to the state lab this afternoon," Chief Terry said. "Until then, I agree with Landon. It's just a mask until we know it's something else."

"See, I told you," I said to Sam. "Landon will figure it out."

"I'm glad to see you have faith in me," Landon said. "We're still going to talk about your little white lie this morning."

My face fell. "Fine."

"We can do it over lunch at the fair," Landon said. "I wasn't joking when I said I wanted an elephant ear."

"**WHAT** DO YOU REALLY THINK?"

Landon, Chief Terry and I sat at a picnic table in the town square, assorted carnival goodies spread before us.

"I think what I already said," Landon said. "I don't think Sam is stupid enough to leave evidence out like that. If he were guilty, he would have burned the mask. He wouldn't have thrown it in the bushes."

"Sam isn't stupid," Chief Terry said. "The question is: Who would want to set him up?"

"I think the question is: Who would know enough about Sam to set him up?" I countered. "He doesn't spend a lot of time with anyone except Clove."

"He used to be tight with Brian Kelly," Landon pointed out.

"He did," I agreed. "I don't think they spend much time together now, though. Sam is kind of a loner."

"Which brings me to the argument portion of today's festivities," Landon said. "What were you thinking going out there alone?"

"I thought I was talking to my cousin's boyfriend about shutting her out," I said. "Clove can't take that. I was trying to make him understand how upset she was."

"I admire your love for Clove," Landon said. "I really do. I'm fond of her myself. That doesn't mean I think it was a good idea for you to go out there alone. Sam is still a person of interest in a bank robbery that resulted in a murder."

"How did you know Sam wouldn't hurt you when you found the mask?" Chief Terry asked.

"I didn't," I admitted. "I just ... it was a feeling."

"Bay, you have a lot of feelings," Landon said. "Most of them are spot on. You can't walk into danger because you have a feeling that everything is going to be all right, though. It drives me crazy."

"I didn't think I was doing that."

"I know," Landon said, holding up his hand. "Just be careful. For me."

"Oh, you two are so cute I could slap you both silly," Chief Terry said, rolling his eyes. "Well, I would never slap Bay. I could slap you twice, though, Landon."

"I'll keep that in mind." Landon's tone was dry, but the hard edge to his shoulders started to give way. "I'm going to spank her later."

"See, that will be just about enough of that," Chief Terry said.

Landon ignored him. "What else are you going to do today?"

"I'm not sure what else there is to do right now," Chief Terry said. "Until we have more information, we're stuck."

"Oh, look who it is!"

I cringed when I heard the voice. Lila, her face painted like a beauty pageant contestant, slipped into the open spot on the other side of the table from Landon and fixed everyone with a bright smile.

"How is everyone today?"

Chief Terry pressed his lips together while I lowered my face to keep from laughing. The situation was surreal, and Lila clearly didn't pick up on social cues.

"We were actually having a private discussion," Landon said. "Police business. I'm sure you understand."

Lila was unfazed. "How can you talk about police business in front of a civilian?"

"She's part of the investigation," Landon said, not missing a beat. "She's a … ."

"Private consultant," Chief Terry finished. "She helps us with a lot of investigations."

"Oh, I've heard about that," Lila said, reaching over and grabbing a French fry from Landon's plate. Her proprietary nature with him was irksome. "Do you involve Bay in your investigations because she won't keep her nose out of your business?"

"We involve Bay because she's invaluable to our investigative team," Landon said, sliding his plate from Lila and giving her a dirty look. "She has a specific skill set that we like to utilize."

"I have skills," Lila offered.

"That's what the football team wrote on the bathroom wall senior year," I grumbled, causing Chief Terry to snicker and Landon to struggle to keep from laughing out loud.

Lila ignored me. "Are you going to the festival this afternoon?"

"We are," Landon said. "We're looking forward to it."

"Oh, good," Lila said. "Maybe we can go on a few rides together."

"I'll be the only one giving him a ride," I snapped. This time Landon couldn't swallow his laugh, while Chief Terry cleared his throat uncomfortably.

"There's no need to get all … territorial," Lila said, rolling her eyes for Landon's benefit. "She's terrified I'm going to steal you away from her. I understand her worry. She's really not the type of woman who could hold on to a man like you for very long. Still, she's bordering on embarrassing."

Landon glanced at me, his eyes filled with mirth. "Is that true? Are you feeling territorial?"

He had no idea. "I'm feeling something. I think it might be indigestion."

Landon smirked. "There's no need for Bay to feel territorial, Ms. Stevens," he said. "No one is capable of encroaching on her territory." He got to his feet and started gathering the containers of half-eaten food. After discarding them in a nearby trash receptacle, he returned to the table and extended his hand. "Now, I believe I promised my girl a day at the festival."

I took his hand, color rushing to my cheeks as Lila glared at me.

"Have a nice day, Ms. Stevens."

SEVENTEEN

"What do you want to do first?" Landon asked, linking his fingers with mine as he studied the carnival. "Do you even like rides?"

"That's all you're going to say?"

Landon shifted to meet my gaze head on. "What do you want me to say?"

"You're my hero. You know that, right?"

"Because I'm handsome and manly?" Landon teased.

"Because you refuse to play Lila's game," I answered honestly. "You have no idea how ... great that is."

"Bay, I'm not putting Lila off because I'm worried about your self-esteem," Landon said. "Although, if I'm being honest, I wish you would yank her hair out of her head and call it a day.

"I don't have any interest in Lila," he continued. "I don't have any interest in anyone who isn't blonde and drives me to distraction."

I pursed my lips, pleasure washing over me. "That's the nicest thing anyone has ever said to me."

"Then you need to hang around nicer people," Landon said, his cheeks coloring slightly under my praise. "I'm not interested in Lila.

Even if there was no you, I would never be interested in Lila. You're more than I can handle. Trust me."

"Are you angry with me for going out to talk to Sam?"

"I'm not angry with you, Bay," Landon said. "I just don't like worrying about you. I know you don't purposely go looking for trouble – well, most of the time – but it does seem to find you. That's what I don't like."

"I honestly didn't think anything would come of it," I said.

"I know," Landon said. "You still didn't tell me what you were doing this morning."

"I figured you would demand I not go … or say you were going with me," I said.

"I probably would have," Landon conceded. "Why do you think that is?"

"Because you like being manly?" I tried, going for levity.

"Because I like knowing you're safe," Landon countered, although he graced me with a small smile. "I can't control a lot in our world, Bay. I like to think I can keep you safe, though."

"Sam didn't threaten me."

"That doesn't mean he couldn't have threatened you," Landon said. "He could have hurt you."

"He didn't."

"And that's why I don't have to kill him," Landon said. He leaned over and gave me a quick kiss. "I don't want to fight today. It's a carnival. Let's put it behind us."

"That sounds like a good idea," I said, rubbing my nose against his cheek briefly.

"Don't do it again, though," Landon cautioned. "Until we've officially cleared Sam, I don't want you alone with him."

"What about Clove?"

"Do you think we can keep her away from him?"

"No one could keep me away from you," I said.

"Then we'll have to watch her," Landon said, tugging on a strand of my hair. "If it's any consolation, I don't think Sam would be stupid enough to hurt Clove. He'd be the prime suspect if something happened to her."

"That doesn't make me feel any better."

"I know," Landon said. "I don't know what to tell you. For now, let's just enjoy the festival. Did you find out if they have that kissing booth?"

"They don't. I already told you."

Landon's smile was rueful. "I guess I'm going to have to settle for copping a feel on the Ferris wheel then."

"I'm sure you'll survive."

"Come on," Landon said, tugging my hand and dragging me deeper into the whirl of music, grinding gears, diesel fuel, game barkers and shouting children wheeling around the sky. "Let's try to enjoy a few hours without any drama, shall we?"

That sounded pretty good to me.

"**I NEED** you to explain this to me," Landon said, studying the sculpture curiously. "What is this supposed to be?"

I tilted my head to the side. "A ghost?"

"It doesn't look like a ghost. It looks like a ... blob."

As part of the anniversary celebration, each business in Hemlock Cove had been tasked with creating a sculpture. The one the library members erected was ... interesting. "I think they let the kids in the afternoon reading group create it. Annie mentioned something about it. She was bummed she wasn't going to be able to see it at the festival."

"Well, if that's the case, I'm sorry for making fun of it," Landon said. "If an adult made that, though, they need to go to the eye doctor and get a new prescription."

While Landon was adapting to life in a small town, there were still times he seemed dumbfounded by the quaint absurdity of Hemlock Cove.

"I think it's kind of cute," I said.

"Then you need glasses."

"My eyesight is perfectly fine, thank you," I said. "Why do you think I started dating you?"

Landon grinned. "If you wanted to get some glasses and play 'naughty librarian' I'm totally up for it, by the way."

"I'll consider it."

"You should feed me bacon at the same time."

"You're sick."

Landon slipped his arm around my waist. "If all the businesses made one of these, did Clove and Thistle do one for Hypnotic?"

I nodded.

"Where is it?"

I narrowed my eyes and scanned the fair. "I think it's over there."

Landon led me in the direction I pointed, and when he caught sight of Thistle's sculpture he let loose with an impressed whistle. "Wow."

The witch sculpture was simple, and yet Thistle had still gone all out. When she'd announced she was going to weld something, our mothers were understandably nervous. Most of Thistle's artistic endeavors as a child doubled as fire hazards. What Thistle accomplished in a simple week, though, was breathtaking.

"Did Thistle do this herself?" Landon asked, moving forward so he could run his hand over the dark metal.

"She's really amazing when she wants to be," I said.

"She could sell these."

"When the festival is over, she's taking it out to The Overlook," I said. "Twila wants to put it in that area by the big oak in the front yard."

"It's ... beautiful." Landon shifted his eyes to me. "Can you weld?"

"My idea of art is putting whipped cream on a cookie."

"We'll play with the whipped cream later," Landon said, winking at me.

"Oh, this is just so ... tacky."

My shoulders slumped when I heard Lila's voice. Was she following us? I turned and glared in her direction. "You're tacky."

Lila ignored me. "Don't you think that's ugly?" she asked, sidling up to Landon. "It's so ... depressing."

Landon shot me a reassuring look. "I think it's beautiful," he said. "I think Thistle could be a world-famous artist someday if she wants to be. I had no idea she was capable of this. I knew she could paint, and her candles are really cool, but this is a whole other level."

"You should see her stained glass," I said.

"She can do stained glass?" Now Landon was doubly impressed.

"She did the windows in the stairwell at the Dandridge."

"Why didn't you tell me that?"

"I didn't think Sam was in the mood to talk about interior design when we were out there yesterday," I said.

Lila's gaze bounced between us, her nose clearly out of joint for being ignored. "So, Landon, tell me about yourself."

"Well, I'm with the FBI," Landon said. "Oh, and I have a girlfriend."

"Are you an only child?"

Landon moved away from Lila and back to my side. "What do you want to look at next?"

"Oh ... um ... ."

"I want to go to the funhouse," Lila announced.

"Have fun," Landon said, keeping his gaze focused on me. "How about some ice cream?"

"I'm still kind of full from lunch," I said, watching Lila's face turn ever more crimson out of the corner of my eye.

"Then we'll share," Landon said.

Lila took a step toward us. "I would love some ice cream." She lurched forward, offsetting her balance, and tumbling to the ground. "What the ... ?"

"Walk much?" I fought the urge to laugh.

"I ... I must have stepped into a hole or something," Lila said. She extended her hand in Landon's direction. "Help me up?"

Landon sighed, but he reached forward and pulled Lila to her feet. When she tried to cling to his hand, he yanked it away. "Better?"

"I don't know what happened," Lila said. "Maybe it's just being in your presence."

"Then you should probably avoid being around me," Landon said. "Come on, Bay. Let's get some ice cream."

We turned to leave, but Lila was close on our heels. "Chocolate is my favorite. What's your favorite? Oomph!"

Lila pitched forward again. She managed to maintain her balance, but only because she grabbed onto a nearby bench to stop from falling.

"Are you drunk?" I asked.

"Of course not," Lila said. "I ... there must be a lot of holes around here. Maybe the town has a mole infestation."

I furrowed my brow as I watched Lila straighten. Something was off here – other than the obvious. "Maybe you should sit down on the bench and rest," I suggested. "The sun must be getting to you." Or karma was finally catching up with her.

"I want ice cream," Lila said. "We can all get it together. It will give me a chance to get to know Landon better."

"Oh, I can't wait for that," Landon deadpanned. He grabbed my hand and started leading me toward the food trucks. "This wasn't what I had in mind when I suggested an afternoon at the fair together."

"Do you think ... ?" I broke off when Lila suddenly raced forward and bumped into a tree on the far side of the path.

"What is happening?" Lila's face was red with exertion.

Uh-oh. I scanned the area. I wasn't one-hundred percent sure what I was looking for, but I had an idea. A hint of movement behind the photo booth caught my attention. "Um ... stay here," I told Landon. "Watch her."

"Why do I have to watch her?" Landon raised his eyebrows. "She's acting crazy."

"I have a feeling I know why," I said. I started to move toward the photo booth. "Oh, if she touches you, I'm going to break her hand," I warned. "She's starting to drive me crazy with the touchy-feely stuff."

"If you're gone too long, I might not be able to fight her off," Landon said. "Women can't help themselves around me."

"She'd better be able to help herself," I said. I increased my pace, and when I rounded the corner of the photo booth, I wasn't surprised to find Thistle and Aunt Tillie kneeling on the ground and laughing maniacally. "What are you two doing?"

"I ... nothing," Aunt Tillie said, trying to hide something in the folds of her shirt.

I glanced over my shoulder when Lila grunted again, watching as her arms flung out wide as she tilted to the side. I realized what Aunt Tillie had hidden in her shirt. "Is that the poppet you made with the hair you stole from Lila the other night?"

"That is a horrible thing to accuse me of," Aunt Tillie sniffed.

I waited.

Aunt Tillie sighed and rolled her eyes. She withdrew the poppet from its hiding place and held it up so I could see. The doll was simple, nothing more than some hay tied together with yarn and long strands of dark hair affixed to the top.

"What did you do to it?" I asked, genuinely curious.

"I just cast a motion spell on it," Aunt Tillie said.

"So you can make Lila do things?"

Aunt Tillie nodded, her eyes sparkling. "Do you want to try it?"

Of course not. That would be ... . "Give it to me." I took the doll and studied it for a second. "How do I make it work?"

"What do you want her to do?" Thistle asked.

"I don't know. Can we make her dance like Michael Jackson?"

Aunt Tillie furrowed her brow. "He did that moon-walking thing, right?"

I nodded.

"I don't know. Let's see." Aunt Tillie took the doll back and scissored the legs back and forth.

I turned back to watch Lila. She didn't look as though she had rhythm, but she did appear to be dancing. Kind of.

"Oh, make her bend over and try to look through her legs," I suggested.

Aunt Tillie obliged, and the sight was so hilarious to Thistle that she fell backward with laughter.

Landon had apparently tired of watching Lila because he was heading in our direction.

"Uh-oh," I said.

"Don't worry. It's not like he can arrest us," Aunt Tillie said. "No one would ever believe him."

"Do you want to tell me what's going on here?" Landon asked, rounding the corner and pulling up short when he saw the three of us together. "Is that the puppet thing you said she was going to make?"

"Poppet," I corrected.

"Whatever," Landon said, glancing down at the doll. "Is that why she's acting that way? She looks drunk."

"That's the point," Aunt Tillie said. "She's causing a scene. People will be making fun of her all day."

"She could be hurt," Landon chided. "Can't you think of something that's a little more ... I don't know ... less dangerous and yet equally as funny?"

He's such a killjoy sometimes.

"I can," Aunt Tillie said. She dug into her purse for a moment, returning with a pin.

"What are you going to do with that?" Landon asked. "Is it like a voodoo doll? Can you kill her with that?"

"I'm not going to kill her," Aunt Tillie said. "That would ruin all of my fun." She flipped the doll over and ran the pin up the backside of it before peering around the side of the photo booth.

Landon followed her gaze. "What did that do?"

The sound of fabric ripping moved across the small area.

"Was that ... ?"

"Omigod!" Lila wailed and grabbed the back of her pants. "What is happening?"

"Holy crap! That lady just split her pants."

I couldn't hear who yelled the observation, but Lila's face was murderous as she swung around. Her antics had drawn a crowd, and a small group of people were laughing and pointing at her as she tried to cover her ... um ... assets. When Lila's gaze landed on me, she scorched me with enough hatred to set the town ablaze.

"I know you did this," she hissed. "I don't know how, but you're going to pay."

Lila turned and ran from the fair, her hands covering her exposed panties as she made a beeline for the parking lot. When she was gone, Landon focused on me. I expected him to yell. I expected him to tell us how immature we were. I expected something – anything really – other than what he said.

"So where did we land on that ice cream?"

EIGHTEEN

"So he didn't say a word about it?" I leaned back on the couch in the middle of Hypnotic and shook my head as Thistle passed me a glass of iced tea. "Not one word."

"Do you think he's waiting until later to fight about it?" Thistle asked, settling next to me.

"I can usually tell when he's holding something inside and trying not to explode," I said. "That's not how this felt."

"Is that how it felt this morning out at the Dandridge?"

I frowned. "That's exactly how it felt. Have you talked to Clove?"

Thistle shook her head. "She got a call this morning and took off without saying a word. I'm assuming it came from Sam."

"I hope that's a good thing," I said.

"Well, maybe they're spending some quiet time together," Thistle suggested.

"Sam said he was going to take her to the fair before … well, before I ruined his day."

"It wasn't your fault, Bay," Thistle said. "What were you supposed to do?"

I shrugged. "I don't know. It still felt … disloyal."

"Were you worried when you found it? Did you think he was going to try to keep you from calling Landon?"

"For a second," I admitted. "He never got overtly angry. He did snap at me a few times, but I think he was frustrated more than anything else. I don't blame him."

"Do you think he did it?"

"No."

"Are you saying that because Clove is going to spend six months in bed if he's guilty?" Thistle asked.

"Listen, I'm not going to lie; I really want Sam to be innocent," I said. "He was ... worried this morning. While I'm sure part of him was worried for himself, the other part was worried for Clove. He didn't want her to be upset."

"Is that why he separated from her last night?"

"Yes. He said he wanted some time alone. And, let's face it, spending the night at the guesthouse with the rest of us would have been ridiculously uncomfortable."

"That's putting it mildly," Thistle said. "What did you tell him this morning?"

I shifted uncomfortably, averting my eyes. "What do you think I told him?"

"I think you told him that Clove is sensitive and he has to be careful with her heart," Thistle said. "I think you told him that in his efforts to protect Clove, he should be careful not to hurt her at the same time."

"How did you know that?"

"Because I was considering going out there and having the same conversation with him," Thistle said, getting to her feet and pacing in front of the register. "I'm really afraid Clove is going to be ... ruined ... in all of this. If Sam is guilty, she's never going to get over it."

"I know."

"I know I like to tease her ... ."

"And bully her," I added.

"I don't bully her," Thistle protested.

I arched an eyebrow.

"Fine. I bully her a little. It's fun, though."

"It's only fun for you," I said. "It's not fun for Clove."

"After everything that's happened the past year, I think losing Sam would be too much for her," Thistle said.

"I agree."

"So, we have to try to prove Sam's innocence," Thistle said.

Where had that come from? "We do?"

"Do you have any other suggestions?"

"That seems like something outside of our wheelhouse," I said. "If we had a direction to look, I would say it's a great idea. We don't have anywhere to look."

Thistle ceased her pacing. "Who do we know in town who is having money problems?"

"I don't know anyone in town who is having money problems," I said. "That's not something people generally volunteer. And there are too many tourists in Hemlock Cove to possibly narrow down a manageable search list."

"We could do a spell," Thistle suggested.

That was an interesting idea. "What kind of spell?"

"I don't know," Thistle said. "We could try to modify a locator spell."

"You want to conjure a ball of light and follow it to a murderer?" That sounded like a terrible idea.

"Do you have a better idea?" Thistle challenged.

I swished my lips around as I thought. I finally gave in. "No."

"Then I think this is what we have to do," Thistle said.

"Fine. I think we should ask Aunt Tillie for help, though."

Thistle balked. "Why?"

"Because our spells always go awry if she doesn't help us." That was hard to admit, but it was the truth.

"Fine," Thistle said. "We're never going to live this down. You know that, right?"

Unfortunately, I did. "Let's go out to the inn and talk to her as soon as you're done here."

"Where is Landon?"

"He's checking in with Chief Terry and then meeting me back at the inn."

"What are you going to tell him?" Thistle asked.

"The truth."

Thistle rolled her eyes. "What are you really going to tell him?"

"The truth," I repeated. "I'm not going to lie to him. I told a tiny one this morning. It was miniscule. He was still upset by it. I'm not going to lie. We're not doing anything wrong."

"What if he wants to come?"

"Then he can come."

"Wow. You're growing as a person and a girlfriend," Thistle teased. "I'm shocked at the maturity you're showing."

"Two hours ago we were trying to make Lila dance like Michael Jackson," I reminded her.

"That was mature fun," Thistle said. "Even Landon didn't have a problem with it."

"Yeah. I'm still trying to figure that one out."

"I think we're a bad influence on him."

"I think you're right."

The door flew open and Clove stormed into the store. When she caught sight of me on the couch, she headed straight for me. "You!"

Uh-oh. "Me what?"

"I know what you did," Clove said, her long dark hair flying as she stomped her foot on the ground. "Sam told me everything."

This was a slippery slope. Was she angry because I talked to him behind her back or because I found the mask? "I ... you'll have to be more specific."

"The mask, Bay!"

"It was an accident," I said. "I saw something in the bush and I just went over to look at it. How was I supposed to know what it was?"

"You didn't have to call Landon," Clove said. "You know Sam is being framed. Instead of helping him, though, you turned on him."

"I couldn't not tell Landon," I said. "He has a right to know – and I'm not going to lie to him. That's not fair to him."

"It's also not the right thing to do," Thistle said. "I know you're upset, Clove, but you can't blame Bay for this. She was in a no-win situation. She had to tell Landon."

Clove crossed her arms over her chest. "No, she didn't. She could have pretended she didn't find it."

"That's not fair," I said. "You know I couldn't do that. That would have been a betrayal of Landon."

"Oh, so it's okay to betray my boyfriend as long as yours is happy," Clove said. "Is that what I'm getting?"

"You're out of control right now," Thistle said. "You need to go home and ... I don't know ... relax or something. Get a drink. Take a bath. You're going to say something you regret."

"No, I'm not," Clove said. "I couldn't possibly regret telling the truth. That's Bay's stance, so it's going to be mine now as well."

"Take a breath, Clove," Thistle instructed. "You're talking like a crazy person."

"I'm not crazy," Clove said, lowering her voice. "I finally see what's going on here. You guys don't want me to be happy, so you're purposely going after Sam to make sure I'll never be happy."

"Oh, yeah, that sounds just like us," Thistle said. "We don't want you to be happy."

"You don't," Clove said, her lower lip trembling. "That's why Bay thinks it's perfectly okay to force Sam to break up with me."

All the air in my lungs escaped with an auditory *whoosh*. "What?"

"That's right," Clove said. "Sam broke up with me this afternoon." The tears that had been threatening to fall finally broke free.

"No," I said. "I talked to him this morning. He said he just needed some time alone. He didn't want to worry you."

"That was before you found the mask," Clove said. "Now he knows he's in real trouble."

"That doesn't mean he wants to break up with you," Thistle said. "It only means he's having a rough week."

"A rough week?" Clove's voice climbed an octave.

"Hey, we've all been there."

I knew Thistle was going for levity, but now was not the time. Clove was beyond reason, and she was very close to losing it.

"Clove, what did Sam say exactly?" I asked.

"He said that he didn't want me to be near him while the cops were sniffing around," Clove said.

Well, that didn't sound so bad. It sounded as though he was trying to protect Clove. "He's trying to make sure you aren't hurt."

"He also said that he doesn't think it's a good idea that we see each other right now," Clove said. "He said that he couldn't take care of me and himself. He said he's sorry, but for right now I have to stay away from him."

My heart sank. "Oh, Clove, I'm so sorry."

"Don't talk to me," Clove snapped. "Don't you ever talk to me again! You are officially dead to me, and I'm not just saying it this time." She turned on her heel and stalked out of the store, blowing past Landon as she did.

Landon let her go, wisely taking a step back instead of engaging, and then he fixed his gaze on me. "Do I even want to know?"

"Sam broke up with her," Thistle said.

Landon's face was unreadable. "Did he say why?"

"He said it wasn't good for her to be around him with all of this going on," I said.

"That sounds to me like he was trying to protect her," Landon said. "He's rising in my estimation."

"And Clove has a broken heart," I said.

"Clove is hurting right now," Landon said. "She's also safe. We'll just have to deal with the ... moodiness."

Thistle and I scrunched our faces up in twin looks of disapproval, causing Landon to blanch. "What?"

"Moodiness?" Thistle asked. "Is that your way of saying you think Clove is being a silly female?"

"That's not what I said," Landon said. "I said she's safe. If she wants to be depressed for a few days, I think she's earned it. Sam is doing the right thing."

"Sam is doing the wrong thing," I countered. "He's doing exactly what I told him not to do."

"Maybe that's why he's doing it," Thistle mused.

"What?"

"Maybe it's payback to you for calling the police when you found the mask," Thistle said.

The thought was sobering. Would Sam be that petty? Landon must have read my mind, because he immediately shook his head. "Don't do that," he said. "You can't blame yourself. You did the right thing. If Sam is doing this to hurt you, then he's a jackass."

"You just said you had more respect for him," I said.

"That was before I thought he might be doing it to punish you," Landon said, his expression dark.

I exchanged a look with Thistle. "Well, we definitely have to go ahead with the plan now," I said.

"What plan?" Landon asked, exasperated. "Wait! I don't want to know. No, tell me. Wait! No, I definitely don't want to know. Oh, crap, just tell me."

Thistle smiled at him. "It's going to be a fun night," she said. "You'd better get something to eat now to bolster yourself."

"How did a day that was going so well go down the toilet so fast?" Landon asked.

"I think it's us," I replied. "We somehow do it to ourselves and everyone around us."

Landon reached over and pulled me in for a hug. "Just tell me the plan. I'd rather know now than spend the rest of the afternoon worrying about it."

"We'll tell you on the way to the inn," Thistle said, grabbing her purse from behind the register.

"Why are we going to the inn?"

"We need Aunt Tillie," I said.

"I was wrong," Landon said. "Things just got worse."

NINETEEN

"I can't believe I'm doing this," Landon said, peering through the front window of his Explorer as he followed the ball of light speeding ahead of us. "I said after the last time that that would be the last time. Now, I'm here doing it again. Unbelievable!"

"Stop your bellyaching," Aunt Tillie barked from the backseat. "You love this stuff and you know it."

From the passenger seat, I risked a look at Landon. There was a small smile playing at the corner of his lips. "Is she right?" I hadn't meant to say the words out loud.

Landon arched an eyebrow. "Does it look as though I'm having fun?"

"Kind of."

Landon shook his head. "I must be crazy," he said.

"You didn't have to come with us," I said. "We could have done it on our own."

"Do you really think I would have rewarded you for telling me the truth by abandoning you?"

"I don't think truth is something that should be rewarded," I muttered.

"You've had a rough day," Landon said. "You'll feel better when this is over. I might even be convinced to give you a massage ... if things don't completely blow up in our faces in the next hour."

"How has my day been rough?"

"You thought you were helping Clove and then you ended up hurting her," Landon said, his eyes trained on the road. "You could've pretended you didn't find the mask."

"No, I couldn't have done that," I said. "I wouldn't betray you that way."

Landon darted his eyes to me briefly. "I know. That's not what I meant. You could have tried to protect Clove by doing the wrong thing. You didn't."

"Clove will understand that," Aunt Tillie said. "She's all caught up in her own head right now."

"I hope so," I said.

"Trust me," Aunt Tillie said. "She won't be able to stay angry with you. It's not in her. She's not mean and vindictive like this one." Aunt Tillie gestured to Thistle, next to her in the backseat.

"I am not mean and vindictive," Thistle protested.

"Hey, those are the reasons I like you," Aunt Tillie said. "You remind me of me."

"That's the meanest thing you've ever said to me," Thistle pouted.

"Not even close," Aunt Tillie replied, unruffled. "You probably don't remember, but when you were six I told you there was a lion living in the woods and it wanted to eat you."

"I do kind of remember that," Thistle said. "You said it was only after little girls who lied and that it was waiting for me because I stole your gold necklace. I was afraid to leave the house for a month."

"See, you had it coming," Aunt Tillie said.

"There's just one problem with that," Thistle said. "I didn't steal your gold necklace. Bay accidentally broke it and then blamed it on me."

Aunt Tillie swiveled, and I could see her fixing me with a look in the rearview mirror. "Is that true?"

I shrugged. "I was trying it on and it broke. It was an accident."

"And you let your cousin take the fall for you?"

"Oh, please! She'd probably done six other things to you that week and gotten away with them," I said. "She was probably due to get in trouble."

Aunt Tillie considered the statement. "You're probably right." She pointed at the glowing orb as it made a sharp left. "There."

"I see it," Landon grumbled. "Hey, isn't this the road to the Dragonfly?"

He was right.

"Is anything else out here?" Landon asked.

"Not really," Thistle said. "There are some old cabins, but I don't think they're decent enough to stay in right now. I heard some developer was looking at them."

"Are you sure?" Landon asked. "If the Dragonfly is the only thing out here then … ."

"Then it means whoever robbed the bank lives there," Aunt Tillie said.

"It could be a guest," I reminded her. "It could be someone farther down the road and we forgot someone lived down there."

"It could be," Aunt Tillie said. The ball of light zoomed to a stop – right over the Dragonfly. "Or it could be someone at your fathers' inn."

This sucked.

"We don't know anything yet," Landon said. Instead of parking in the lot he pulled up the road a bit and shut off the Explorer's lights. "Let's not panic until we know something. Can you kill that light?"

Aunt Tillie snapped her fingers and the orb dissipated.

Landon swiveled in his seat. "What do you guys want to do? Do you want to spy on them?"

"Spy? That's undignified," Aunt Tillie said.

"So, what do you want to do?" Landon asked.

"We're going to cast a truth spell on them and then spy," Aunt Tillie said.

Landon pinched the bridge of his nose. "Truth spell? Isn't that what backfired on you guys when my family was in town?"

"Technically yes," Thistle said. "That was because we were working against Aunt Tillie, though. This time we're working with her."

"What does that mean?"

"It means no one is better at casting a truth spell than me," Aunt Tillie said, shoving open the door and hopping out. "Now, come on. I don't want to be here too late. Thor is supposed to be on Jimmy Kimmel."

"Thor?"

"That blond guy who plays Thor in those movies," Aunt Tillie said.

"Chris Hemsworth?"

"If you say so."

"Why do you want to see him?" Thistle asked.

"He's the sexiest man alive."

"Says who?"

"*People* magazine."

Landon shot me a look. "Seriously? We're following the woman setting her schedule around a talk show guest?"

I shrugged. "He is really sexy."

Landon narrowed his eyes.

"For a blond," I corrected hastily. "I prefer my men dark and handsome. Like you."

"Nice save," Landon grumbled. He pushed open his door. "Well, come on. We can't keep Thor waiting."

"**WHAT** ARE THEY DOING?" Aunt Tillie asked, peering through the window at the side of the Dragonfly.

"They're talking," Thistle said. "Aren't you going to cast your spell?"

"Hold your horses, you big nag," Aunt Tillie said. "Give me a second."

Landon leaned against a tree a few feet away and watched us. "You know we're technically breaking the law, right?"

"No, we're not," Thistle said. "We're just … taking a walk."

"Right," Landon said. "We're hunting for mushrooms."

"That's a real thing," Aunt Tillie snapped. She started chanting under her breath. I couldn't make out the words.

"I have a question," Landon said, crossing his arms over his chest. "I understand casting a truth spell. I really do. How does that do us any good if we're not in there to ask the people inside questions?"

Huh. That was a really good question. "Well ... ."

"We're going inside," Aunt Tillie said, clapping her hands as she finished her spell.

"We are?" Thistle raised her eyebrows dubiously.

"We are," Aunt Tillie confirmed.

That sounded like a really bad idea. "How are we going to explain why we're here?"

"Do I have to do everything?" Aunt Tillie was exasperated.

"What lie can we possibly come up with that explains what we're doing out here?" Thistle asked.

"That's a pretty good question."

We all froze when we heard the voice, turning in unison to face my father. "Hi, Dad," I offered lamely.

"Way to go," Aunt Tillie chided Landon. "If you can't act as lookout, what good are you?"

"I didn't realize I was supposed to be the lookout," Landon said. He didn't appear to be upset by my father's appearance. "I thought I was acting as your chauffeur."

"And you did a crappy job at that," Aunt Tillie said.

"How did I do a crappy job at that?"

"You drive like an old lady with cataracts."

"You would know," Landon said.

"Other than arguing and insulting each other, can you tell me what you're doing here?" Dad asked.

"We came to visit you," I said with faux brightness. "Doesn't that make you happy?"

"If I thought you were actually here to visit me, it would," Dad said. "Unfortunately, I know you're up to something witchy."

My mouth dropped open. "What makes you say that?"

"I'm not stupid."

"Wait a second," Thistle said. "Shouldn't he be ... ?"

"Telling the truth?" Landon supplied. "What makes you think he isn't?"

"What are you guys talking about?" Dad asked.

"Let's test him," Landon said. He moved in front of my father. "What do you really think about me?"

"I think that you seem far too affectionate with my daughter and I don't like it, because if you die in the line of duty she's going to be broken for the rest of her life." Dad shook his head, stunned by the words. "I ... I don't know why I said that."

"You're saying you don't dislike me. You're saying you're worried I'll die and hurt Bay," Landon said. "Is that right?"

"I don't particularly like how you're always touching her, but I have nothing personal against you," Dad said.

"This could work," Landon said, moving around my father. "Let's go inside."

"You still haven't told me why you're here," Dad said.

"We're here to spy on you for our mothers," I lied.

"Why?"

"Because they're worried you're going to steal business from them," I said. "We told them it wasn't true, but they want to know whether you're doing something special to wow your guests."

"That does not sound like your mother," Dad said.

I was surprised he was taking up for her. He didn't go out of his way to badmouth her, but he was bitter where their breakup was concerned. I decided to take advantage of the situation.

"Why did you leave?"

Thistle's eyes widened. "Now? You want to get into that now?"

"Can you think of a better time?"

Thistle shrugged. "Actually, no. Why did you leave?"

"It was just too hard," Dad said. "I didn't want to leave you. None of us wanted to leave you. Living in Hemlock Cove was like living under a microscope. People were always talking about your mothers, and especially Aunt Tillie, and it started causing problems.

"It had nothing to do with any of you," he continued. "We were fighting all the time, and you were all so unhappy. Marnie and Warren were even talking about putting Clove in therapy because she had taken to chewing her hair.

"At a certain point, we had to make a decision," Dad said. "We either had to stay and watch you guys suffer or leave."

"You still could have seen us," I said.

"We wanted to," Dad said. "It became harder and harder as you got older. The more time we spent away, the harder it was to come back. I think I convinced myself that you didn't even miss me."

"That wasn't true," I said.

"I know." Dad's face was a mask of concern. "I tried to see you as often as I could."

"It wasn't enough."

"I ... I have no idea what's going on here." Dad looked miserable.

"Don't worry about it," Aunt Tillie said. "It was a long time coming."

"I guess it was," Dad said. "Wait, what are you doing here?"

"Spying," Aunt Tillie said. "Keep up." She turned toward the front of the building. "We might as well go inside. We've already been discovered."

"What are you going to do inside?" Dad asked, worried.

"We're going to have a nightcap with your guests," Landon said. "We're going to converse, and everyone is going to get along. Then we're going to go and everything is going to be fine."

"Who are you trying to convince when you say that?" Thistle asked. "Is it Uncle Jack or yourself?"

"Both," Landon said. He held out his hand to me. "Come on. Let's get this over with."

"What should we ask when we get inside?"

"Let me do the talking," Landon said. "I'm a professional."

"You can't even drive your truck," Aunt Tillie countered. "Let me do the talking. I'm better at it."

"Just ... get inside."

I raised an eyebrow as Landon led me toward the front porch. "Are you still glad you came?"

Landon was beaming when he turned to me. "I hate to admit it, but she's right. I do love this stuff."

TWENTY

"Who should we start with?" Aunt Tillie asked, rubbing her hands together.

My gaze landed on Lila. "I'm going to let Landon do the heavy lifting," I said, patting his arm. "He's a professional, after all. He's going to be a lot better at this than we will be."

Landon narrowed his eyes suspiciously. "Okay, suck-up, what are you going to do?"

"What makes you think I'm going to do anything?" I asked, hoping my face looked innocent despite the evil intentions running through my mind.

"I know you," Landon said. He scanned the room. When he saw Lila heading in our direction, he groaned. "What are you going to ask her?"

"Just a few simple questions."

"Fine," Landon said. "Go nuts. Just don't leave this room. Can you do that?"

"Sure."

Landon gave me a soft kiss. "Just keep her away from me."

"Landon." Lila practically purred as she approached us. "I had no idea you were coming here tonight. You just can't stay away, can you?"

Landon furrowed his brow. "Do you really believe that, or are you just trying to annoy Bay?"

I arched an eyebrow.

"What? I want to play, too," Landon said. "Answer the question, Lila."

"I just don't see what you could possibly see in her," Lila said. "She's not very pretty, and she's a total ... freak."

I frowned. Apparently this wasn't going to be as much fun as I initially thought. "I'm not very pretty?"

"Oh, sure, if you like that corn-fed bland thing you do so well," Lila said. "When men look at me, they see a fine wine. When they look at you, they see a bottle of stale beer. It's not your fault. You were born that way."

My mouth dropped open.

"You honestly think you're prettier than Bay?" Landon asked.

"Of course," Lila said. "I was the most popular girl in high school."

Landon shook his head. "Is that why you still live in high school?"

"I miss high school," Lila said. "That was the best time of my life."

"How sad for you," Landon said. He glanced at me. "Do not let her get to you," he directed. "She's not worth one second of your time. She's not worth one second of doubt. Promise me."

"I promise."

"Okay," Landon said, running his hand down the back of my head to smooth my hair. "I'll be close." He cast a disparaging look in Lila's direction. "It's not high school. The sooner you realize that, the sooner you'll have the opportunity to become a real person."

Once Landon was gone, Lila fixed me with a wide-eyed look. "He really is something, isn't he?"

"Yeah," I agreed. "He's my something."

"For now," Lila said.

"You don't even live here," I said. "You're in town for a week. How do you possibly think you're going to snag Landon?"

"Oh, I plan on putting the full-court press on him," Lila said. "That's a sports metaphor, by the way. Besides, I'm not leaving town. I'm staying."

"Why?" I was horrified.

"I lost my job at the real estate agency," Lila said. "Wait, no I didn't. What ... why did I just say that?"

"I have no idea," I said. "Why did you lose your job?"

"I was having sex with my boss, and his wife found out," Lila said. "Seriously, why did I just tell you that?"

"Maybe you want to get it off your chest," I said. "Did you know your boss was married when you started sleeping with him?"

"Of course," Lila said. "His wife was pregnant, though, and I knew she was too fat to satisfy her husband. He was an easy mark. He told me he was going to leave her so we could get married, but then he fired me and stopped taking my calls."

"What did you do?"

"I left a photo of us in bed on her car windshield."

Nice.

"What's going on here?" Thistle asked, moving up beside me.

"Lila was just telling me how she got fired from her job as a secretary at a real estate office because she was sleeping with her married boss," I said.

"I thought you were a very important person," Thistle said. "Isn't that what you told us?"

"Of course I told you that," Lila said. "I didn't want you to think I was a loser. You two are losers. I need to be better than you guys." Lila's hands flew to her mouth. "What is going on? Does this have something to do with what happened to me this afternoon?"

"What do you think happened to you this afternoon?" I asked.

"I think you cast a spell on me," Lila answered matter-of-factly.

Thistle arched an eyebrow. "A spell?"

"Everyone in this town knows you're real witches," Lila said.

"How do they know that?"

"I don't know. They just do."

Thistle and I exchanged a look. "If you believe that we're real witches, why would you mess with us?" Thistle asked.

"I can't stop myself," Lila said. "It's a compulsion. I hate freaks, and you guys are freaks."

"Well, here's a little truth for you," I said. "We may be freaks, but we're employed and we don't have to lower ourselves to sleeping with married men to try to get ahead in this world. We believe in a hard day's work."

"That's something all losers say," Lila said. "Why would you work if you didn't have to?"

"She's kind of sad," Thistle said. "I thought she was just mean. She's pathetic, too."

"I know," I agreed. "I thought this was going to be so much more fun than it is."

"Oh, I can still make it fun," Thistle said. "Hey, Lila, how old were you before you needed a bra?"

"Sixteen."

"I knew you stuffed," Thistle said.

"I didn't stuff," Lila said. "My mother bought me a water bra. It enhanced. It wasn't fake."

"It's fake when you fill it with Lake Michigan."

"Whatever," Lila sniffed. "I was a late bloomer."

"How much work have you had done?" I asked.

Landon, who was moving between guests, paused behind us. "Are you having fun yet?"

"It's getting better," I said.

"I had my boobs and nose done," Lila said. "I also get Botox injections every three months."

"How can you afford Botox?" Thistle asked. "You said you were fired from your job at the real estate agency."

"I'm sleeping with the doctor, and he gives it to me for free because he doesn't want me to tell his wife," Lila said. "Wait … that's not true … well, it's true but I really shouldn't be telling you that … seriously, what is going on?"

"I think you have a guilty conscience," I said.

"Evil doesn't have a conscience," Aunt Tillie said, popping from behind Lila. "Has she told you anything good?"

"Not really," I said. "Some of it is funny. Most of it isn't, though."

"It's just sad," Thistle agreed. "Where have you been?"

"Questioning your fathers," Aunt Tillie said.

Uh-oh. "About what?"

"How they really feel about me."

"And?"

"It's not good," Aunt Tillie said. "I'm happy."

"You're happy?"

"They live in fear of what I'm going to do to them," Aunt Tillie said. "I'm happy."

We all looked up when the front door opened to allow Chief Terry entrance. "What's he doing here?" I asked.

"Oh, I called him when I saw you guys spying from the window," Lila said. "He's here to arrest you for trespassing. Don't worry, I'll keep Landon warm for you."

"Listen, you … walking herpes donor … stay away from Landon," I said.

"What are you going to do if I don't?" Lila asked.

"I'm going to fill your mouth full of dirt and kick you in your filthy lady bits," I said.

"Nice," Thistle said. "I'm glad to see you're getting some of your spunk back."

"I can't believe I was ever afraid of her," I said.

"Me either."

"Do you want to give her herpes?" Aunt Tillie asked, her eyes bright.

"You can't get rid of herpes," I said. "Give her ringworm or something. That will make her hair fall out."

"Oh, that shows what you know," Lila said. "I have a weave."

"So, wait, you stuffed all through high school and you had fake hair? I knew it!" Thistle practically crowed.

"Of course she stuffed," Aunt Tillie said. "Her mother is flat as a board."

"My mother has a concave back," Lila said.

"Oh, she's like a hunchback," Thistle said.

I kept one ear on the conversation and the other on Chief Terry as he discussed something with my father. I couldn't make out what they said to each other, but things looked heated between them. My father gestured wildly.

"I'll be right back," I said, moving across the room. I tugged on Chief Terry's coat when I got close. "What's going on?"

Dad's face was red.

"Your father was giving me an earful," Chief Terry said. "I got a call that there was a prowler here. He says it was you."

"It wasn't only me," I said. "It was Aunt Tillie and Thistle, too." I figured throwing Landon under the bus wasn't the best way to go.

"Why were you spying?"

"We were bored."

Chief Terry tilted his head to the side. "Do you really want to tell me what you were doing?"

That was a thorny question. "Well ... ."

"I'll handle this," Landon said, stepping between Chief Terry and me. "Let's go over here and talk."

"You're a prowler, too?" Chief Terry was beside himself.

"I'm the chauffeur," Landon replied. "Come over here."

Once they stepped away, I shot my father a rueful smile. "I'm sorry we invaded you tonight."

"Why did he have to come?"

"Who?"

"Terry."

I frowned. "Lila said she called him when she saw us lurking outside," I explained. "She was hoping we would get arrested. She wants Landon."

"Oh, please," Dad said. "Landon would never fall for the likes of her. Don't worry about that. He's utterly devoted to you."

Finally the truth spell was making me feel better. "Do you really think so?"

"Unfortunately, yes," Dad said. "I have a feeling he's going to be the father of my grandchildren."

That was a sobering thought. "I don't think you have to worry about that right now," I said. "We're nowhere near that point."

"Good," Dad said. "I'm not ready to be a grandfather. Although, to be honest, the idea of your mother becoming a grandmother makes me kind of happy."

"Why?"

"I want the kid to call her 'Granny.' Can you promise me that?"

I smiled, despite myself. "I can try."

I watched Dad as he stared at Landon and Chief Terry for a moment. "Why do you have such a problem with Chief Terry?" I asked.

"I don't like that you're so close with him."

"Why?"

"You treat him more like a father than me."

"In some ways he was more of a father than you," I said. "That doesn't mean you're not my father."

"You don't have to say that," Dad said. "I know I was a terrible father."

I felt helpless. "You were the best father you could be. You came back. That counts."

"He was there for you when you needed someone."

"He was." There was no way I would ever say anything bad about Chief Terry. "He was always there for me. That doesn't mean you're in competition with him."

"Isn't your mother involved with him?"

I pursed my lips. "My mother and aunts compete for his affection."

"Do you think one of them will win?"

"I think he's afraid to let one of them win," I said. "If he does, the other two will get hurt. Besides, I'm not sure any of them really want to win. They like competing with each other more than anything else."

"Some things never changed," Dad said, smiling sadly. "Still, I want your mother to be happy. She's a good woman. She drove me crazy for ten years, but she's a very good woman."

"She is. She's also a rampant pain in the ass."

Dad smirked. "She's definitely a pain in the ass."

Landon and Chief Terry approached us warily.

"Is everything okay?" I asked.

Landon's face was a mask of worry as he regarded me. "I questioned everyone here. I questioned your father and uncles, too, and if you're going to have a fit about that wait until we get back to the guesthouse."

"I expected you to question them," I said.

"Question us about what?" Dad asked. "The robbery? Did you really think one of us did it?"

Landon ignored the question. "Everyone here denies being involved."

"But ... how is that possible?"

"I don't know. Maybe the spell didn't work."

"Oh, it worked."

"What spell?" Dad asked, mortified.

"It's not important," I said. "It will be over soon."

"It's still going on?" Now Dad looked angry. "You cast a spell on us?"

"Don't even get all uppity with her," Aunt Tillie said, pushing past me and glaring up at my father. "I cast the spell. Blame me."

"She came with you."

I felt caught. "Dad ... I ... ." What could I say?

"I think you should all be going," Dad said.

"Dad, I'm sorry."

His face was immovable. "Have a nice night."

TWENTY-ONE

I woke up the next morning with a killer headache and Landon breathing down my neck. He was practically on top of me, snoring like a freight train.

I tried to wriggle out from under him, exasperated, but he snagged me around the waist and held me still. "Good morning."

"You're awake? Why were you snoring?"

"I was trying to wake you up without being a jerk," Landon said.

"So you thought snoring in my ear was the best way to go?"

"You're crabby this morning," Landon said, rolling away slightly but not loosening his grip on me. "Do you want to talk about what happened last night?"

"What do you want me to say? Do you want to talk about how Lila is even worse than I thought?"

"Not particularly."

"Do you want to talk about how my father essentially kicked us out of his inn because he thinks we betrayed him?"

"That's what I was talking about." Landon stretched languidly and then ran a hand through his sleep-tousled hair. "You were pretty quiet after we left."

"What do you want me to say?" I was angry. Sure, most of my ire was directed at me, but I was furious with Landon, too.

"Why are you angry with me?" Landon asked, his eyes wide. "What did I do?"

"You let us get completely out of control," I said.

Landon rolled his eyes. "I let you? When have I ever let you do anything? I think you're really angry with yourself and you're taking it out on me."

I threw the covers back dramatically. "That just shows how little you know." I started to move out of the bed, but Landon grabbed my arm.

"You're not getting out of this bed yet," he said. "I want to talk about this."

"What is there to say?" I asked, my voice bordering on shrill. "I managed to make my relationship with my father even worse than it already was."

"I think we all had a hand in that," Landon said. "Why don't you call him and make up? The spell is over now, right?"

"Yes."

"So call him," Landon prodded.

"I can't," I said. "I don't know how to interact with him."

"Why not?"

"I'm afraid of saying the wrong thing." I studied my fingernail beds so I wouldn't have to look him in the eye.

"You're afraid that if you tell him how you really feel he's going to take off again," Landon said. "Is that it?"

"I ... ."

"Bay, I think that's a reasonable fear," Landon said. "You were young when your father left. You saw him only a couple of times a year after that. You probably blamed yourself.

"I'm not saying you were to blame, mind you," he continued. "Kids always blame themselves – and you have a martyr complex as it is."

"I do not have a martyr complex," I grumbled.

"You do," Landon said. "You can't go through life afraid to tell your father how you really feel. He deserves the chance to hear some honesty. If you want to unload on him, unload on him."

"And if he leaves again?"

"Then he was never worth your time," Landon said. "As someone who ... walked away for a little while ... you should know that being away from you is a miserable experience. I think he knows that. He's not going to run if you yell ... and you've been bottling this up for so long you're ready to explode."

I scrunched my nose up as I regarded him. "Were you really miserable when you were away from me?"

Landon grinned. "Why did I know that was the thing you would focus on?"

"Because I'm so transparent."

Landon kissed the tip of my nose. "I was definitely miserable."

"Did you cry?"

"No."

"Did you want to?"

"Don't push your luck, Bay."

"WHAT'S GOING ON?"

Thistle arose in the middle of the living room, hands on hips. Marcus sat on the couch, a dumbfounded look on his face as Landon and I exited the bedroom.

"Clove moved out."

"Yeah, right. What's really going on?"

"She really moved out," Thistle said. She pointed to a sheet of paper on the coffee table. "She packed her clothes and left."

I narrowed my eyes and snatched the sheet of paper from the table. It was definitely a goodbye note. She must have been in a hurry – or drunk – because half of the words were misspelled. "But ... where would she go?"

"Maybe she's at the Dandridge," Marcus suggested.

"Sam broke up with her. Keep up." Thistle was beside herself.

"Hey! Don't take your bad morning out on me," Marcus said. "I'm trying to help."

"I'm sorry," Thistle said. "I just ... I can't believe she did this." She turned on me. "This is your fault."

"What?"

"You shouldn't have called Landon when you found that mask."

"You said I did the right thing," I said. "Now this is my fault?"

"You broke her heart."

"I'm going to break your face if you don't shut up," I snapped.

"Everyone calm down," Landon instructed. He took the note from me and scanned it. "This reads like an eight-year-old wrote it. Are you sure it's her handwriting?"

"Who else would leave a note calling us the 'worst cousins ever?'"

"A really dramatic middle-schooler," Landon replied, nonplussed.

"You're on my list," Thistle said, pointing at him.

"Right back at you," Landon said. "Let's look at this logically, shall we? Where could she go? We know she's not out at the Dandridge. All the inns in the area are booked because of the festival. She has nowhere to go. She probably slept in her car."

"Or she's just up at the inn," Marcus muttered, running his hand through his hair.

We all stilled. How did the one man in the room without any investigative experience come up with the only plausible answer? We were all off our game.

"Everyone get showered and dressed," Landon said. "We'll go up to the inn together. You two can apologize to Clove, and everything will be back to normal in five minutes flat."

"That's right," Marcus said. "Just be nice to her. I know you can do this if you set your minds to it."

Thistle made a face. "I'm always nice to her."

Landon and Marcus exchanged dubious looks.

Thistle turned to me for support. "Do you want to chime in here?"

"Just be nice," I said.

"This is still your fault," Thistle said.

"It's no one's fault," Landon said. "Stop screeching at each other. You're giving me a headache."

"You're giving me a headache," Thistle shot back.

"You're both giving me a headache," I said.

"Get in the shower, Bay," Landon said. "You're on my list."

OKAY, everyone, try to remain calm and be nice," Marcus said, his hand hovering over the backdoor handle. "If we all stand together, we can do this. We're a team."

"Who are you talking to?" Thistle asked.

"You."

"I know what I'm doing," Thistle said. "You just need to calm down."

Marcus didn't look convinced. "You look as if you're going to make things worse." He turned to Landon. "Right?"

"Oh, no, you're on your own," Landon said. "This is one fight I don't want to referee."

"You're saying that because you and Bay made up in the shower before we came here," Thistle said.

"How did you know that?" I asked.

"You just told me," Thistle said. "Plus, Landon has a lazy grin right after you guys ... you know. He's had it for the past five minutes."

I studied him for a moment. He did look a little self-satisfied. "I think he's handsome," I said finally.

Landon smiled down at me and gave me a quick kiss.

"I'm going to be sick," Thistle griped.

Marcus opened the door, and when Thistle began to move past him he stopped her with a hand on her arm. "Why don't you ever say nice things like that to me?"

"Because you already know you're handsome."

"Do you think I'm better looking than Landon?" Marcus asked.

"Of course."

"Hey! No one is better looking than me," Landon said.

We filed into the back of the inn, pulling up short when we found Clove staring at us from the entry that led into the kitchen. Her expression was murderous. "What are you doing here?"

"Having breakfast," Thistle said.

"And we came to find you," I added. "We were worried."

"You realize I heard everything you said while you were arguing by the back door, right?" Clove's face was pale, and dark shadows rimmed her eyes. "You didn't sound worried. You sounded like you all had a great morning together ... without me."

Of course she'd been listening. If I didn't have bad luck, I would have no luck at all these days. "Why are you down here?"

"Because I can't trust the two of you," Clove said.

"What did I do?" Thistle asked. "Bay's the one who betrayed you when she turned Sam into Landon. She's dead to you, but I'm still alive."

I scorched her with a look.

"Every witch for herself," Thistle shrugged.

"Why is it that my life is coming to an end and yet it's business as usual for the two of you?" Clove asked.

"Let's not get dramatic," I said. "You're going through a rough patch, but your life isn't coming to an end."

"Thanks to you," Clove said.

"Stop fighting right now," Aunt Tillie said, flouncing out of the hallway and fixing us with a look of disappointment. "You're acting like children."

It was an interesting insult coming from a diminutive elderly woman wearing combat boots and pink camouflage pants.

"Where did you get those pants?" Thistle asked. "And are those ... sparkles ... on the knees?"

"I ordered them on line, and they're not sparkles. They're ... glitter flecks. They're rated four and a half stars on Amazon. All the kids are wearing them."

"Well, good," I said. "This won't end poorly for me."

"Oh, suck it up," Aunt Tillie said. "They're pants. What's the big deal?"

"Has Mom seen those yet?"

"Of course not," Aunt Tillie said. "I was saving them for a special occasion."

"Why did you decide to wear them when the inn is full of people?" I asked.

"I plan my offensives against your mothers very carefully," Aunt Tillie said. "This happens to be a perfect time to irritate them."

"Why?"

"Because they're going to give me anything I want to get me to change my clothes."

"What do you want?"

"I can't tell you in front of ... him." She inclined her head in Landon's direction.

"Why?" I asked.

"Because he's the fuzz, and he'll turn me in."

Now it was Landon's turn to be suspicious. "What are you up to?"

"What makes you think I'm up to something?"

"You just said you couldn't tell them what you were up to because I was here. I want to know what you're doing."

"I'm old," Aunt Tillie said. "You can't expect me to remember everything I say. My mind is like Swiss cheese."

Landon narrowed his eyes. "Tell me what you're up to."

"I'm not up to anything. If I didn't know any better, I would think you're paranoid." Aunt Tillie knows exactly how to get under Landon's skin. If it were an Olympic sport, she'd claim the gold, silver and bronze medals.

"I'm not paranoid," Landon said. "You're always up to something."

"Maybe you always think I'm up to something because you're paranoid," Aunt Tillie countered. "Have you been smoking the wacky tobacky? You know that's illegal, right?"

Since Aunt Tillie had her own pot field, and she magically cloaked it so Landon couldn't find it and burn her crop, that was a pointed jab.

"I'm going to find out what you're up to," Landon warned. "You're not getting ahead of me on this one. I won't let you."

"You do what you have to," Aunt Tillie said. She grabbed her gardening hat from the nearby desk and plopped it on her head. She'd glued fake flowers – and what appeared to be a rubber spider – to it since I'd last seen it.

"What's with the hat?" I asked, confused.

"It matches the pants."

It really didn't.

"Are we done here?" Aunt Tillie asked.

"We're just starting," Landon said.

"You're cute," Aunt Tillie said. "You're like a puppy with a bone. Or, even better, a kitten that sees its reflection in a mirror and gets paranoid enough to believe it's another cat."

Landon scowled. "I'm going to find out what you're doing."

"I should hope so," Aunt Tillie said, shuffling through the room. "You're a professional investigator, after all. There's no way a little old lady like me could outsmart you. None at all."

When she turned to push through the swinging door, I saw what I had missed on first inspection of the garish pants. There was a message written across the rear end. It was one word, but it was enough to induce simultaneous aneurisms when my mother and aunts saw it.

"Hurry up," Aunt Tillie said. "If you're late for breakfast, you're going to get in trouble."

Once she was gone, Thistle turned to me. "She had writing on her butt. You saw that, right?"

"I saw it."

"What did it say?" Marcus asked. "I was afraid to look for too long. She's still convinced I tried to feel her up when we shared that bed together at the Dragonfly. I didn't want to give her more ammunition."

"It said 'juicy,'" Landon said, wearily.

Thistle, Clove and I were already moving toward the kitchen door.

"Why are you guys in such a hurry all of the sudden?" Landon asked. "I thought you were fighting."

"Oh, we're still fighting," Clove said. "We can't miss this, though."

"She's right," I said. "This could be the best breakfast ever."

"It's going to be legendary," Thistle said.

"Omigod!" The screech flew from the kitchen.

"We're missing it," Thistle said, pushing through the door. "Come on. Someone make sure to video it on a phone. I don't ever want to forget this moment."

TWENTY-TWO

"You are not wearing that to breakfast." Mom vigorously waved her spatula as she rolled up and down on the balls of her feet.

"I have no idea what you're talking about," Aunt Tillie said, her face blasé. "What's wrong with my outfit?"

"You know very well what's wrong with that outfit."

"I'm at a loss."

Mom shifted her gaze to the five of us, a mixture of helplessness and rage washing over her face. "Tell her what's wrong with that outfit."

"I love it," I said, not missing a beat.

"I think the color is really good for her skin tone," Thistle said, her eyes sparkling.

"I think she could sell those hats on Etsy," Clove said.

Mom glowered at us. "I know what you're doing."

"That's a horrible thing to say," I said, grabbing Landon's hand and pulling him through the kitchen and toward the dining room. "We're just calling it like we see it."

Mom smacked me on the arm with the spatula. "We're going to have a talk about this later."

"I can't wait," I said.

I pushed Landon through the door in front of me, managing to keep from laughing out loud until we were on the other side.

"You're going to Hell. You know that, right?" Landon looked as though he was enjoying the situation.

"It's going to be fun," I said. "If we're lucky, Aunt Tillie is going to monopolize the entire breakfast conversation this morning."

"Which means you don't have to deal with Clove," Landon finished.

"I ... ." He knows me too well. I decided to change tactics. "That's a horrible thing to say. You're really hurting my feelings."

"That doesn't work on me."

I kissed his cheek softly.

"That works better," Landon conceded. He wrapped his arms around me and gave me a hug. "You're very manipulative."

"I learned from the best."

"Aunt Tillie?"

"Actually ... they all taught me a lesson or two."

"Good to know," Landon said, making his way to his usual seat. "What are you going to do today?"

This was a test. "I'm going to try to find Amy." I kept my voice low. Only a few guests were sitting at the table, and they were talking amongst themselves, but I didn't want them to overhear me admitting I was trying to find a ghost.

Landon arched an eyebrow. "Really?"

"She's our best option to clear Sam."

"Where are you going to look?" Landon asked.

"I'll start downtown," I said. "If she's not there, I'll check her house."

"I have to check in with Chief Terry," Landon said. "If you want to wait for me, I'll go with you."

"Are you worried I'm going to get in trouble, or are you worried I'm not telling you the truth?" It was a pointed question.

"Neither," Landon said. "Maybe I just want to spend some time with you. Did you ever consider that?"

I rolled my eyes. "Now who is playing who?"

Landon gave in and grinned. "Just be careful. If you could text me a couple of times while you are out and about it would make me feel better."

"Dirty texts?"

"Those would make me feel great."

The sound of scuffling in the other room assailed our ears.

"What do you think?" Thistle asked.

"I think they're wrestling," Clove said.

"Are you still angry?" I asked.

"I'm not talking to you," Clove said, crossing her arms over her chest.

"Oh, good, it's starting." The brunette at the middle of the table looked excited as she glanced between us. "Do you guys work from scripts?"

The guests were starting to get to me with all their talk of dinner theater. "No."

"Oh, improv," the woman said. "That makes it even better."

"We're glad to be able to entertain you," Thistle said.

"Oh, good, I'm not late." Nick rounded the corner and headed for the open chair next to me. "You look nice this morning, Bay. You look nice every morning, though."

"Thank you."

"I'm going to punch him," Landon grumbled under his breath.

"Did you say something?" Nick asked.

"He was wondering where breakfast is," I answered smoothly. "His blood sugar is low."

"There'd better be bacon," Landon said.

Something clattered in the kitchen, causing everyone to shift their attention in that direction. "You are not going out there!" It sounded as if Marnie was working against Aunt Tillie now.

"Don't ever tell me what I can do," Aunt Tillie said.

"We're not telling you what you can do," Mom said. "We're telling you what you can't do."

"Why are they starting the show in there?" The brunette wrinkled her nose, disappointed.

"I think they're warming up," I said.

"Oh, that makes sense," the woman said. "You're probably right."

"She's not right," Clove said. "Trust me. She's not right."

"Really, Clove? Now you're ready to talk about this?" She was starting to tick me off.

"I'm not talking to you."

"No, you're just talking about me," I countered, "while I'm sitting at the same table."

"Did someone hear something?" Clove asked, lifting her chin higher. "It's like there's this ... annoying buzzing ... and I can't figure out where it's coming from."

"That's mature," I grumbled.

"You are not going out there in that outfit." Mom was obviously still struggling with Aunt Tillie in the next room.

"I don't think it's that bad," Twila said. "It's a nice color."

"Leave it to Twila to turn on them," I said.

"She's always the one who gives in to Aunt Tillie," Thistle agreed.

"Maybe it's just that she's loyal to the aunt who helped raise her," Clove suggested. "I know loyalty is a weird concept for some of us, but I admire it."

"How was I disloyal to you?" I snapped.

"You got me dumped," Clove said.

"You're single now?" Nick looked interested, and that bothered me for some reason. I didn't like him flirting with me – well, kind of – but I didn't want him moving in on an impressionable Clove. She could only deal with so much at one time.

"She's not single," I said.

"He said he didn't want to see me," Clove said. "And he said it right after you stuck your big, fat nose into the middle of our business."

"Oh, that's not what happened."

"It's exactly what happened," Clove said. "You got me dumped. Admit it."

"Are you single or not?" Nick asked. "I'm lost."

"Then stay out of it," Landon said.

"Are you dating both of them or something?" Nick challenged.

"No."

"Then why do you care whether I'm interested in Clove? Shouldn't you be focused on Bay?"

"I am focused on Bay," Landon said. "I'm focused on her being happy. You romancing anyone in this family makes us all unhappy."

"You're a bundle of joy," Nick said.

"And he has no say over what I do," Clove said. "He didn't want me to date Sam, and yet I dated him."

"So, would you like to go out?" Nick asked.

"No," Clove said, making a face. "I have a boyfriend."

"I thought he dumped you?"

"Because of Bay."

"Let go of me!" Aunt Tillie muscled her way into the dining room, clutching her hat as she gained entrance. Everyone at the table shifted to stare at her. "Good morning."

"Good morning," everyone replied in unison.

Mom, Marnie and Twila followed her into the room, their faces red with exertion.

"Come back here," Mom growled.

Aunt Tillie ignored her and primly sat in her chair. "What's for breakfast? I'm starving."

IT TURNS out I didn't have to go too far to find Amy. She was waiting for me on the back porch of The Overlook when Thistle, Marcus and I let ourselves out of the inn an hour later.

"Your family should be committed," she said.

"Oh, you saw that?"

"Who is she talking to?" Marcus asked.

Thistle shrugged. "Probably a ghost. Anyone I know?"

"It's Amy Madison."

"Does she have any news?" Thistle asked.

"I've talked to her for exactly five seconds," I said. "How would I know?"

Thistle stuck out her tongue and blew a thick raspberry.

"Nice."

"Family therapy might help all of you," Amy said. "I've never seen a display like that in my whole life ... or afterlife, for that matter."

"Oh, I'm starting to hear her," Thistle said.

For some unknown reason, while Thistle and Clove couldn't see ghosts on their own, if they were around me when I was talking to one they could eventually hear them. It was a strange quirk in our genetic makeup that we hadn't quite figured out.

"She can see ghosts, too?" Amy asked.

"No," Thistle replied. "I can hear them when I'm around Bay, though."

"You people are freaks," Amy said, crossing her ethereal arms over her chest.

"Do you want us to help you or not?" Thistle asked.

Amy rolled her eyes. I was thankful Thistle couldn't see her. We were all on edge, and I had no idea how far Thistle could be pushed right now.

"Did you remember something?" I asked.

"I did," Amy said. "I remembered that people around town are always whispering about you guys."

I made a face.

"You're really witches, aren't you?"

"We're ... hard to explain," I said. "It's a long story."

"We're witches," Thistle said.

I shot her a look.

"What?" Thistle was nonplussed. "Who is she going to tell?"

"Do you cast spells on people?" Amy asked.

"No."

"It depends on whether they piss us off," Thistle said.

"Can you cast a spell on my ex-boyfriend?"

"No," I said.

"What did he do?" Thistle asked.

"He dumped me for some eighteen-year-old who works at a Dairy Queen in Traverse City. She doesn't wear a bra."

"Sure," Thistle said. "What do you want? We could shrink his testicles."

"No one would notice," Amy said. "Can you make his hair fall out?"

"Sure."

"Thistle!"

"What? The guy sounds like a turd," Thistle said.

I rolled my eyes. "Do you remember anything about the robbery?" I asked, changing the subject.

"That's all I think about," Amy said. "It's like a running loop in my head. And I've been thinking about Tom Burton a little. What are the ethics involved if I drop into his house as a ghost and look at him naked?"

I pressed my lips together, unsure how to answer.

"I think that's fine," Thistle said. "It's not as though he'll ever know."

"Thistle, you cannot tell her to spy on a naked man," I said.

"What naked man?" Marcus asked.

"He's hot," Thistle said. "I'm sure he'd be flattered."

"Who is hot?" Marcus asked.

"You're hot, baby," Thistle said, rubbing his arm.

"She wants to see me naked?" Marcus was lost.

"No," I said.

"I wouldn't mind seeing him naked," Amy said. "He's even better looking than Tom."

"You can't see him naked," Thistle said. "I'm the only one who can see him naked."

"I accidentally saw him in the bathroom last week," I admitted. "You're a lucky woman."

Marcus' cheeks colored. "We said we weren't going to tell her."

"It's not a big deal," I said. "It's not as if she thinks something is going on between us."

Thistle pinched my arm viciously. "Don't ever look at him again."

"Ow!" I yanked my arm away. "It was an accident. It happened to you, too. Landon said you walked into my bedroom two weeks ago and saw him naked. Thanks for knocking, by the way."

"You saw Landon naked?" Marcus was horrified. "Does he have a better body than me?"

"No one has a better body than you," Thistle said, distracted. "Do you really think Marcus is better looking than Tom?" she asked Amy.

"Oh, definitely," Amy said. "He's one of the hottest guys in town."

"Hotter than Bay's boyfriend, right?"

Amy shook her head. "I don't know. There's something mysterious about him. Plus, he's always doting on Bay. People are always talking about him. We can't figure out how Bay snagged him."

"Hey! I'm desirable," I said.

"I think we need to put new locks on all the doors in the guesthouse," Marcus said.

"Sure, honey," Thistle said.

"And we need to lock the doors," Marcus said.

"Sure," I said. I returned my focus to Amy. "So, about the robbery …"

"Yeah, yeah, yeah," Amy said. "That's why I came out here. I wanted to tell you that I thought I recognized the voice."

"Who was it?" Thistle asked, intrigued.

"I have no idea," Amy said. "It was familiar, but I can't quite place it."

"You came out here to tell us you think you might've recognized the voice of the robber but you don't know who it is?" She was starting to bug me.

"Yes."

"Okay. Well … thanks."

"Is that all?" Amy asked.

"For now," I said.

Amy smiled in Marcus' direction.

"You know he can't see you, right?"

"Oh," Amy said. "I forgot. I still wouldn't mind seeing him naked."

"And we're going," Thistle said, lacing her fingers with Marcus' and tugging him down the pathway. I could hear them talking as they walked away. "Sometimes I think you're too hot for me."

"You're hotter than the sun, honey," Marcus replied. "You're too hot for me."

"See, you're the perfect man," Thistle said. "You know when I'm fishing for a compliment."

"I'm still angry you saw Landon naked."

"Don't worry," Thistle said. "You have a better body." She cast a look at me from over her shoulder and silently shook her head. "You have the best body ever, baby."

TWENTY-THREE

"Is this the best plan we can come up with?" Thistle asked, scanning the festival dubiously.

"Do you have a better idea?"

"We could cast a truth spell on the entire fair," Thistle suggested. "We'll cast the spell and then walk up to everyone and ask whether they're a murdering robber."

"Absolutely not."

"You're still upset about what Uncle Jack said to you last night, aren't you?"

I bit the inside of my cheek and pretended I didn't hear the question. "Should we split up or work together?"

"Bay, he was just upset," Thistle said. "He didn't mean it. We didn't technically do anything wrong."

"We cast a spell on our fathers and all of their guests," I said. "This was after we spied on them and before we let Landon question them."

"We are trying to find a murderer," Thistle said. "They should understand our intentions were good."

"I don't think that's how they see it."

"They're going to have to get over it," Thistle said. "It's not like they've earned our loyalty."

"They're our fathers. They deserve our loyalty because we wouldn't be here without them."

Thistle rolled her eyes. "We owe them respect," Thistle said. "We don't owe them loyalty. Loyalty is earned."

That brought up an interesting conundrum. "Do I owe Clove more loyalty than I owe Landon?"

Thistle sighed. "Is this about what I said at breakfast? You know I was trying to make sure Clove still liked me, right?"

"I got that. Thanks. That's not an answer, though."

"You owe Clove loyalty," Thistle said. "You also owe Landon loyalty. He's done a lot for us. He could have turned on us a hundred different times. He could have turned on you. He could have abandoned you.

"He didn't do any of those things," she continued. "In fact, he's made you a better person. He listens to you. He makes you laugh. He tries to protect you. He puts up with Aunt Tillie, for crying out loud."

"Yeah, he does deserve an award for that," I said. "I still feel as though I chose him over Clove."

"Well, there's a problem with your logic," Thistle said. "We don't know that Sam isn't a robber and murderer. We know Clove likes him, and we want her to be happy, and we want him to be a good guy. We don't know that he is, though."

"Shouldn't we trust her intuition?"

"She's only ever been attracted to losers her entire life," Thistle reminded me. "The odds are actually against her on this one."

She had a point. Still .... "I want her to get a win so badly it hurts."

"I want her to get a win, too," Thistle said. "I don't want her to win a murderer, though. You did the only thing you could do. You can't turn back time. We can only move forward."

"That means we have to prove Sam is innocent," I said.

"Then let's do it," Thistle said, gripping my hand briefly. "Let's get Clove a win."

THISTLE, Marcus and I regrouped two hours later.

"Have you found anything?" I asked, sucking from my malt dejectedly.

"I found out that Martha Morrison hasn't had an orgasm in ten years and she's interested in having Marcus break her streak," Thistle replied dryly. "She promises it will only be once and we never have to talk about it again."

"Martha Morrison?" Marcus made a sour face. "She's like ... fifty."

"Age is just a number," Thistle said. "You shouldn't turn anyone down just because they're old. That's ageist."

"Oh ... um ... ."

"You should turn her down because I'm the best lover you've ever had and you can't imagine being with anyone but me," Thistle said.

"That's what I meant."

"There you go."

I smirked.

"How about you?" Thistle asked.

"I found out that Ned Thompson has an abnormal lump in his groin," I said. "He doesn't think it's cancer, but he wanted me to check it for him. Just to be sure."

"Didn't Ned Thompson teach biology when we were in high school?"

"Yes."

"He was also the guy who married two of his former students, right?" Thistle was grossed out.

"Yes."

"He's sick."

"Yes."

We both turned to Marcus expectantly.

"I found out that I'm afraid to talk to people," he said.

"What?" Thistle dipped her spoon into the banana split they were sharing.

"I walked up to five different people," Marcus said. "I didn't know what to ask any of them, so I asked them about the weather. I think Maddie Johnson thinks I was hitting on her."

"Maddie Johnson is thirteen," I countered.

"I know. I was very uncomfortable with the way she talked to me. She kept asking me whether I wanted to go to a One Direction concert. She said her mother would drive us down to Detroit."

Thistle and I giggled.

"I think you're just shy by nature," I said. "I can't believe you ever asked Thistle out."

"I couldn't help myself," he said. "She was always so pretty, and she kept coming in for feed she didn't need. I knew why she was coming in, and I also knew she would stop coming in if I didn't ask her out.

"When I finally got up the courage to ask her, I thought I was going to puke," he continued. "She was so … gorgeous, and she was wearing this skirt that had my mind spinning. I just kind of blurted it out. I thought for sure she was going to laugh at me because I was such a … spaz.

"She didn't laugh, though," he said. "Her face got all red, and I could tell she was as nervous as me, and it was like this weight was lifted off my shoulders. I knew at that moment that everything was going to work out."

I'd always liked Marcus. When Thistle first expressed interest in him, I was surprised and intrigued. She was a loudmouth and overbearing. He was shy and sweet without being a pushover. I couldn't decide whether they would be a good match. The time they'd been together had been a growing experience for her and an expanding experience for him. I knew now they were a perfect match.

"You're so sweet," I said. Thistle's eyes shined with unshed tears as she gazed at him, which made me choke up. "So sweet."

"Are you crying?" Thistle asked, brushing a tear away hastily. "Don't cry. It's so … stupid."

"You're crying," I shot back.

"I am not."

"You are so."

Marcus rolled his eyes. "You guys are a trip."

Thankfully for all of us, the conversation was cut short when someone screamed. We all swiveled as a woman ran out of the bakery down the street. She yelled for help.

We all started moving in unison, running to the woman's side and leaving our treats behind without hesitation. As we approached, I realized I recognized the woman. Sarah Stillman. She'd been two years ahead of me in high school – and leagues ahead of me in the popularity department.

"What's wrong?" I asked, gasping for breath as I stopped at her side.

"I ... Mrs. Gunderson ... she's been ... someone hurt her." Sarah was beside herself.

I pushed Sarah toward Marcus and ran inside bakery, finding Mrs. Gunderson on her side on the floor. I moved to her and knelt, touching her arm lightly. "Mrs. Gunderson?"

She held her head, and her eyes were glassy as she tried to focus on me. "Tillie?"

Well, that was disconcerting. Do I look like Aunt Tillie? Shoot me now. "It's Bay. Bay Winchester."

"I ... what happened?"

She was confused. Blood pooled around a wound on the back of her head.

"I'm not sure," I said. "What do you remember?"

"What's going on?" Thistle asked, running into the bakery. "I ... crap. What happened?"

"Call for help," I instructed. "She's kind of out of it."

Thistle pulled her phone from her pocket. "Should I call 911 or Landon?"

"Both," I said. I forced a smile as I focused on Mrs. Gunderson. "What do you remember?"

"I was pulling a tray of rolls out of the oven," she said. "I ... oh ... I didn't get them out. They're probably burning."

"I'm on it," Marcus said, moving past me and toward the ovens. I had no idea when he'd gotten here. I thought he was still outside comforting Sarah.

"Marcus is saving the rolls," I said. "What else do you remember?"

"I heard the bell over the door," Mrs. Gunderson said. "I ... I remember yelling that I would be right out. Then I heard the buttons on the register being pushed."

"Can anyone open the register, or do they need a key?"

"It's an old register. If you push the right buttons you can open the drawer."

"Did you come out to see what was going on?"

Mrs. Gunderson nodded, grimacing as she reached for the back of her head. "I came out and … there was a man behind the counter."

"Did you recognize him?"

"He was wearing a mask," Mrs. Gunderson said. "It was one of those masks people wear to ski."

Well, that was interesting. That meant that the person who dumped the mask at the Dandridge had more than one. "How do you know it was a man?"

"Broad shoulders. Narrow waist."

"Go on," I prodded. "What happened?"

"He pulled all of the money out of the till," Mrs. Gunderson said. She was slurring her words and struggling to remain conscious. "I tried to stop him. He was strong."

"What happened then?"

"I … he hit me. He hurt me."

I pursed my lips. Mrs. Gunderson spent years married to an abusive man. Floyd Gunderson drank without reservation, and beat her without reason – or mercy. His death freed a tormented woman, only to have her hurt again now. "You're going to be okay," I said.

"I know how to take a punch," Mrs. Gunderson said. "Floyd taught me that."

My heart constricted. "What happened then?"

"I tried to grab the money," she said. "I knew it was stupid even as I was doing it, but it was instinct. I couldn't stop myself."

"You're going to be okay."

"I grabbed his arm," Mrs. Gunderson said. "I really dug in there. He pushed me, and I slammed into the corner of the doorframe. I hit my head."

"Did he take the money?"

"Yes."

"Did he ... I don't know ... say anything to you?"

"Just that he was sorry," Mrs. Gunderson said, closing her eyes. "He said he was sorry and that he needed the money for the Dandridge."

My heart stuttered. "For the Dandridge?"

"Yes."

"I ... did it sound like Sam?"

"I have no idea," Mrs. Gunderson said. "I've talked to him a few times, but I don't know him well enough to know whether it was him."

"Do you think it was Sam?"

"He said he was Sam." Mrs. Gunderson's voice trailed off. "He said he was Sam and he needed the money. He said he was sorry."

This was a nightmare.

"Floyd always said he was sorry, too," Mrs. Gunderson murmured. "He never was."

Mrs. Gunderson slipped into unconsciousness.

"Well, this is not good," Thistle said.

"This is the worst thing ever," I said.

"What's the worst thing ever?"

Landon and Chief Terry stepped into the store.

"I was wrong," Thistle said. "This is the worst thing ever."

TWENTY-FOUR

Landon stepped out of the bakery, making room for the state police crime scene team, and pulled me in for a hug.

"Is Mrs. Gunderson going to be all right?" I asked, raising my face and resting my chin against his chest.

"I don't know for sure," Landon said. "Her head wound is pretty serious. The paramedics were hopeful, but they couldn't be sure until a doctor looked her over."

"I ... did she wake up again?"

"No."

I bit my lower lip. "She was beaten by Floyd for years," I said. "This is so ... unfair. To have this happen to her after everything she's gone through, it's just so wrong."

Landon pressed a kiss to my temple. "Floyd was an ass. I remember his poltergeist well."

"You really hated that poltergeist."

"That's what happens when a jerkoff goes after the woman you ... care about." Landon kissed my forehead again. "I probably shouldn't be doing this."

"Hugging me?"

"I need to ask you a few questions," Landon said. "This isn't usually how I collect my witness statements."

"I hope not."

Landon smiled, but the expression didn't make it all the way up to his eyes. "You're the only one I question with kisses. Don't worry about that." This time he pressed his lips to mine softly. "Still, I have to be a professional."

I ruefully pulled away from him. "Ask away."

"Are you two done cuddling?" Chief Terry asked, moving up next to us. "I'm starting to feel uncomfortable."

"You'll live," I said, rubbing the spot between my eyebrows.

"Are you okay?" Chief Terry asked. "You look ... sad."

"I'm sad for Mrs. Gunderson," I said. "I think she's gone through enough. This is just ... wrong."

"She's going to be okay," Chief Terry said.

"Did you hear from the hospital?" I was hopeful.

"No," Chief Terry said. "I have faith. You should try it someday."

"I have faith."

"You're a defeatist sometimes," Chief Terry countered. "Don't take it personally. I don't think you can help yourself."

"I'm not a defeatist."

"You're a total defeatist," Thistle said, stepping up on the curb. "What's going on?"

"We have a few questions," Landon said. "How did you guys end up in the bakery?"

"We were eating ice cream at the table over there," I said, pointing. "We heard Sarah scream and ran over."

"What did she say?"

"She said someone hurt Mrs. Gunderson."

"What was the first thing you noticed when you went into the bakery?"

"I didn't notice a lot," I replied honestly. "I saw her on the ground and I went to her."

"What did she say?" Landon asked.

"She … she seemed a little confused," I said. "She thought I was Aunt Tillie."

Landon pressed his lips together.

"Oh, that must have killed you," Thistle said. "I missed that."

"I don't look like Aunt Tillie, do I?"

"If any of us look like Aunt Tillie, it's Clove."

"That's exactly what I thought," I said.

"Don't ever tell her I said that," Thistle said. "She'll never forgive me … and she's got enough to deal with now."

Landon's gaze bounced between us. "What is that supposed to mean?"

The moment of truth was upon me. Would I lie for Clove? Could I? "I want to stress that Mrs. Gunderson seemed confused," I said carefully.

Landon waited.

"She said the robber told her he needed the money for the Dandridge."

Chief Terry and Landon exchanged a look.

"Is that all she said?" Chief Terry asked.

I opened my mouth … and then shut it.

"Bay," Landon prodded me. "What else did she say?"

I glanced at Thistle, hoping she could save me from the one thing I didn't want to say. I knew she couldn't, and yet I still hoped. All Thistle could do was shrug.

I steeled myself. I couldn't lie to Landon. I didn't have it in me. "She said the man identified himself as Sam."

Landon reached for me again, pulling me close. "Thank you for telling the truth."

"I … ." Tears started falling. I had no idea I was about to cry.

Landon kissed the top of my head. "It's okay."

I didn't think Clove was going to feel the same way.

"**ISN'T** THERE something else we can do?"

I was in the backseat of Landon's Explorer, and we were heading to the Dandridge.

"What do you suggest?" Chief Terry asked from the passenger seat. "Do you think we can ignore this?"

"No," I said. "Mrs. Gunderson said she didn't see his face, though. Anyone can say they're Sam."

"Bay, we know that," Landon said, his eyes focused on the road. "We still have to take him in. Mrs. Gunderson identified him."

"What if she changes her mind when she regains consciousness?"

"Then we'll cut him loose."

"That doesn't seem fair to him," I said. I was grasping at straws. I kept picturing Clove's face, though. Sam's arrest was going to wreck her.

"We don't have a choice," Chief Terry said. "She identified him."

"She didn't identify him," I countered. "In fact, she said she didn't know Sam well enough to say that it was his voice."

The two men in the front of the Explorer remained silent.

"She said the robber wore a mask," I said. "I found a mask at the Dandridge. That can't be a coincidence."

"No," Landon agreed.

"Someone is setting him up." I tried again, desperate. "Someone is trying to make Sam look guilty to cover their own tracks."

"I'm not disagreeing with you, Bay," Landon said.

"Our hands are still tied," Chief Terry said. "We have to follow the evidence. We have to … follow the letter of the law."

I knew they were right. It still hurt. I focused on the landscape as it sped by. After a few minutes of quiet, Landon couldn't take my silence any longer. "We'll do what we can for him, Bay."

"I know."

"We'll make sure he has a lawyer."

"That will make everything perfect," I said bitterly.

"We can't ignore this."

"I didn't say you could."

Chief Terry reached over and put a hand on Landon's arm to still him before he could say anything else. "What are you worried about, Bay?"

"What do you think I'm worried about?"

"I think you're worried about Clove," Chief Terry said. "Do you think she's so weak that she can't take this?"

Weak? Clove wasn't weak. In a way, she was stronger than the rest of us. "I think she's going to be crushed."

"And you blame yourself," Chief Terry said. "Bay, I've known you for most of your life. I've loved you for all that time. You are the type of person who tries to fix things. You can't help yourself.

"When you were a kid, it was Thistle who always swooped in to fight your battles," he continued. "She was the brawler ... and she liked to do it. You were the brave one, though, because you took all the abuse so Thistle wouldn't have to fight.

"Clove was always different," he said. "She was amiable and pleasing, and she was desperate for approval. I always knew how to handle you and Thistle. I never knew how to handle her. It was as though she was searching for something, and I had no idea what that was."

"She wanted to be loved," I said, my voice small. "That's all she's ever wanted."

"Everyone wants to be loved," Chief Terry said. "Clove is desperate for it, though. As hard as this is going to hit her, she does have love. You and Thistle love her. Your mothers love her. Hell, Aunt Tillie loves her. She's not going to go through this alone."

"She's still going to be ... broken."

"I don't happen to believe you can break a person," Chief Terry said. "I believe you can hurt a person. I believe you can wound a person. I believe you can kill a person. I don't believe you can break a person."

I didn't respond. I couldn't find the words.

"Look at Mrs. Gunderson," Chief Terry said. "Floyd terrorized her for years. He broke her jaw. He broke her arm. He didn't break her spirit, though. She didn't give up. She wasn't broken inside."

"Are you sure?"

"Aren't you?"

I rubbed my forehead, uncertain. "She's strong."

"Clove is strong," Chief Terry said. "She's strong because she was born that way ... and she has all of you."

"This is still going to crush her."

"No one has been convicted yet," Chief Terry said. "We're arresting him. That doesn't necessarily mean he's guilty."

"Then why arrest him?"

"You know why," Chief Terry said. "I know you're going through it right now. You're terrified that Clove is going to fall. She can't fall while she has all of you. You won't let her."

I opened my mouth to reply, but the only sound that escaped was a broken sob.

Landon parked in front of the Dandridge, and my door was open before I realized what was happening. He unfastened my seatbelt and pulled me to him, cupping the back of my head and forcing my gaze to meet his.

"We'll figure this out," he said. "I promise."

I nodded.

"Stay here."

I nodded again.

Landon kissed me, his lips soft and his arms strong as he pressed me close. "We'll be back in a few minutes. I'm so sorry for all of this."

"**WHERE** IS HE?"

Landon and Chief Terry had been gone about fifteen minutes when I realized something was wrong. I fought my inner urges and remained standing by the Explorer, even though I was desperate for information. When they returned – alone – I knew things were about to hit rock bottom.

"The Dandridge is empty," Landon said.

I pointed to Sam's car. "He has to be here."

"It looks like someone collected some clothes quickly," Chief Terry said. "The front door was open, but nobody was home."

"What does that mean?" I knew what it meant. I needed them to say it, though.

"It means he ran," Landon said, collecting my hand before I could run it through my hair.

"But ... how?"

"Maybe he got the money he was looking for and put this town in his rear-view mirror," Landon said.

"I don't believe he's the robber," I replied. "Only an idiot would admit to it. I don't believe Sam is an idiot."

"I tend to agree with you," Landon said. "We can't ignore the facts, though. The facts state that Mrs. Gunderson identified him."

"If he wasn't guilty, how did he know to run?" Chief Terry asked.

That was a very good question. "I don't know."

"You didn't ... you didn't call Clove, did you?" Landon was reluctant to ask the question.

"Of course not!" I jerked my hand from his. "Do you really think I would do that?"

Landon sighed. "I think you love your family," he said. "I wouldn't blame you if you did do it."

"I didn't."

"Okay," Landon said, holding up his hands in mock surrender. "I didn't really think you did. I had to ask."

"If you believed I hadn't done it, you wouldn't have asked."

"That is not true," Landon said, pointing at me. "I know you didn't have time to call Clove. We walked in before you had the chance. You haven't been out of my sight since."

"That's how you know?" My voice was shrill, even to my own ears.

"No," Landon said. "I also know because you're the best person I've ever met. I still had to ask. It's part of my job."

My head told me he was telling the truth. My heart still hurt. "Fine."

"Don't," Landon said. "I trust you more than I've ever trusted anyone. Don't shut me out. Don't ... do whatever it is you're about to do."

His words warmed me, but I was still upset. "I would never do that."

"I know," Landon said. "We have to cover our bases. I'm sorry."

I pinched the bridge of my nose. "What happens now?"

"Now we stake out the Dandridge and ... put out a BOLO."

A BOLO? That stood for "be on the lookout." This was officially serious. "They won't shoot him if they find him, will they?"

Landon and Chief Terry exchanged a look.

"Not unless he gives them a reason," Chief Terry said.

That made me feel better. Kind of. Sam wouldn't give them a reason. Would he? No, seriously, would he? I needed to get home.

TWENTY-FIVE

"Where's Clove?" My mother's face was drawn when Landon and I walked into The Overlook. "She's in the kitchen."

"Does she know?"

"She knows."

"How?"

"Thistle told her when she got here about an hour ago," Mom said.

"How did she take it?"

"She didn't believe her at first," Mom said. "Then we saw the news."

I hadn't even thought about that. The local television stations – always starved for stories – would have aired Mrs. Gunderson's assault and robbery as the lead story. "Is she okay?"

"No."

I turned to Landon, conflicted. "I … ."

"Go," he said, bringing my hand to his lips and kissing it softly. "I'll be in the dining room."

I glanced at Mom.

"Go," she said. "Your cousin needs you now. I'll take care of Landon. We have fresh bread. He'll be happy."

My feet were leaden as I moved through the house. A few of the guests called out to me, but their greetings barely registered and I didn't acknowledge them. I could hear Landon making excuses in my wake – something about preparing for the next show – but I didn't absorb his words. I had to get to Clove.

I found her in the kitchen. She was on the floor, her back pressed to the wall and her knees drawn up in front of her. Her cheek rested against her knee. Thistle sat next to her, a hand on her arm, but she was silent, too.

"What's going on?" I asked.

Thistle didn't bother looking up. "She's not saying much."

"Has she said anything?"

"She called me a liar," Thistle said. "Then she saw the news."

"I heard." I stepped lightly as I closed the distance between us. Without a better idea to bolster me, I pressed my back against the wall and sank down on the floor next to Clove. "I'm so sorry."

"You didn't do it." Clove's voice was small, her eyes red from crying. "He did it."

I glanced at Thistle, helpless. "We don't know that."

"Mrs. Gunderson identified him."

"Mrs. Gunderson didn't technically identify him," I said. "Mrs. Gunderson said the masked man identified himself. That doesn't mean it was Sam."

Clove shifted her head so she could focus on me for the first time since I'd entered the room. "Do you really believe that?"

It was truth time. I searched my heart. "Yes."

"If it's not him, who is it?"

"Someone trying to frame him," I said. "Mrs. Gunderson was very confused when we were with her."

"How do you know?"

"She thought I was Aunt Tillie."

Clove snorted, the sound offering me the first moment of levity I'd felt in hours. "That must have killed you."

"It wasn't my finest moment."

"What did she say?"

I recounted my conversation with Mrs. Gunderson, making sure to leave nothing out, and then rubbed my hand over Clove's knee. "I still think he's innocent."

"Then why did he run?"

That was a very good question. "I'm more interested in how he found out," I said.

Thistle narrowed her eyes. "That's a pretty good point."

"Landon asked me whether I called Clove," I admitted.

"Is he still alive?" Aunt Tillie asked, shuffling into the room. Her usual bravado was absent as she focused on Clove. Her outfit was ... however ... unique.

"Where did you get a Batman costume? And where did you get one that's a dress?"

"I ordered it on line," Aunt Tillie said, moving toward Clove. "It's technically a theme dress. It's meant for costume parties."

I could see that. "Where did you get it?"

"Hot Topic."

I wanted to laugh, but the noise died on my lips. We could use a superhero about now.

"Do you want to tell us what you're trying to blackmail our mothers in to letting you do?" Thistle asked.

Aunt Tillie was unruffled. "I want to build a still."

It shouldn't have surprised me, but her admission tipped me over the edge. "Seriously?" I burst into uncontrollable laughter.

"It's nothing to laugh at," Aunt Tillie said, primly. "I have a vision for my future ... and it involves a still."

"You already make wine," Thistle pointed out. "Why do you need a still?"

"Because your mothers don't want me to have one."

"You're a piece of work," I said.

"We all are," Aunt Tillie said, leaning over and resting her chin on top of Clove's head briefly. "Don't worry. Sam will be vindicated."

"How can you know that?" Clove asked.

"I have faith in him," Aunt Tillie said, pulling away and straightening. "You should, too."

"What if he's found guilty?" Clove asked.

"Then we'll fix it."

"What if he's killed before he can be arrested?"

"He won't be," Aunt Tillie said.

"What if ... ?"

"Don't," Aunt Tillie said, extending a gnarled finger in front of Clove's face. "Things happen as they're supposed to happen. There's always a reason. That's our faith, and that's our lot in life. The only thing you have to question is your resolve."

"I want to believe in him," Clove said. "It's just so ... overwhelming."

"Life is overwhelming, kid," Aunt Tillie said. "The strong survive. I have no idea whether Sam is strong enough to survive, but you're strong enough for the both of you."

On a regular day, Aunt Tillie exasperated me. Today, though? Today she was my hero. She'd given Clove the one thing she needed: faith.

"I am strong enough," Clove said, grabbing Aunt Tillie's outstretched hand and pulling herself to her feet. "We can fix this. We will fix this."

"Of course we will," Aunt Tillie said. "You should never doubt that." She led Clove out of the kitchen and into the dining room.

Thistle rolled her head to face me. "Does it bother you that we're supposed to be the ones closest to Clove but it's Aunt Tillie who made her feel better?"

"Of course not," I said. "That would make me petty."

"I guess I'm petty then."

She wasn't the only one. "I kind of wish she had a Robin dress," I said. "I would be proud to be her sidekick tonight."

Thistle pushed herself off the floor. She moved in front of me and extended her hand so she could pull me to my feet. "I'm Robin," she said. "You're Batgirl."

"I don't want to be Batgirl."

"No one wants to be Batgirl," Thistle said. "That's just your lot in life. Suck it up."

"**THIS IS AMAZING**," Nick said, sucking a noodle from the seafood Alfredo dish into his mouth like an enthusiastic child with an obnoxious slurp. "I've never had pasta this good."

I tried to rein in my disgust. "Our mothers are the best cooks in the state."

"I totally agree."

I scratched the back of my head and forced my gaze to Landon. His eyes were kind ... and concerned. "Are you okay?"

I nodded.

Landon inclined his head in Clove's direction. She wasn't talking, but she wasn't hiding either. "Is she okay?"

"Aunt Tillie fixed her," I said, reaching for a breadstick. "She fixed her when we failed."

Landon rubbed my knee under the table. "She has a special brand of magic."

I glanced at my great-aunt, who was reveling in the dirty looks my mother and aunts shot in her direction as she lorded over her spot at the head of the table. "She's Batman."

Landon snickered. "How much money is she spending on these outfits?"

"I have no idea," I said. "She seems to be enjoying herself."

"And what does she want?"

"A still."

Landon faltered, a forkful of pasta halfway to his mouth. "Seriously?"

"I don't think she really wants it," I said. "I think she wants it to irritate our mothers."

"Why don't they want her to have it?"

"It's a fire hazard."

"Is that the only reason?"

I leaned my head over and rested it on his shoulder. "Yes."

Landon pressed his lips to the side of my head. "I can't let her have a still. You know that, right?"

I did know that. "I'm kind of looking forward to her trying to build one," I admitted.

AMANDA M. LEE

"I'll have to arrest her," Landon said. "I'll have to have to the still confiscated."

"You'll have to find it first."

"You have a lot of property here," Landon said. "That doesn't mean she can hide a still."

"She's hiding a pot field," I pointed out.

Landon scowled. "Magically."

"What makes you think she won't do the same with a still?"

That was a sobering thought, and I could see the ramifications of my question wash over Landon's face as he considered it. "Crap."

"What are you guys talking about?" Nick asked, leaning his head in our direction. "Are you talking about Batman?"

While his tone was teasing, and his attention had previously been flattering, given our new circumstances Nick's presence was irksome. "We're talking about something private," I said.

Nick wasn't put off by my admonishment. "Did Clove's boyfriend really kill that teller and attack Mrs. Gunderson?"

I frowned.

Landon grabbed my hand under the table and gripped it tightly. "We have no idea who robbed the bank or the bakery," he said. "It's an ongoing investigation."

"The news said Mrs. Gunderson identified him," Nick said. "That sounds pretty open and shut to me."

"I guess that's why you're not an investigator," Landon replied dryly. "We go on evidence ... not what the news says."

Nick's face was awash with surprise. "I thought Sam was a suspect."

Landon gritted his teeth and poured himself a glass of wine.

"He is," I said carefully. "He's not the only suspect, though, and there are some problems with the accusations against him." I had no idea why I said it.

"That's interesting," Nick said. "The television news made it sound as though the case was closed."

"You shouldn't believe everything you see on television," Landon said, pouring the rest of the wine bottle into my glass.

"You'll find that television news makes assumptions that aren't always correct."

"Do you believe this guy is innocent?" Nick asked.

"I believe in a proper investigation," Landon countered. "I don't rule anything out ... or in ... until I have proof."

"Are you just saying that because of Clove?"

Nick's questions were starting to irritate me.

"Of course he's not," I said. "Landon's relationship with Clove ... and with me ... has nothing to do with his work ethic. He doesn't let personal feelings infringe on his profession."

Nick didn't look convinced. "Do you expect me to believe that he's sleeping with you and working against your cousin?"

I scowled. "I ... ."

Landon reached over and grabbed the sleeve of Nick's shirt roughly. "I'm not sleeping with her," he said. "We're in a relationship. That doesn't mean I don't do my job."

"I ... I'm sorry," Nick said, flustered. "I didn't mean anything by it."

I put my hand on Landon's and unclenched his fingers from Nick's shirt. "We're all tired," I said. "It's been a long day."

Landon collected himself. "I'm sorry," he said. "Bay is right. We have a lot on our plates." He focused back on his dinner. "I shouldn't have touched you. That was wrong."

"It's okay, man," Nick said. "I shouldn't have pushed."

Landon's cellphone rang. He pushed away from the table, sent me a reassuring look, and then pulled it from his pocket. "Michaels," he answered.

I watched him walk into the front lobby for privacy.

"He's intense," Nick said.

"He's a good man," I replied. "He's ... the best man I've ever met."

"You love him," Nick supplied.

I ignored the statement. "He's a good man, and a good agent. He always finds the truth. He doesn't know how to fail when it comes to a case."

"I guess you're lucky that you've found someone you have faith in," Nick said. "I've never been that lucky."

"Maybe you haven't earned the gift of an honest person," I countered, distracted by Landon's silhouette as he paced the lobby.

"Maybe," Nick said.

Landon returned to the dining room, his face unreadable. "I have to go."

"Why?"

"Mrs. Gunderson has regained consciousness."

I moved to get to my feet, but Landon stilled me with a hand on my shoulder. "You can't come," he said.

I understood why, but it still hurt. "Okay."

Landon leaned down and gave me a quick kiss. "I'll be back at the guesthouse as soon as I can," he said. "Eat. You need the fuel. I'll be back with you as soon as is humanly possible."

I nodded. I feared conversation would betray me.

"It's going to be okay," Landon said. "I'll … it's going to be okay."

Landon kissed me again and then turned to Clove. "I'll call as soon as I have any information."

TWENTY-SIX

After dinner, Thistle, Clove, Marcus and I hung out long enough to watch Aunt Tillie use her Batman dress – including fighting invisible bad guys while yelling "kapow" and "bang" at the top of her lungs – to irritate my mother until she developed a bizarre facial tic, and then we called it a night.

The walk back to the guesthouse was mostly quiet until Clove felt the need to fill in the conversational gaps.

"Are you sure you don't have a problem with me moving back home?"

Now that she'd put her meltdown behind her and was bolstered by a good meal, Clove regained some of her personality, along with the color that had been missing from her cheeks when I found her in the kitchen. Now she needed sleep to eradicate the shadows under her eyes. I considered drugging her. She needed eight uninterrupted hours, and she wasn't going to get it as long as her mind kept churning.

"You didn't move out," Thistle said. "You threw some clothes in a bag and walked a hundred yards to sleep on a couch for a night. You basically had a really boring slumber party."

Clove smiled. It was weak, but heartfelt. "I guess I should thank you guys for not trying to make me feel bad about how I've been acting."

"We don't ever want you to feel bad," I said.

"I want you to feel bad sometimes, but not right now," Thistle said. "Now you just need to get some sleep. You look as if you haven't slept in days."

"I've slept," Clove protested.

"How long?" I asked.

"I … a couple hours."

"Total, or each night?" I asked.

"Total." Clove lowered her dark eyes sheepishly. "I've had a lot to think about."

"We know," I said. "It's been a rough three days."

"You should probably prepare yourself," Thistle said. "I think things are going to get worse before they get better."

"How could they get worse?" Clove asked.

"Something could happen to Sam when they try to take him into custody," Thistle replied.

I smacked her arm, the sound echoing throughout the quiet night air. "Ow," Thistle said, jerking her arm away from me. "That hurt."

"It was supposed to," I said. "What were you thinking? She doesn't need to hear things like that."

"I … it was an accident," Thistle said.

"It's fine," Clove said. "I've already figured out how bad things could go on my own."

"Sam is smart," I said. "If he's caught, he'll surrender without incident. He won't risk being shot. That's not like him."

"I hope so," Clove said. "I didn't think it was like him to run either."

She had a point. "Are we sure he ran?" I asked. "Maybe he was just out."

Thistle rolled her eyes. "His car was at the Dandridge."

"Maybe he went for a walk."

"When did you become such a Mary Sue?" Thistle asked.

"About the same time you became Nellie Oleson," I shot back.

"You're such a geek," Thistle said. "Who makes a *Little House on the Prairie* insult?"

"Someone with great taste in television," I replied. What? I have a thing for that show. I keep catching the repeats on the Hallmark Channel. It's completely ridiculous, and the continuity is non-existent, but I can't stop myself from watching. I keep picturing Aunt Tillie in Walnut Grove. We all know she would be Harriet Oleson. Don't pretend you weren't thinking it. "That show is heartbreaking and poignant."

"Doesn't it bother you that Charles Ingalls was shaving his chest in the 1800s?"

Huh. I had never considered it. "Maybe he was follicly challenged."

"He had a huge mullet."

She was ruining my fun. "Oh, just stuff it."

"You stuff it."

"Both of you stuff it," Marcus said.

Thistle's mouth dropped open as she turned to face him. He wasn't watching us, though. His gaze was focused on the greenhouse. "What did you just say to us?"

"Shh." He held his finger to his lips, his eyes trained on the greenhouse.

"Did he just shush me?"

"We all wanted to do it," I said. "He was just the first one to say it."

"There's a whole pile of dirt right there," Thistle said, gesturing to a nearby flowerbed. "I'm going to make you eat it." Thistle leaned over to grab some of the dirt, but Marcus stopped her with a hand on her arm.

"Don't you guys hear that?" Marcus hissed.

"Thistle never stops talking," I said. "I spend half my day listening to it."

"Like you have room to talk," Thistle snapped.

"Not that," Marcus said. "And, for the record, you both never shut up. That's not what I was talking about, though. There's someone in the greenhouse."

We turned in unison, focusing on Aunt Tillie's special building.

The unmistakable sound of shuffling – and pots being moved around – wafted to us.

"Maybe it's Aunt Tillie," Clove said, nervous. "Maybe she's practicing being Batman."

"She was still at the inn when we left," I said. "She's sneaky like a cat – a really mean one that waits until your back is turned before attacking – but she can't move that fast."

"She's more like the cat who kills animals and leaves their half-eaten corpses on the porch looking for praise," Thistle said. "Plus, let's be honest, there's no way she's gardening after dark. She doesn't believe in gardening unless she can bully Marcus into doing it for her."

"She doesn't bully me," Marcus argued. "I like to help her."

"Why?"

"Because she knows a lot about gardening," Marcus replied. "I've learned a lot from her."

"You help her with her pot field," Thistle said. "Has she taught you a lot about cultivating bud?"

"Michigan is a medical marijuana state," Marcus said.

"The only thing she's treating with that pot is boredom," I said.

"Is now really the time for this conversation?" Clove asked. "Someone is rummaging around in the greenhouse. What if it's a robber?"

"It's probably a guest," I said, hopeful.

"What if it's Sam?" Thistle asked.

"It's not Sam," Clove said, although she didn't sound convinced.

We all shared a look. "Well, now we have to check it out," I finally said.

"I don't think Landon would like that," Marcus said. "I think we should go to the guesthouse and wait for him. Then we'll all check it out together."

"Are you afraid?" Thistle asked.

"I'm not afraid," Marcus said. "I'm the only man here, though. You … women … are vulnerable if there's a crazy person in there."

"We were raised by crazy people," Thistle said, stepping off the stone walkway and heading toward the greenhouse. "There's nothing in there worse than Aunt Tillie. It's impossible."

I followed her, while Clove hung back and Marcus remained rooted to his spot. "I think this is a bad idea," he hissed.

"Then stay there," Thistle said, nonplussed. "We'll be right back."

I caught up to Thistle, and once we were outside of the greenhouse our bravado slipped.

"Do you think we should go in there?" I whispered. "What if it is Sam?"

"We can't turn around now," Thistle replied. "We'll look like cowards."

"I thought for sure Marcus and Clove would come with us," I said. "Four on one are much better odds than two on one."

"We're witches," Thistle reminded me.

"Who don't work out," I added.

"We have magic."

"Which always backfires on us."

"Are you seriously going to wuss out on me?" Thistle challenged.

I swallowed. "No."

"Good," Thistle said. "We are not wusses. We're the brave ones. We're going to be able to lord this over Clove and Marcus for months."

I think that was more important to her than it was to me. "Let's just do this," I said. "The more we sit out here, the more we're going to freak each other out."

"I'm not freaked out," Thistle said.

"You look freaked out."

"Well, I'm not."

"Are you two going in or what?" Marcus appeared behind us, Clove beside him, making us jump in unison.

Thistle slapped Marcus' arm. "Don't ever sneak up on me again," she said.

"I thought you were big and brave?" Marcus countered.

"I am brave," Thistle said.

"Then what were you two waiting for?"

"I ... we were waiting for you to catch up," Thistle said.

"You realize that whoever was inside probably already left, right?" Clove's face was grim. "You two were loud enough to wake the dead."

"We were stealthy," I said. "We could be ninjas."

"Only in a *Teenage Mutant Ninja Turtles* movie," Marcus said. He reached forward and grasped the door handle. "Now ... stay behind me."

"What are you going to do?" I asked.

"I'm going to be our first line of defense."

"I think we should be playing offense," Thistle said.

"I think this is the dumbest conversation we've had in weeks," Clove said.

"That's not true," I said. "We spent an hour Sunday talking about whether or not Aunt Tillie could fly."

"We were drunk," Clove said.

"We were barely drunk," I said. "And, let's face it, we spent most of the time talking about what kind of broom she would ride."

"I still maintain she would fly on a vacuum cleaner instead of a broom," Thistle said. "She doesn't like manual labor. She wouldn't even know where to find a broom."

"I really hope there's someone inside here and he kills me," Marcus said, throwing open the door. "Anything would be better than continuing this conversation."

Marcus strode into the greenhouse while Thistle and I exchanged a dubious look.

"He's crabby," I said.

"I'll make him feel better later."

"What are you doing in here?"

We froze at Marcus' question. Someone was in the greenhouse. Until now, I'd actually convinced myself we were imagining things. What? It wouldn't be the first time, and it certainly won't be the last.

Thistle and I pushed our way in, pulling up short when we caught sight of Nick. He had an empty pot in his hand, and there were several others strewn about on the potting bench.

"Nick," I said. "What are you doing out here?"

"Oh, hey," Nick said. He was nervous. I didn't blame him. He put the pot on the bench and ran a hand through his hair as he smiled brightly in our direction. "What are you guys doing out here?"

"We were on our way back to the guesthouse when we heard the noise you were making," I said. "Do you want to tell us what you were doing?"

"I'm afraid if I do you're going to tell your mothers to kick me out of the inn," Nick said, his expression rueful.

"We're probably going to do that anyway," Thistle said, shifting when Clove kicked her ankle. "What? He's out here sneaking around like a ... sneaking around guy."

"Nice one," I said.

"Don't tell on me," Nick pleaded. "I just ... I was looking for your Aunt Tillie's pot."

Did he think that made things better? "Why were you looking for her pot?"

"What she means is, why do you think Aunt Tillie has pot?" Clove corrected. Thistle may have referred to me as a Mary Sue, but we all knew Clove was really the Mary Sue of our group.

"Everyone in town knows she grows pot," Nick said. "I was hoping to ... I don't know ... take a really small amount of it. I'm a little tense. I need to relax."

If he was lying it was a really stupid way to go. Who admits to trying to steal pot from a woman who could curse his manhood into a real twig and berries? "She doesn't keep pot in the greenhouse," I said.

"What Bay means is that Aunt Tillie doesn't grow pot," Clove said, causing me to roll my eyes. "He could be a narc," she whispered.

"You know I can hear you when you whisper, right?"

"I did not know that," Clove said.

"If you can hear us, why didn't you run while we had the world's lamest conversation outside?"

"I didn't hear that," Nick said.

I narrowed my eyes. "There's no pot here," I said.

"Good to know," Nick said, straightening. "I guess I should be ... ."

"Going back up to the inn? Yeah, that would be a good idea," Thistle said.

We watched as Nick shuffled toward the door, turning back to us before exiting. "You're not going to tell Aunt Tillie, are you?"

"We're going to have to give it some thought," I said.

"That's right," Thistle said, hands on hips. "You should go to bed and think about what you've done."

"If it helps, I'm sorry," Nick said.

"It doesn't," Thistle said. "Quite frankly, I feel violated."

A sheepish Nick turned and exited the greenhouse. Thistle moved to the door and watched him go. When she was sure he was well on his way back to the inn, she turned to us. "Do you believe him?"

"I don't know," I said, moving to the potting bench and glancing at the mess Nick left behind. "Why else would he be out here? There's nothing here but plants."

"How does he even know about the pot?" Clove asked.

"Everyone knows about the pot," Thistle said. "It's the worst-kept secret in town."

"Maybe he was telling the truth," I said.

"That would be a nice change of pace in our life right now," Clove said.

It certainly would.

"Well, there's nothing else we can do out here," I said. "Let's get back to the guesthouse. Maybe Landon will have some information when he gets back."

TWENTY-SEVEN

I woke up to a warm body draped over mine and tried to clear my morning-muddled mind. We waited for Landon to return until well after midnight, but finally gave in and retired to bed. I had no idea when he'd returned, but I didn't want to wake him. He was probably exhausted.

I shifted slightly, but Landon instinctively held on to me in his sleep. It was kind of sweet, but I really had to go to the bathroom. I tried again.

"Are you trying to escape?" Landon murmured without opening his eyes.

So much for him being sweet in sleep. "I didn't want to wake you up," I said. "What time did you get back?"

"A little before two," Landon said.

"Why didn't you wake me up?"

"Because you were snoring like a freight train and I figured you needed your sleep," he said.

"I don't snore."

"You do when you're exhausted," Landon said. "It's fine. I find it cute."

"I don't snore."

"Fine. You don't snore." His eyes were still closed.

"Thank you."

"You just breathe really loudly when you're sleeping."

"And to think I was just thinking how sweet you are when you sleep," I grumbled.

Landon finally opened his eyes and focused on me. "Is that really what you were thinking?"

"Yes."

"Then I'm genuinely sorry," he said. "You don't snore. I was making it up."

I didn't believe him. "You snore, too."

"You didn't even know I was in bed with you," Landon scoffed.

"I knew there was a man in bed with me," I said. "I just wasn't sure it was you."

Landon grinned. "You're cute."

"You're kind of cute, too," I said, giving in and snuggling back up to him. My bladder could hold a few more minutes.

"I'm handsome," Landon said. "There's a difference."

"Fine. You're handsome."

"I'm the handsomest man in the land," he said.

"Don't push it," I said. I ran my fingers over his stubbled chin. "Did you find out anything last night?"

"Mrs. Gunderson told the same story you did," Landon said.

"Did you expect her to tell a different story?"

"No. But I was hoping she would remember something else when her mind was clearer," Landon said.

"You were hoping she would be able to tell you something to clear Sam," I said.

"I was."

"I guess that didn't happen."

Landon sighed. "Sam is officially a fugitive, Bay. Every police agency in the state is on the lookout for him. His photo has been circulated to every border crossing, too."

"Does that mean they'll shoot him on sight?"

"That means that he needs to turn himself in," Landon said. "The longer he stays out there, the worse he's making things for himself."

That was a sobering thought.

Landon brushed his thumb over my cheek. "How is Clove?"

"She's better," I said. "We managed to cheer her up a bit."

"How did you manage that?"

I told him about the dinner he missed, which caused him to break out in hearty guffaws.

"I'm sorry I missed that," he said. "I really wish I had seen the fight reenactments."

"I think my mother was on the verge of a stroke."

"Do you think she'll give in and let Aunt Tillie have her still?"

"I don't think Aunt Tillie really wants a still," I said.

"Then why is she asking for one?"

"She's asking for something really big and bad, and then acting up to get it," I said. "She's trying to wear them down to the point where it will seem a relief to give her what she really wants."

"Which is?"

"I have no idea," I said. "I just know it's not a still. She doesn't need a still. She likes making her wine."

"The real thing she wants is still going to be bad, isn't it?"

"Oh, yeah."

"I can't wait," Landon said, rolling on his back and running his hand through his hair. "Did anything else happen?"

"Actually, yes." I told him about our excursion to the greenhouse, making sure to leave out the bits of the story that made us look like idiots. I expected him to explode when I was done, but his expression was thoughtful.

"Do you think he was telling the truth?"

"There's nothing else in that greenhouse," I said. "We searched around a little bit after he was gone, but there's nothing in there but plants. She's not dumb enough to put pot in that greenhouse. Anyone can walk in there."

"I know," Landon said. "I've searched that greenhouse eight different times trying to catch her with contraband."

I smirked. "What would you do if you found anything?"

"Burn it."

"Would you arrest her?"

"As a duly sworn law enforcement representative, I should say yes," he said. "You and I both know that's not the truth, though."

"Now I really think you're sweet."

Landon cocked an eyebrow. "Really? Do you want to reward my sweetness?"

"What did you have in mind?"

Landon's smile had a hint of angel and a whole lot of devil when he flashed it. "I'm glad you asked."

"DO THE POLICE have any idea where Sam is?" Clove asked. Her face was drawn, and she gripped her fork so hard her knuckles paled.

After a round of coffee in the guesthouse that involved Landon repeating everything he'd already told me, we found ourselves back at the inn for breakfast. We seriously have nothing but liquor in our cupboards right now. It's a little sad, and if our mothers knew they would pitch a righteous fit.

"I already told you we don't know where he is," Landon said, patiently. "The second I know something I will tell you."

"I know," Clove said. "I just can't stop thinking about him."

"Try," Landon said. "This could go on for days. You're going to drive yourself crazy if you keep dwelling on it."

"It's nice that you're worried about me," Clove said.

"I am worried about you," Landon said. "I'm also worried that if you're worked up Bay is going to be worked up, and that's going to seriously cut down on my fun quota this weekend."

Clove shot him a dark look. "That's great."

Landon was unruffled. "Eat your breakfast. You need to take care of yourself." I leaned over and rested my chin on his shoulder, batting my eyelashes as he glanced down at me. "Oh, you're going to ask me for something big, aren't you? You only do that eyelash thing when you want something. Just for the record, I don't think it's as cute as you seem to think it is."

I frowned. "What makes you think I was going to ask you for something?"

"I know you," Landon replied. "What do you want?"

"I ... I don't want anything," I said, pulling my head away from him. "I only wanted to cuddle for a second."

"You're a horrible liar," Landon said. "Tell me what you really want."

"I don't want anything."

"If you tell me, I might give it to you."

"I ... ." Crap. "I was just wondering how busy you were going to be this afternoon."

"Why?"

"I was hoping we could finish our afternoon at the festival."

"Why really?"

I pressed my lips together. "It's just ... there's a special picnic for people who graduated the same year I did."

Landon waited.

"I wasn't going to go," I said, "but then I thought better of a few things you and Thistle have been saying to me and I thought maybe ... ."

Landon tilted his head to the side, but remained silent.

"Fine," I said. "I want all the girls who thought they were better than me to see me with you."

Landon snorted. "All you had to do was ask. I'm sure I can go to the picnic with you. I can be your trophy boyfriend. I've always wanted to be able to add that to my resume."

I made a face. "You're loving this, aren't you?"

"Yes."

I turned back to my breakfast. "Do you think less of me?"

"Why would I? This whole thing makes me look good."

"You're not that good looking."

"Of course I'm not," Landon said. "That's why you want to parade me around like a prize bull."

"You're never going to let me live this down."

"Probably not," Landon agreed. He tapped the edge of my plate.

"Eat your breakfast. You need to take care of yourself, too."

"Why?"

"Because I like you healthy," Landon said. He leaned over and gave me a quick kiss on the cheek. "And don't worry; when my high school reunion comes around I plan to parade you in front of everyone, too."

Sadly, I was just pathetic enough for that to make me feel better.

"Oh, good grief. Do you two walk around pawing each other every chance you get?"

I froze when I heard Lila's voice. Lila Stevens was in my family's home. Lila Stevens was ... wait ... why was she here?

I shifted in my seat. "Lila."

"Bay."

Aunt Tillie chose this moment to walk out of the kitchen. She was dressed normally, which made me wonder whether she'd worked out an agreement with my mother after we left the previous evening. The second she saw Lila, her façade slipped. "Be gone, demon!"

"Oh, stuff it," Lila said, shooting Aunt Tillie a dark look. "Your theatrics don't work on me."

Unfortunately for Lila, Aunt Tillie took that as a challenge. "I could amp it up a notch."

"Don't you have some dentures to sharpen or something?"

Everyone at the table sucked in a breath.

"Oh, good, they're adding new actors," one woman said. "It was starting to get old with the same faces every day."

"The only thing I'm going to sharpen is the stake I'm going to drive through your heart," Aunt Tillie said.

"Sit down," Landon ordered.

"Don't tell me what to do," Aunt Tillie countered.

"Sit down now."

"You sit down."

"I'm already sitting down."

"Then ... well ... keep doing it."

Landon growled, and I patted his arm to soothe him. "What are you doing here, Lila? We don't want you here, and I have a hard time believing you want to be here."

"I'm looking for Nick."

"Nick?"

"Yes, Nick Spencer. My old boyfriend."

"Are you trying to suck more life from his husk?" Aunt Tillie asked.

"You shut your mouth," Lila snapped, pointing her finger in Aunt Tillie's direction. "I've had just about enough of you."

"Are they trying to say that woman is a vampire?" The guests watched Lila with interest. "I don't think vampires are supposed to walk around during the day."

"She's not a vampire," Aunt Tillie said. "She's a succubus."

"What's that?"

"A demon who lives off the life force of others."

"Oh, fun."

"I am not a demon!" Lila stamped her foot on the floor. "These people keep making up horrible lies about me. They're witches. You know that, right?"

"Isn't that the whole point of this town?"

"Yes, but they're real witches," Lila said. "They keep casting spells on me. You didn't think I knew that, did you?"

"Actually, it took you longer to figure it out than we thought it would," Thistle said. "We overestimated your intelligence."

"Shut your filthy mouth," Lila said.

"This is getting out of hand," Landon said.

"Good," Lila said. "Arrest them."

"You're the one trespassing," Landon said. "You weren't invited here, and no one wants you here. I think you should be going."

"You can't be serious," Lila said. "You're taking the side of these … freaks?"

"These freaks are my family," Landon said. "Now get out."

"You can't kick me out," Lila said. "This isn't your property."

"It's my property, though," Aunt Tillie said. "I can kick you out."

Lila narrowed her eyes. "You can try."

That was all the challenge Aunt Tillie needed. Her face was pinched, and I could feel the crackle of energy as magic licked at the edges of the room. Oh, no. This wouldn't be good.

"What's going on?" Landon couldn't feel magic, but he knew Aunt Tillie well enough to know that something very bad was about to happen.

"I have no idea."

"She's not going to set her on fire, is she?"

I certainly hoped not. The fire extinguisher was in the kitchen. "Probably not."

"I ... crap ... what is she doing?"

Lila screeched and her hands flew to her face. "What's happening?"

I was still trying to figure that out myself, so when Lila finally shifted her fingers so I could see a hint of her upper lip, memories of high school graduation came rushing back. I leaned closer to Landon. "Don't worry. She's just giving her a mustache."

Landon looked concerned for a moment, his eyes trained on Lila, and then he shrugged. "I can live with that."

Lila desperately tried to cover her lower face. "I knew you were responsible for this the first time it happened."

"Responsible for what?" Aunt Tillie asked, faux innocence flitting across her face. "I'm not doing anything. Did anyone here see me do anything?"

The guests all shook their heads in unison, mesmerized.

"You know what you did," Lila hissed, refusing to move her hand so her words came out muffled. "I'm going to make you pay."

"That will be a neat trick," Aunt Tillie said. "I can't wait to see it."

Lila focused on Landon. "This is assault," she said. "You have to arrest her."

"I have no idea what you're talking about," Landon said. "By the way, I think it's an improvement."

Lila whimpered and stamped her foot on the floor once more. Then she turned on her heel and fled. "This isn't over."

"Have a nice day," Thistle called to Lila's fleeing back. "Who's the freak now?"

Landon arched an eyebrow. "I think we can all safely hide under that umbrella. Can someone pass the bacon?"

TWENTY-EIGHT

"What time does your picnic start?" Landon asked, linking his fingers with mine as we walked through the festival.

"In about an hour," I said. "Do you need to stop in at the police station?"

"Chief Terry said he'll text me if something pops up," Landon said. "Right now, we're just looking for Sam. We can't do anything until we find him. I'm all yours."

"That's just how I like you."

Landon smiled. "How about we play some games?"

I wrinkled my nose. "What kind of games? I don't think we have time to play naked hide-and-seek."

"I only suggested we play that because I was drunk when it came up," Landon said. "You know that, right?"

I cocked an eyebrow.

"If you want to play, I'm willing. I don't want to hear any complaints if we get caught, though."

"I was joking," I said. "I didn't realize you like carnival games. Actually, I didn't realize anyone liked carnival games. They're all rigged."

"Only people who can't win say they're rigged."

I think carnival games must be a man thing. I've never seen the appeal of throwing money away to win a cheap stuffed toy or a Jack Daniels mirror. Still, he was doing me a favor by going to the picnic. If he wanted to play a few games, I had no problem watching him waste his money. "What do you want to play?"

Landon glanced around the midway. "What do you want me to win you?"

Was that a trick question? "You're going to win me something?"

"That's what a man does at a carnival," Landon said. "He wins his woman a prize."

That was kind of demeaning, but I let it slide. I pointed to the stuffed witch at a nearby booth. "I want that witch."

"You don't think I can win it, do you?"

Was that a trick question? I was so confused. "Let's just say I've never seen anyone win a carnival game."

"Well, you're about to," Landon said, tugging my hand. "One stuffed witch coming up."

"I HONESTLY CAN'T BELIEVE you won this." I clutched the witch against my abdomen as we walked through the fair. "I ... how did you know you could do it?"

Landon rolled his eyes. "I had to throw three balls through a hoop," he said. "It's not like I solved the debt crisis."

I pursed my lips, trying to keep from smiling, and failed. "No one has ever won anything for me before. This is amazing."

Landon's cheeks colored. "Really?"

"Really."

"Why not?"

"I have no idea," I said. "I guess no one ever wanted to."

"That makes me a little sad," Landon said. "Do you want me to win you something else? There are plenty of stuffed animals to choose from."

It was an interesting offer, but I already felt like I'd won enough for one day. "I'm good."

"See ... now I kind of want to win you ten things."

"How many girls have you won things for?"

"A few," Landon conceded. "I was very popular in high school."

That didn't surprise me. "Are you saying the popular boys in high school won the popular girls stuffed animals at carnivals?"

"I feel like you're trying to trap me."

"I'm not," I said. "I honestly ... this is the best thing that's happened to me all week."

"No, what I gave you this morning was the best thing that happened to you this week," Landon teased. "This is just ... a stuffed toy."

"It still means something to me. I'm going to put it on my bed."

"Yeah, now I have to win you something else," Landon said, glancing around for inspiration. "I have to make up for your entire high school existence."

"You've already done that."

Landon cupped the back of my head and gave me a sweet kiss. "Yup. Now you're getting as many prizes as you can carry. Come on. We only have a half hour for me to win you as many things as I can."

MY ARMS WERE LADEN with stuffed animals and toys by the time the picnic rolled around. Landon had been so earnest in his efforts I almost wanted to cry. I figured that would send him over the edge and there wouldn't be room to walk in the guesthouse by the time he was done trying to eradicate all of my high school memories if that happened, so I fought back the tears.

"Wow, someone has been busy."

I forced a smile onto my face as I regarded Heather Dempsey. She'd been one of Lila's cohorts a decade ago, and I'm not going to lie, I was a little happy to see she'd gotten fat. What? I'm petty. I know it.

"Hello, Heather," I said, shuffling the prizes in my arms. "It's good to see you."

"You, too," Heather said. "You look exactly the same. Who is your friend?"

"This is Landon."

Landon extended his hand. "It's nice to meet you."

Heather shook his hand flirtatiously. "Well, aren't you just ... handsome."

"I've been told," Landon said.

"I'll just bet you have." Heather reluctantly turned her attention back to me. "Did you win all those stuffed animals yourself?" she asked, laughing. "How much money did you spend? Did you think those would impress us if we thought he won them for you?"

I frowned. "I ... ."

"I won them," Landon said, taking an instant dislike to Heather.

"For Bay?"

"She's my girlfriend," Landon said, slipping an arm around my waist. "I wouldn't win them for anyone else."

"You're with Bay?" Heather wrinkled her nose. "How did that happen? Is she like ... paying you? It wouldn't surprise me. She never could get a date in high school unless he was drunk."

Landon frowned. "Why are we here again?"

I was surprised by the question. "I ... ."

"Oh, is that a hard question to answer?" Heather said. "Could you go to jail if someone finds out she hired you?"

"I'm with the FBI," Landon said.

"Of course you are."

Landon gritted his teeth and turned to me. "Why don't you let me take those to the car? You can ... catch up here ... and I'll be back in a few minutes. I need a little air."

"No," I said.

"I'll be back, Bay," he said. "I promise."

"I don't want to stay," I said. "Let's take these to the car together and then get some ice cream."

He was surprised by the offer. "But I thought ... ."

"I did, too," I said. "It turns out I wanted to impress people I don't even like – and that seems like a waste when I could spend the afternoon with someone I already like."

Landon smiled. "Come on. I'm going to buy you eight ice cream cones."

Heather's face fell. "Are you leaving? Lila isn't even here yet. She's going to be sorry she missed you."

Somehow I doubted that. "I'm not sorry I'll miss her," I said. "Have a good life, Heather."

"**DO YOU** want to tell me what kind of epiphany you had this afternoon?" Landon asked, licking his melting ice cream cone as he watched me.

We sat at a picnic table, the warm sun radiating down on us, and he seemed to be enjoying himself. "Epiphany?"

"This morning you were desperate to impress these people," he said. "You were desperate to impress them with me, which I'm going to reward you for later. You were still desperate to impress them. Five minutes with one woman turned that all around. Why?"

"I ... it wasn't the time with Heather," I said. "Don't get me wrong, that wasn't a highlight of my day, and I got perverse pleasure in seeing she's gotten fat, but it wasn't her."

"What was it?"

"You."

Landon's eyebrows shot up. "Me?"

"You know I was miserable in high school," I said. "You've already heard way too much about it. Today, though, you tried to make up for all of it."

"I won you some stuffed animals."

"It's not about the stuffed animals," I said. "I'm going to keep them forever, though. You should probably know that. It was about you wanting to win them for me." I could feel my cheeks burning under his studied gaze.

"I wanted to win them for you because you're my girlfriend," Landon said. "That's what you do when you have a girlfriend."

"It was more than that to me," I said.

"You're making me want to strip you naked and spend the day in bed," Landon said. "I don't think that was your intention."

"I'm about to get mushy," I said. "I don't want you to comment on it."

Landon waited.

"I never thought anyone – especially someone like you – would be able to accept me."

"Why?"

"You've met my family."

"I like your family," Landon said.

"Even Aunt Tillie?"

"Even Aunt Tillie."

"I always thought the reason I never connected with someone earlier was because of them," I said. "Now I'm starting to think it was because of me."

"Bay, I know you don't want me to comment, but I'm going to," Landon said. "I knew the second I saw you at that stupid corn maze that there was something different about you. I told myself that I was under cover and there was nothing I could do about my attraction to you, but that didn't stop me.

"I wasn't following you around because I thought you were up to something," he said. "I was following you around because I couldn't stop myself. That didn't change after I met your family.

"Now, your family is work," Landon said. "I'd be lying if I said otherwise. They're fun, though. You're fun. I wouldn't want to be anywhere else. I think you worry about that sometimes. I see your face when Aunt Tillie does something crazy. You're afraid. You don't have to be. I'm not going anywhere."

Hot tears flooded my eyes. "I ... ."

"Don't you dare cry," Landon warned. "I can't take it."

"You're really my favorite person in the world right now," I said, choking back a sob.

Landon slung an arm over my shoulder and brushed a quick kiss against my forehead. "Right back at you."

"Did you mean what you just said?"

"I don't say things I don't mean."

"What about ... everything else?"

"Everything else?"

I glanced around, making sure no one was listening. "The magic."

Landon exhaled heavily. "If you had ever asked me whether I thought I would be with someone who could ... do the things you do ... I wouldn't be able to say yes. I didn't know those things existed. I didn't believe those things existed.

"Even when I thought I was handling what you are, I realize I was just going through the motions until ... Erika," he said.

I was surprised. Erika was a Civil War-era ghost who led us to a boatful of children being shipped to Canada as part of a child-trafficking ring several months before. At a time when my life was in danger, Landon showed a hint of power himself when Erika appeared to him and told him where to find me. We'd never really talked about what happened, or the fact that Landon was able to see Erika when she reunited with her mother and passed on, but I could tell now it weighed on him.

"You don't usually want to talk about that."

"That's because I don't understand it," Landon said. "Well, I didn't understand it. I think I do now."

"You do?"

"I think I could see Erika because, if I didn't, you would have died."

That wasn't the explanation I was expecting. "I don't understand."

"Have you ever asked yourself how Erika knew to come to me?"

"All of the time."

"She could have gone to the inn and had a better chance talking to your mother," Landon said. "She came to me, though. She came to me because she knew I could never let anything bad happen to you if it was in my power to stop it."

"You haven't seen a ghost since."

"Maybe I never will," Landon said. "I just know that Erika saved us both that night, and I've learned not ignore a gift like that. I have no problem with what you are, and I'm proud of you."

The tears were back, and this time one managed to slide down my cheek.

"Oh, good grief," Landon said, pulling me in for a hug. "You're such a girl." His voice cracked.

I decided not to comment on that. Neither one of us could take it if I did.

TWENTY-NINE

My romantic afternoon with Landon was cut short when Chief Terry called a few minutes later. Landon didn't look any happier with the call than I felt.

"I have to go to the station for a little while," Landon said. "Terry has something he wants to show me. Do you want to come?"

On a normal day, nothing could have dragged me away. Landon mentioning Erika gave me an idea, though. "I think I want to check something out."

"What?"

Lying would be a terrible idea right now. "I want to look in the cove."

Landon stilled. "What cove?"

"The one Erika led us to," I said. "The one where the trafficking boat was hidden."

"Why do you want to go there?"

"Sam knows where it is."

Landon rubbed the back of his neck, unsure. "Why don't you come to the station with me and then we'll go together?"

He didn't want me to go alone. I got that. "I'll just look," I said. "I'll text you if I see anything."

"Bay ... ."

"Landon, you have to trust me on this stuff sometimes."

"I do trust you," Landon said. "I just don't want anything bad to happen to you. I thought we covered that this afternoon."

"We did," I said. "I'm fully capable of walking to the cove and looking around, though."

"I didn't say you weren't."

"I swear, if I find something, I'll call you."

"If you find Sam, you're not going to approach him, right?"

"Right."

"Okay," Landon said, giving me a quick kiss. "Text me when you get there and text me when you're leaving. If you're good, I'll take you out to a private dinner tonight. I think we could both use a night away from the crazy."

I couldn't believe he was agreeing to this. "That's it? You're not going to argue?"

"No."

"Why?"

"Because we moved to a new level today," Landon replied. "I won you stuffed animals and you put high school behind you. You're an adult. You're fully capable of taking care of yourself."

"Thank you."

"If you get hurt, I'll never let you live it down."

I smiled. "Don't worry. Even if Sam is there – which is doubtful – I don't believe he would hurt me."

"Neither do I," Landon said. "That's the other reason I'm letting you go. Just ... be careful."

"I'm always careful."

"Be more careful than that."

TWENTY MINUTES later I parked in front of the Dandridge. It looked lonely. The patio garden was already wilting without Clove's attention. I could practically imagine her here with Sam. Long nights with wine on the patio, quiet walks in the woods, shared smiles and heated whispers.

Clove wasn't the only one who needed Sam to be innocent, I realized. I needed it, too.

I texted Landon that I had arrived and waited for his reply. When it arrived with another admonishment to be careful, I pocketed my phone.

It didn't take long to hike to the cove. The reason the Dandridge had been erected in its specific location was because of the slave trade. Abolitionists needed a spot from which to signal oncoming ships when it was safe to move into northern waters to ferry runaway slaves to safety in Canada. The spot offered a hidden bonus: the cove.

You couldn't find it unless you knew it was there. We'd only discovered it thanks to supernatural intervention. The genius of the cove was that it could only be seen from the water. That's what made me think there was a chance – even if it was slight – that Sam fled there.

I picked my way through the heavy underbrush, having to change my direction twice. I'd been out here before, but my memory wasn't set in stone. Finally, I found myself staring at the distinctive rock outcropping that hid the cove from prying eyes.

I was quiet as I moved forward, my eyes busily scanning the beach. It looked empty, but the shadow from the rock cliff hid the beach at a certain angle. I had to be sure.

I was moving forward when a voice interrupted my internal reverie.

"I shouldn't be surprised."

I froze, my heart dropping. I recognized the voice. "Sam?"

"I'm not going to hurt you, Bay. There's no reason to panic."

I turned slowly, taking in Sam's grizzled countenance with a worried eye. He looked … rough. He hadn't shaved in days, and his skin was sallow. He clearly didn't thrive in the outdoors. I didn't blame him.

"How are you?"

"How did you find me?" Sam asked, resigned. "Is Landon on his way?"

"Landon is at the police station," I replied. "I'm alone."

"How did you know I would be out here?"

"Just a hunch," I said. "I didn't think about it until this afternoon. Landon brought up Erika, which made me think of the cove. I thought there was a chance you would try to hide here."

"I'm not guilty."

I nodded my head. "I know."

"You do?" He looked hopeful.

"I do," I said.

"How?"

"I searched my heart," I said. "I can't believe the man who listens to Clove and tries to make her happy would kill a bank teller and beat an old lady who has already spent years being abused."

Sam pinched the bridge of his nose. "This is all so ... ."

"Crazy," I finished for him. "It's crazy. We have to figure out who is framing you."

"You're going to help me?"

"I'm going to find out who is framing you," I said. "I'm not going to help you do ... this."

"I can't turn myself in," Sam said. "If I do, it will all be over. I'll be locked up forever."

"I don't believe that," I said. "Landon and Chief Terry are working to clear you. They just haven't caught a break."

"You expect me to believe that Landon is working to clear me? He hates me. He wants me away from Clove ... and you."

"I expect you to believe that Landon is the best man I've ever met," I said. "He doesn't believe you're guilty."

"Then why is he trying to arrest me?"

"He doesn't have a choice," I said. "Mrs. Gunderson said the robber who attacked her identified himself."

"As me."

"She said she couldn't be sure. She said she didn't know you well enough to know either way. They're doing the best they can."

"That doesn't make me feel better," Sam said. "I'm the one who is going to lose my freedom. I'm the one who is going to lose ... Clove."

"You already lost Clove," I snapped. "You broke up with her."

"I did not."

"She says you did."

Sam's face contorted. "Are you kidding me?"

"Yeah, I thought I would hike out here to find you and then play a big joke at your expense," I said.

"No one needs your sarcasm."

"Clove said you broke up with her," I insisted.

"I didn't break up with her," Sam said. "I told her it wouldn't be good for her if she spent so much time around me while everyone thinks I'm a killer. You know very well the townspeople will turn on her – and turn on Hypnotic by extension – until I'm cleared."

Well, crap. Now I liked him even more. He was taking her business into account. Murderers don't do that, do they? "She didn't see it that way."

"She's just ... emotional," Sam said. "How is she?"

"Worried," I said. "She's trying to put on a brave face, but she's not sleeping and she's barely eating. She's a nervous wreck. She thinks you're going to be shot on sight by the police."

"Do you think that's a possibility?"

"Not if you turn yourself in."

"I'm not turning myself in," Sam said. "I can't clear myself if I'm in a jail cell."

"You can't clear yourself camping in the woods either," I said. "Everyone in town knows the cops are looking for you. How can you possibly run an investigation when you're the prime suspect?"

Sam looked helpless. "I don't know."

His admission tugged at my heart. "You probably don't want to hear this, but I've learned a lot about myself this week."

"Oh, good," Sam said, rubbing his forehead. "Now we're going to talk about you."

"Shut up."

Sam rolled his eyes.

"I spent my entire high school existence hating myself and hiding from people who thought they were better than me," I said. "Do you know what I learned today?"

"That you're better than all of them?"

I faltered. "Well ... kind of."

"High school is for losers," Sam said. "Popularity is a figment of people's imagination. In the grand scheme of things, it doesn't matter. It doesn't matter who was prom queen. It doesn't matter who was the class geek. It just doesn't matter. Do you want to know why it doesn't matter?"

Not really. I was starting to feel a little silly.

"It doesn't matter because who you are in high school has nothing to do with who you really are," Sam said. "It has nothing to do with who you grow up to be. You're awesome. Clove and Thistle are awesome. Thistle is mean, but she's still awesome. I don't give a rat's ass who you were in high school. The only one who cares who you were in high school is you."

"Don't be ... you."

Sam smirked. "Fine. Tell me what you learned today."

"I learned that I have everything I've ever wanted," I said. "When I was in high school, I dreamed about the life I'm living now. I realized I'm happy, and high school doesn't matter. It never mattered. I learned that the people who think it mattered are the sad ones now."

"Isn't that what I just said?"

"Yes. I still wanted to say it myself."

"Bay, you're a great person," Sam said. "You're loyal, and you have a huge heart. The people from high school who didn't want to know you lost out."

"I know."

"I'm surprised Landon didn't tell you this himself."

"He did," I said. "I just wasn't listening when he said it. He had to win me fifteen stuffed animals at the carnival before I realized he was telling me the truth."

"He won you fifteen stuffed animals? Carnival games are rigged."

"That's what I said!"

"I missed the carnival with Clove," Sam said, rubbing his forehead. "I ran and ruined the anniversary celebration for her."

"You were going to be in jail anyway," I said. "You couldn't have enjoyed the carnival."

"Thanks for the upbeat news tip."

I smiled, rueful. "You have to turn yourself in, Sam. If you don't, things will only get worse. Look at it this way, if you turn yourself in and there's another robbery, you'll automatically be cleared."

Sam opened his mouth, and then snapped it shut. "Oh."

"You didn't consider that, did you?"

"Nope."

We were both silent, the only sound encroaching on our wooded sanctuary coming from chirping birds.

"What are you going to do?"

"I guess I'm going to turn myself in," Sam said.

"Do you want to go back with me?"

"I need to pack up my stuff," Sam said.

I didn't want to be suspicious, but I couldn't help myself. "Are you trying to get me to leave so you can run again?"

Sam smiled, his eyes lighting up for the first time since he'd approached me. "No. I'm going to pack up my stuff and drop it off at the Dandridge. Then I'm going to call Chief Terry and have him pick me up."

"I can only give you an hour," I said. "I have to tell Landon after that."

"I know," Sam said. "I'll do it."

"Thank you."

"No, thank you," Sam said, squeezing my hand briefly. "Tell Clove what's going on. Ask her to come see me at the station in a few hours. I want to see her."

"Okay," I said. "You're doing the right thing, Sam."

"I hope so," he said. "I hope this is all going to work out."

"Have faith. Everything works out the way it's supposed to. It's karma. You're a good man. You'll get a happy ending."

TWENTY MINUTES later I was back at my car in the parking lot of the Dandridge, and the vise previously gripping my neck disappeared. I texted Landon to tell him I was okay, leaving out my discovery of Sam. I'd promised him an hour. I could keep that promise.

I was waiting for Landon to text back when the sound of a snapping branch behind me caught my attention. I swiveled. "Sam?" I was surprised he managed to pack up so quickly. He had to be motivated.

It wasn't Sam, though. I didn't get the chance to register the approaching face fully before pain ratcheted up the side of my head and darkness claimed me. I dimly remember falling toward the ground, and then everything winked out of existence.

I was in trouble. Again.

THIRTY

The darkness morphed into a faint red, but my eyes refused to open when consciousness finally reclaimed me. That was probably a good thing. It allowed me to ascertain my surroundings without letting my assailant know I was awake.

I felt I was closed in, a smothering feeling plaguing me. The ambient noise was familiar. I just couldn't put a name to it. I was still too fuzzy.

I racked my memory, trying to put a face with the dim edges invading my memory. I knew who had attacked me. I also knew it wasn't Sam.

"I know you're awake."

The voice jolted me. Nick. I kept my eyes shut, hoping he would think I was still out.

"I saw you shift, Bay," Nick said. "I know you're awake. If you sit up, you'll probably be more comfortable. You look like you're folded up on that seat."

Apparently he wasn't as dumb as I initially thought. I wrenched my eyes open, the dashboard of a car swimming into view. That would explain the motion sickness. We were in a car, and it was moving.

"How are you feeling?" Nick asked. "I didn't mean to hit you so hard. I didn't have time to think about what I was doing."

"You're the robber." My voice was thick, and I wet my lips as I straightened in the passenger seat of Nick's car. My head screamed, agony washing over me, but I tried to keep the evidence of pain from my face.

"I didn't have a choice," Nick said. "I need the money."

I touched my head tentatively, thankful there was no blood on my fingertips when I pulled them back and studied them. "Why do you need the money?"

"I'm in debt," Nick said. "I ... people are after me."

"Debtors? You know you can just change your phone number, right? Bankruptcy laws are really lenient now."

"Not debtors," Nick said. "Well, debtors. They're not my main concern. I know they're going to take my house. They're not enough to make me rob a bank, though. I'm not insane."

All evidence to the contrary. Instead of saying that, though, I waited.

"I need money to pay off a loan shark."

I should've been surprised, but I wasn't. I'd sensed something "off" about Nick. This had to be it. "Do you have a gambling problem?"

"How did you know that?"

"Just a guess," I said. More like witchy intuition, but he didn't need to know that. "How much do you owe?"

"Half a million."

Good grief. "Why would they let you borrow that much?"

"It's more than one loan shark."

Of course it was. "What were you thinking?"

"It's a sickness," Nick said. "I can't help myself. Those horses were just so ... pretty."

"You lost that much money gambling on horses?"

"Gambling addiction is a real thing."

"I know it is," I said. "I just don't understand how you could get that far into debt without admitting you needed help."

"I kept telling myself that I would win big and fix everything," Nick said. "Every time I told myself that I borrowed more money and made things worse. And worse. And worse. They can't get much worse now."

"And yet you never stopped."

"I couldn't," Nick said. "Do you have any idea what the guys loan sharks send out to collect debts look like?"

"I've seen it in movies."

"It's worse in real life. They don't shower ... or brush their teeth."

Well, that was a nice picture. "I don't understand how you thought robbing a bank would be the answer."

Nick shrugged as he navigated the country road. I recognized our location. We were heading back to The Overlook. Why? What was Nick's ultimate goal?

"I needed money," Nick said. "I thought about leaving the country, but they have ways to find you if you're not careful. Plus, you need a passport. Did you know that?"

"Did I know you needed a passport to the leave the country?" He was dumber than I remembered. "No. I had no idea." It doesn't hurt to play along with crazy people.

"Well, you do," Nick said. "That costs money, and it takes weeks to get one. It's so stupid."

"So you decided to come home and rob the Hemlock Cove Savings & Loan? That doesn't seem the best idea."

"I had no intention of ever coming back here," Nick said. "My parents moved away, and let's face it, this is the most boring town ever. They don't even have a Starbucks. When I got the invitation, though, I got an idea. It made so much sense. It was as if everything finally fell into place. I couldn't ignore it and it could turn my luck around."

"What made you think the town bank had enough in cash to pay down a debt that big?"

"I thought all banks had millions of dollars. That's what it shows on television."

Was he this stupid in high school? "How much did you get from the bank?"

"Don't you know? I would think your FBI boyfriend would have told you."

Funnily enough, I'd never asked. That one was on me. "He doesn't tell me the specifics of his job. It's none of my business."

"But you're so close," Nick said. "He's obviously into you."

"I should hope so. We're dating. I would hope you wouldn't date someone who you're not 'into.'"

"I've never dated anyone I was into," Nick said. "I guess you're lucky."

"I guess so."

"How did you two meet?"

He was so ... blasé. It was as though we were two old friends catching up. I decided to play along. "He was undercover. There was a murder in a corn maze. We just kind of ... connected."

"I heard about that murder," Nick said. "You solved it, didn't you?"

"Kind of."

"Is he the guy who was shot?"

"He is."

"Wow. I've always wondered what it was like to be shot. Did he say whether it hurt?"

I rolled my eyes, and the movement caused my head to throb. "He was shot. He could have died. It hurt."

"Does he have a scar?"

"Yes."

"Is it ugly?"

I often found myself running my fingers over the scar as Landon slept, wondering how close I had come to losing him before I could really know him. There was no way I was sharing that with Nick. "It's not so bad."

"He's tough, isn't he?"

"He is."

"Does he treat you right?"

"Well, he doesn't hit me over the head with ... whatever it is you hit me with ... and throw me in a car," I said. "I guess it depends on how you look at it."

WITCH ME LUCK

"Listen, I didn't want to attack you," Nick said. "I wasn't lying when I said you grew up to be hot. In fact, I was going to invite you on a great trip when I got enough money to run away. I realized that wouldn't work when I saw you with your boyfriend."

"Is that when you shifted your attention to Clove?"

"She's hot, too," Nick said. "Actually, you're all hot."

"Thanks … I guess."

"Thistle is hot, but she looks mean. Is she mean?"

"You have no idea."

"How does Marcus put up with her?"

"They're good together," I said, aggravated with the conversation. It was as if Nick had ADD. I guess, upon reflection, he was this way in high school, too. Live and learn. "Where are we going?"

"Back to The Overlook."

"Why?"

"I need your help."

That wasn't likely, but I was trying to keep him calm. "With what?"

"I can't find my money."

Oh, well, that figured. "Let me get this straight, you stole money from the bank and then you attacked Mrs. Gunderson and stole money from her, and now you've lost it?"

"It's not my fault."

He was officially pathetic. I decided to change my plan of attack "Why did you finger Sam Cornell? How did you think you could get away with it?"

"It was a fluke," Nick said. "I was looking for an outsider. He didn't seem to have any friends. I was talking to Jesse Wharton and he told me that Sam was sprucing up the Dandridge. I thought he was a perfect patsy. He didn't have a lot of ties. That was before I found out about Clove, but even after I found out it didn't matter. I had to do what I had to do."

"So you made an anonymous call to the police and fingered Sam after the robbery?"

"I honestly didn't mean to hurt anyone," Nick said. "Someone screamed, and I jumped and the gun went off. I never wanted to hurt anyone. I don't even remember the woman who was shot."

"She died. You know that, right?"

"I know," Nick said. "I feel bad. I can't fix it, though. She's already gone. Dwelling on stuff like that only makes you depressed. You have to let it go. I think that's your problem. You dwell on things. You know, if you let it go you'll feel better. You know that, right?"

Not entirely. "Why did you go after Mrs. Gunderson?"

"I needed more money," Nick explained. "I thought if I robbed every business in town I might have a chance to buy myself some time. I realize now that was a stupid idea."

At least he was the one who said it. "How much money did you manage to get?"

"Twenty thousand."

I wanted to laugh, but it didn't seem appropriate. "What's your plan now?"

"I have to run," Nick said. "Twenty grand won't last me forever, but I should be able to get away. I only want to start a new life."

"So why did you come after me?"

"I don't have a choice," Nick said. "I need your help."

"I'm not helping you rob someone. You're fresh out of luck there. My boyfriend is with the FBI. He wouldn't like it." And I wouldn't rob someone if my life depended on it – which it technically did in this specific circumstance.

"I know that," Nick said. "I need you to help find my money."

I swiveled so I could face him, ignoring the screaming pain shooting through my neck. I must have hit the ground harder than I thought. "Are you saying you really lost the money?" I thought he was kidding before, or maybe it just didn't register fully. If I didn't think he was stupid before .... "I thought you were just making excuses."

"It's gone," Nick said.

Things started slipping into place. "Did you hide it in the greenhouse?"

"How did you know?"

"Your lie about looking for Aunt Tillie's pot didn't make a lot of sense," I said. "You know very well she would never plant pot in a greenhouse."

"I can't believe she's still planting pot when you have a Fed staying on the premises so often," Nick said, laughing as if he didn't have a care in the world. "She must have a death wish."

"Landon would never arrest her."

"Because of you?"

"Because he loves Aunt Tillie."

"He's a good guy," Nick said. "I still wish you would run away with me, but I can see why you're attracted to him. He's a good-looking guy."

This conversation was getting uncomfortable. "Nick, what do you think I can do for you?"

"I need you to find my money. I hid it in a pot in that greenhouse. I was worried your mother or aunts would find it if I hid it in my room. Now it's gone."

"I don't know where it is," I said.

"Someone had to take it."

"It wasn't me."

"I know that," Nick said. "I just need you to find it."

He wasn't making any sense. "I don't know where it is."

"Yes, but you have ways of finding it."

Now I was definitely confused. "What ways?"

"You're a witch," Nick said, matter of factly. "You can do a spell."

Well, crap. And I thought things couldn't get any worse.

THIRTY-ONE

"What's the big plan now?" I asked, staring at the front of The Overlook from the passenger seat of Nick's car. "Do you expect me to magically divine where your stolen money is?"

"That would be great," Nick said, turning to me expectantly. "The faster you find my money the faster I can get out of this crap town and start my new life."

"You're going to start a new life with twenty grand?"

"I don't think I like your tone," Nick said.

"Oh, well, with the throbbing head wound and back pain I guess I must have lost my charming personality somewhere between here and the Dandridge."

"You need to find it," Nick said. "I'm sick of your attitude. You're treating me like I'm stupid."

I wonder why? "I don't know where your money is."

"Well, you need to find it," Nick said. "I can't leave this place with nothing. I've been through too much."

"You've been through too much? You killed Amy Madison."

"That was an accident," Nick said. "You have to let that go."

"You fingered Sam and ruined his life."

"So what? He's not your boyfriend."

"This whole thing is breaking Clove's heart."

"She's hot. She'll get over it."

He wasn't just senseless, he was soulless. "I don't know how to find your money."

"You're a witch. Do a spell."

"Oh, well, why didn't I think of that?" I grumbled. "Um, let me think." I tapped my chin, irked. "Bibbidi, bobbidi, boo. Money I want to find for you. This is completely moronic. I could use a gin and tonic. Bibbidi, bobbidi, boo."

"Cool," Nick said. "Where is my money?"

I wanted to smack him. If I didn't think he would smack me back, I would totally do it. "It's not here."

"It has to be," Nick said. "I put it in the greenhouse. Maybe we should go out there. If you're closer to where I hid the money your chant might work."

I considered the suggestion. The chant was never going to work – and not just because I didn't want it to – but if I could manage to get out in the open I might be able to escape. The problem was, I had no idea whether Nick was armed. If we ran into a guest – or worse, one of my relatives – there was no way I could guarantee their safety.

"We have to be careful," I said finally. "I don't want anyone else drawn into this. We have to act normal when we walk to the back of the property. We can't draw attention to ourselves."

"See. Now you're thinking." Nick opened his door. "Don't try to run. I'd hate to have to shoot you."

Well, that answered that question. "I won't try to run as long as you leave everyone else out of this."

"Good," Nick said. "Let's get going. No offense to you, but I'd like to find someone fun to spend some time with. You're hot, but you're nothing but a killjoy. How does that Fed put up with you and the constant nagging?"

I hate him.

"**WHERE** DID YOU HIDE THE MONEY?" My head felt two sizes too big for my body, and all I really wanted to do was sleep.

"Over here." Nick ambled to the far corner of the greenhouse and pointed to a stack of pots. "I put it in the one in the middle."

"Did you search through every pot? Maybe you accidentally put it in the bottom pot or something."

"Do I look stupid?"

He didn't really want me to answer that, did he? "When was the last time you saw the money?"

"I put it here the night before last," Nick said. "When I came down here last night, though, it was gone. That's why I was making so much noise. Duh."

Seriously, I hate him. "So it was down here for only a day. That's what you're saying, right?"

"Yes. Someone had to take it. Who has access to the greenhouse?"

"Technically it belongs to Aunt Tillie," I said. "We don't lock it, though. Anyone could come in here."

"I'll bet it's Tillie," Nick said. "She's been mean to me since I checked in. I think it's because she knows you're attracted to me."

Yeah, I was pretty sure that wasn't it. "It wasn't Aunt Tillie."

"Are you saying she's above stealing money? I heard she gave Lila a mustache."

That was still funny. "I don't think she's above stealing money," I said. "I do think she's incapable of keeping quiet about it if she did. She would have bought something big. She's had her eye on a new snow plow for months."

"Oh," Nick said, rubbing his forehead. "I guess you would know best. What about your mother? She looks like she would steal. It's always the prim ones who get down and dirty behind closed doors."

"You should tell her that."

Nick frowned. "Someone stole my money. You have to find out who, and you have to do it right now because I can't spend one more second with you. You're such a downer."

"I'm a downer?"

"You just harp and harp on stuff," Nick said. "You never let anything go. I know it's a woman thing, but you have no idea how annoying it is."

"You're a murderer and you're annoyed with me?"

"See!"

I bit my tongue to keep from screaming at him.

"Now, say your spell again and find my money," Nick said.

"That wasn't a spell. I don't have a spell to find lost money." Actually, I could probably whip one up, but I had no intention of helping Nick.

"Well, you'd better think of one," Nick said, pulling a handgun from his pocket and leveling it at me. "You're running out of time. I think you might need some motivation."

I glared at him. "Do you think a gun is going to motivate me?"

"Treating you like a human being hasn't been working," Nick said. "I'm flexible. I'm willing to try multiple things. I do that in bed, too, just in case you're still interested."

"You hit me on the head and threw me in your car," I said. "You kidnapped me and dragged me to my mother's inn and now you're holding a gun on me. How is that treating me like a human being?"

"You just won't let things go," Nick said. "Do you think you get that from your mother?"

I wish he would hit me over the head again. "What if someone else took your money?" I suggested.

"Who? Oh, do you think your boyfriend took it? Is that why he left you alone today? Do you think he took my money and ran?"

"I wasn't talking about Landon," I said, trying to remain calm. "What about the other guests? Have you told any of them that you were hiding a bunch of money on the property?"

"Only an idiot would do that."

I arched an eyebrow.

"I'm starting to think you're questioning my intelligence," Nick said, the hand holding the gun wavering.

"Nick, you robbed a small-town bank because you thought it would have millions of dollars," I said. "I can't be the first person to question your intelligence."

I should probably be questioning my own right about now. Never verbally poke a murderer when he's holding a gun. It's a basic rule. I know it. I've been faced with the prospect before. Maybe I have brain damage?

"I have an IQ of eighty," Nick said.

"That's impressive," I said, taking a mental step back. It's important to placate crazy people with false platitudes. "I ... isn't one hundred the standard for normal intelligence?" Yup, I definitely have brain damage.

"You're making that up," Nick said. "I'm smart."

"Fine. You're smart."

"I am."

"I believe you."

We lapsed into silence for a moment, the words "leave it alone" running through my mind on a constant loop. Finally, I couldn't take Nick's frustration, or the shaking gun, for one more second. "If you're so smart, why don't you remember where you left your money?"

"I remember where I left it! Someone stole it!"

I was starting to wonder whether that really was the case. "And you're sure it was the pots in that corner?" I asked, pointing.

"Yes."

"You're one-hundred percent positive it wasn't those pots over there, right?"

Nick glanced in the direction I pointed, where another three pots were stacked in the same configuration. I could practically see his mind working.

"You're not sure, are you?"

"I am so," Nick said, although he was already walking toward the pots. "I just ... maybe someone moved the pots over there after I put the money in them."

"Maybe."

Since his back was to me, I took the opportunity to move toward the door. I kept one eye on him as he rummaged through the pots and the other on the door as I turned the handle. It opened quietly, and I cast one more look at Nick before slipping outside. While it's never fun to deal with a madman with a gun, it's markedly easier when he's also an idiot.

I broke into a run as I climbed the low-rolling hill. I could see the back of The Overlook. If I could get inside, I could lock the door. I would have backup. Magical backup at that. Nick wouldn't be stupid enough to take on all of us, would he?

"Bay!"

I didn't turn around. Nick had discovered my trickery, but slowing wasn't an option. I was almost to the back of the inn when a familiar garden hat popped into view. Aunt Tillie was on her knees working in the dirt next to the patio, and Nick's bellowing clearly caught her attention.

"What happened to you?" She asked, getting to her feet. "You look like you've been rolling around in the dirt. Did you and Thistle get into another argument?"

"Get inside," I ordered.

Aunt Tillie didn't move, instead tilting her head so she could look in the direction of her greenhouse. "Is that Nick? Why was he in my greenhouse? I'm going to kick his ... ."

I grabbed her shoulders. "He has a gun."

"So he's been telling everyone at the inn," Aunt Tillie said. "I'm guessing he's packing light if he has to keep talking about it like that."

"He's the robber! He killed Amy Madison."

Aunt Tillie furrowed her brow. "He doesn't have the stones to do that."

"He hit me over the head and kidnapped me."

"Is that why you look like that?"

"Get inside!"

I risked a glance over my shoulder. Nick was almost upon us.

"Don't worry," Aunt Tillie said. "I'll handle this." She took a step forward and extended a gnarled finger in Nick's direction. "Take one more step and I'll blow you up with the power of my mind."

Oh, well, that was convincing. I'm sure that scared the fight right out of him.

Nick stilled, his hand behind his back. He was hiding the gun, but for how long? "Can you really do that?"

"You have no idea what I'm capable of," Aunt Tillie said. "Now, put your gun on the ground and lay down. Put your hands behind your back. I'll cuff you and we'll call the police. This doesn't have to get ugly."

"Cuff him? With what?"

Aunt Tillie didn't move her eyes from Nick as she reached into her pocket and removed a set of steel handcuffs.

"Where did you get those? Actually, why do you even have them?"

"That's none of your concern," Aunt Tillie said. "Suffice it to say, there was a sale on Amazon and I wanted them."

I never should have given her that computer.

Nick's gaze bounced between the two of us. "Listen, I don't want to cause problems, but I need Bay to find my money."

"You lost the money you stole from the bank? What kind of idiot …?"

Nick whipped the gun out from behind his back. "I'm not an idiot!"

"You keep telling yourself that," Aunt Tillie said. "Maybe it will be like a self-fulfilling prophecy. You can take some classes in prison and better yourself."

"I'm not going to prison."

"Of course you are," Aunt Tillie said. "You're out of options on that front. Don't worry. I'm sure you'll find someone to protect you in the big house. It's probably going to be … uncomfortable … for those first few nights, but you'll learn how to satisfy your prison husband."

"That's not going to happen to me." Nick's voice was shrill.

"Oh, honey, you've got 'prison bitch' written all over you."

"Is that helping? We need to go inside and call Landon."

"Shut up," Aunt Tillie said. "I told you I have this under control. You're starting to bug me."

"Well, I'm sorry my kidnapping and head wound are ruining your afternoon."

"You're such a drama queen."

"She is, isn't she?" Nick said. "She's mean, too. I have no idea what that Landon dude sees in her."

"I think it's her butt," Aunt Tillie said. "That's neither here nor there, though. You need to put that gun down."

"I'm not putting the gun down," Nick said. "It's all I have left."

"You still have your head," Aunt Tillie pointed out. "If you don't put that gun down right now, I'm going to blow it off your neck. Then where will you be? I don't think you're going to be very desirable in prison without a head."

"Stop saying that!" Nick waved the gun around. Even from six feet away I could see his finger reflexively pulling the trigger.

I reacted out of instinct, throwing myself in front of Aunt Tillie. I heard the gun go off, but it was hard to register the sound with the pain ripping through my arm.

I hit the ground. Hard.

That's when Aunt Tillie lost her temper and the skies opened up with a lightning strike close enough to make my hair stand on end. At first, I thought the screaming was coming from me. It wasn't. Nick lost what was left of his mind when the lightning struck, and he fled into the newly formed storm.

I leaned back on the ground, gripping my arm as the blood coursed out. "Well, that was interesting," I said, darkness pulling at the edges of my mind.

"I told you I would handle it," Aunt Tillie said, glancing down at me.

"That's good," I said. "I'm trusting you to handle this, too."

"What?"

I didn't answer her. I passed out instead.

THIRTY-TWO

"Let me in that room right now." I recognized Landon's voice, including the fear tingeing it, from my hospital bed.

"Sir, you're going to have to calm down." It sounded as though a nurse was trying to calm him. Given the pain medication I was on, unfortunately I was picturing her trying to do it with her boobs. "Ms. Winchester is being checked by a doctor. When she's stable, you'll be able to go in and question her."

"She's not stable?" Landon pushed past the nurse, pulling up short when he saw me in the bed. "Hey." Relief washed over his face.

"Hey," I said, weary. "You look nice."

"You look like hell," Landon said, moving to my side. "What's going on here?"

"Who are you?" Dr. Ray Hardges had served Hemlock Cove as the primary physician for years. He was used to Winchester drama, although he obviously hadn't been introduced to Landon yet.

"I'm her boyfriend."

"You said you were with the FBI," the nurse said, appearing in the doorway. "It's against the law to pretend to be an agent."

"I am an agent," Landon snapped. "I also happen to be her

boyfriend. I … what are you doing there?" Landon pointed to my arm, which was covered with bloodied bandages.

"I'm going to stitch up her arm," Dr. Hardges said. "If you can remain calm, you can stay with her. If you can't, you have to go out in the waiting room with the rest of her family."

"They were banned," I offered helpfully.

"Banned?"

"Mom was a little hysterical. She kept thinking my arm was going to fall off. She was willing to donate hers if I needed it."

"How bad is it?" Landon asked, putting his hand on my shoulder.

"It's minor," Dr. Hardges said. "She was lucky. The bullet ripped through some flesh. It didn't hit anything important, including bone. In a few days it won't be anything but a minor aggravation and a bad memory."

"Twila thinks I'm going to get lead poisoning," I said.

"You seem a little out of it," Landon said.

"I'm drugged."

"Good." He sat down on the edge of the bed, his hands nervously roaming up and down my body as he checked me over. "Is anything else hurt?"

"Just my head."

"What happened to your head? You weren't shot in the head, were you?" He was back on his feet, his hands clutching at my hair as he tugged it to the side.

"Ow!"

"Sir, you need to stop that," Dr. Hardges said. "She was not shot in the head."

"Then what's wrong with her head?"

"Oh, there are so many answers to that question," I mumbled.

"Sweetie … ." Landon straightened his shoulders, collecting himself. "What happened to her head?"

"She was struck from behind," Dr. Hardges said. "My understanding is that Nick Spencer attacked her in the parking lot of the Dandridge. Everyone was talking at once when they brought her in, though, so I think you should probably talk to them."

"Chief Terry is out there doing that right now."

"Oh, that's good. He knows how to handle them."

"Can anyone handle them?"

"Good point."

Landon forced a smile for my benefit. "How are you feeling?"

"Drugged."

This time the smile that crossed his face was real. "When I got the call that you'd been shot, I honestly think my heart stopped beating."

"It wasn't so bad," I said. "It probably wouldn't have happened if Aunt Tillie hadn't told Nick he had 'prison bitch' written all over him."

Landon scowled. "She got you shot?"

"Not if you're going to be angry with her."

Landon pressed his lips together. "Where is she? Is she in the waiting room, too?"

"I ...."

"It's going to be fine, sweetie," he said, holding up his hand, conciliatorily. "I promise. I just want to have a little talk with her."

"You look like you want to strangle her."

"That might be fun, too," Landon said.

"Who are you going to strangle?" Aunt Tillie popped into the room.

"Tillie, I told you that anyone who shared the same last name with Bay had to sit out in the waiting room," Dr. Hardges scolded. "How did you get past Evangeline?"

"She's not so spry these days," Aunt Tillie said. "I walked right past her."

"Are you going to behave yourself?"

"Yes."

"It's good that you're here," Landon said. "I want to have a talk with you."

"Do you want to thank me for saving Bay's life?" Aunt Tillie was guileless. The innocent look on her face made me want to laugh, but I didn't have the energy.

"Did you get her shot?" Landon's face was grave.

"Of course not," Aunt Tillie said. "Nick wasn't even aiming at us.

He was waving his gun around like a crazy person. I think he pulled the trigger by accident. Bay jumped in front of me so I wouldn't get hit. It's all her fault."

Landon clutched his hands together, furious.

"It's okay," I said. "I'm fine. It's just a flesh wound."

"You were shot!"

I jolted at the anger in his voice and contrition instantly flooded his features. "I'm sorry. I'm sorry." He leaned over and kissed my forehead. "I didn't mean to yell and scare you. I'm sorry."

"You should really learn to control your temper," Aunt Tillie said.

Landon inhaled deeply, the air rasping through his nose. "You're probably right."

Dr. Hardges patted him on the shoulder. "I'm going to go and get a few things for Bay, then we're going to clean up her wound and sew her up. Then you can take her home. I'll give you a few minutes with Tillie. It would be nice if you didn't kill her."

"I'm not going to kill her. Wait. Should Bay be going home? She was shot."

"I'm not staying here," I said. "I want to go home. I'm tired."

"You can sleep here," Landon countered.

"I want to sleep in my own bed. With you."

Landon's face softened. "Is it safe for her to go home?"

"She doesn't have a concussion," Dr. Hardges said. "We're going to give you some pills for pain. She'll probably sleep twelve hours. She'll be much better tomorrow."

"Okay," Landon said. "Make sure you get me all the instructions."

"I'll be back in a few minutes," Dr. Hardges said.

Once Dr. Hardges left, Landon unleashed his fury on Aunt Tillie. "This is your fault!"

"How is it my fault?" Aunt Tillie asked. "I'm the one who saved her."

"I have trouble believing that."

"No, she did," I said. "She told Nick she was going to blow his head off with the power of her mind. Then, when he shot me, she called down a storm and almost struck him with a bolt of lightning. He was so frightened he ran into the storm."

Landon faltered. "You created that storm? You know they're talking about it on television, right? The weather forecasters can't figure out how it even happened. They said the weather conditions weren't right for it. They're calling it an act of God."

"You're welcome," Aunt Tillie said.

"I'm not thanking you."

"She's alive."

"She's got a head wound and she's been shot," Landon argued. "She's lucky to be alive."

"And you've spent the past half hour imagining her dying in a pool of her own blood," Aunt Tillie said, patting his arm. "You're just an emotional pit of despair right now, aren't you?"

Landon pinched the bridge of his nose. "She could have died."

"I would never let that happen," Aunt Tillie said.

"If that bullet had been a few inches off … ."

"It wasn't."

"If she had moved slower … ."

"She didn't."

"If … ."

"She's right there," Aunt Tillie said. "You need to calm yourself. You're starting to embarrass me."

"Get out!"

"You get out!"

"I'm not joking," Landon said. "Get. Out!"

Aunt Tillie pulled herself up to her full four feet and eleven inches, and fixed Landon with a dark look. "I'm only doing this because you're about to blow a gasket."

"Great."

"We're going to have a talk about this later," Aunt Tillie warned, shuffling toward the door.

"I can't wait."

"If Nick wasn't already at the top of my list, and if Lila Stevens wasn't still in town, you would have a tornado of terror heading in your direction," Aunt Tillie said.

"Get out!"

***

"ARE YOU COMFORTABLE?" Landon shifted the pillows under my head, pulling the covers up and tucking them around my shoulders.

"I'm going to pass out any second. You know that, right?"

"Not yet," Landon said. "You have to take those pills Dr. Hardges sent home first. Here."

He grabbed the medication bottle from the nightstand, tipped two pills into the palm of his hand, and passed them to me.

"I don't need these," I said. "I'm ready to pass out now."

"Take them."

"I ... ."

"Take them."

"You're really bossy," I said. I tossed the pills into my mouth and took the bottle of water he handed me so I could wash them down. When he was satisfied, I handed the bottle back and watched through heavy-lidded eyes as he stripped out of his clothes and climbed in next to me.

Mom wanted to stay at the guesthouse to make sure I was all right, but when Landon informed her that my bed was too small for the three of us she reluctantly left me in his capable hands, promises of a catered breakfast tomorrow morning escaping her lips as he pushed her out the door.

Landon switched off the lamp and rolled on his side so he was facing me. "Come here."

I snuggled as close to him as I could, resting the side of my face against his chest. "I'm really tired."

"You're going to be out in a few minutes."

"You'll probably be at work when I wake up tomorrow."

"I'll be right here," Landon said, rubbing the back of my neck.

"What about Sam?"

"He turned himself in," Landon said. "We were processing him when I got the call about you."

"You can let him go now," I murmured. "He's been cleared. We should tell Clove."

"Chief Terry is handling Sam and Clove. Don't worry about that. Go to sleep."

I ran my fingers over the faint scar on his shoulder. "Now we've both been shot."

"Yeah, we're quite the couple." Landon brushed his lips against my forehead. "Go to sleep."

"Will you wake me up if Nick is caught?"

"No. Go to sleep."

"He won't be able to get far, will he?"

"Bay, if I have to track him down and kill him myself, I'll do it."

"I don't want him dead," I said. "He's too stupid for that."

"We'll talk about it tomorrow, Bay. I need you to go to sleep."

"What are you going to do?" I was barely holding on.

"I'm going to watch you sleep and try to pretend that we didn't get really, really lucky today."

"I'm sorry," I murmured.

"Why are you sorry?"

"I told you I would be fine if I went to the Dandridge by myself," I said. "Look what happened."

"You were right about Sam," Landon said. "We had no way of knowing that Nick was following you. We'll talk about it tomorrow."

"Okay."

Landon nestled down under the blankets. "Bay?"

"Hmm."

"You nearly scared the life out of me today."

"I'm sorry."

"Don't be sorry," he said. "If you have nightmares, I'll be right here."

"What if you have nightmares?"

"I have the antidote right next to me," he said, resting his cheek against my forehead. "Now go to sleep. I think I aged ten years today.

I'm exhausted, and you need to rest. We'll figure this all out in the morning."

"Okay." I thought those were the last words I'd utter before sleep claimed me, but something else bubbled out of my mouth. "I love you."

Landon tightened his arms around me. "I love you, too. Now sleep."

THIRTY-THREE

"What do you think they're doing in there?"

"Sleeping."

"Do you think they're naked?"

"I don't think either one of them was feeling particularly amorous last night."

"Do you think we should knock?"

"I don't know. Maybe we should let them sleep longer."

Landon groaned as I shifted in his arms, consciousness slowly claiming me.

"What's going on?" I asked, rubbing my forehead.

"They've been out there for twenty minutes debating whether they should come in," Landon said. "I was hoping they would go away, but I'm not sure that's going to happen."

I smiled. "Who's out there?"

"I think it's all of them."

"Even Aunt Tillie?"

"Not if she knows what's good for her," Landon said. He glanced down at me, pushing my messy hair out of my face. "How do you feel?"

"Well rested."

"How is your arm? Let me see it."

I held it up so he could study the bandage. "It's fine. It barely hurts."

Landon kissed the edge of the bandage and then lowered my arm. "How is your head?"

"It feels normal."

"Normal for you or normal for me?" Landon asked, his eyes twinkling.

"Normal for me."

"Oh, so we're still dealing with abnormal here."

"You're so funny." I poked his side. "How are you feeling?"

"I wasn't shot."

"This time."

Landon sighed. "I'm fine."

"Did you have nightmares?"

"Yes." He watched me for a moment. "Did you?"

"No. It was one big ball of blackness."

"Good." He rubbed my back lightly. "Do you want to pretend we're sleeping or do you want to go out there and deal with them?"

That was a good question. My growling stomach answered it.

"You're hungry," Landon said.

"Aren't you?"

"I'm starving. I still don't want to face … them."

"Do you think they're going to curse you or something?" I asked.

"No. I'm afraid they're going to smother you, and that's my job."

"I'll bet they have bacon," I teased.

Landon smiled. "You know the way to my heart. Let's go."

"ARE there any eggs and pancakes left at the inn?" I asked, studying the feast my mother and aunts had brought. "You know I can't eat all of this, right?"

"You need to keep up your strength," Mom said, combing her fingers through my tangled hair. "You also need to shower. You shouldn't let a man see you looking like this. It will scare him away."

Landon slapped Mom's hand away from my hair. "She looks fine. Leave her alone. Her head is still tender."

Mom glared at him. "I may have let you push me out of here last night...."

"Let me?"

"This is still my property," Mom said. "This is my property, too." She tugged on my hair.

"Ow!"

"Stop being a drama queen," Mom said. "You're fine."

Landon and I exchanged a look.

"Where's the bacon?" I asked, trying to push the chill from the room. "Landon is starving."

"What makes you think I brought bacon?" Mom asked.

"Because you're not mean enough to make him suffer," I said. I lifted the cover off one of the serving dishes, smiling when I saw the huge mound of crispy bacon. "See."

"And that's why you're my favorite," Landon said, rubbing my mother's shoulder.

She shot him a rueful smile. "I'm still angry with you. You kept me away from my daughter last night."

"She slept like a rock," Landon said. "And there was no way all three of us were sleeping in that bed."

"You could have slept on the couch."

"No, I couldn't have."

"Do I smell bacon?" Marcus emerged from Thistle's bedroom, pulling a shirt over his bare chest and smiling as everyone turned in his direction.

"I'm sure that bacon is for Bay and Landon," a bleary-eyed Thistle said, pushing past him. "Where's the coffee?"

"Mom brought more than enough for everyone."

"You should brush your hair," Twila said, pushing her hand down on Thistle's wild pink hair. "This is just...."

"Leave her alone," I said. "We're not used to early-morning guests."

"It's almost ten," Mom said.

"That's early morning for us."

"That's just a waste of a day," Marnie said. "Where is Clove?"

"She's probably still asleep," I said. "She had a big day yesterday. Do we even know she's here?"

"Where else would she be?" Marnie asked.

"Well, Sam was cleared yesterday," I said. "Maybe they made up."

Clove's door opened. Her face was drawn as she took in the scene. "Why is everyone down here?"

Since she was alone, I guessed she and Sam hadn't made up yet.

"In case you missed it, Bay was shot yesterday," Mom said.

"I heard." Clove was grumpy.

Marnie dug around in her purse. Retrieving a hairbrush, she moved behind her daughter. "Your hair is a mess."

"I just woke up."

"You could still brush your hair."

Our mothers have a weird set of priorities.

"Have you talked to Sam?" I asked, settling in one of the dining room chairs and reaching for the plate of eggs.

Landon moved my hand back. "I'll get you a plate," he said. "Rest your arm."

"My arm is fine."

"You were shot. Indulge me."

I rolled my eyes until they landed on Thistle, who watched the scene with amusement.

"Sam was already gone from the police station by the time I got there last night," Clove complained.

"Why didn't you go to the Dandridge?"

"Because he broke up with me."

"That's not what he said." I reached for a slice of bacon, causing Landon to grab my hand and push it back down.

"What did he say?" Clove asked, moving to the chair next to me. When she reached for a slice of bacon, Landon ignored her. Instead of eating it, though, she handed it to me. "You got to talk to him yesterday afternoon, didn't you?"

"Yeah. I talked him into turning himself in." I bit into the bacon.

Landon shot me a dark look. "You can't wait for thirty seconds?"

"I'm sorry."

Landon slid a heaping plate in front of me. "You're going to eat all of this."

I forced a smile onto my face. "If you insist."

"What did Sam say to you?" Clove asked.

"Before you answer that, I have to go," Mom said, dropping a quick kiss on the top of my head. "Clove and Thistle, you're responsible for bringing these dishes back to the inn after breakfast. We have to get lunch ready for the guests, and we haven't cleaned the rooms yet. I'll be so glad when Belinda gets back in a few days."

"Why do we have to bring them back?" Thistle asked. "It's Bay's breakfast."

"Bay was shot," Mom and Landon said in unison. I was starting to feel infantilized.

"Fine. We'll bring the dishes up."

Mom, Marnie and Twila left after sharing two more passive aggressive comments about our hair, and then it was just the five of us. Clove shifted on her chair while I ate.

"What's wrong with you?" I asked.

"I asked you what Sam said," Clove said. "You were shot, though, so I don't feel like I can badger you until you've finished your breakfast."

"You're not badgering her at all," Landon said. "She's going to eat her breakfast and then she's going back to bed."

"I'm fine," I said.

"You were ... ."

I cut him off. "Shot. I know. You need to take a chill pill. I feel fine. My head barely hurts. My arm is numb. It's going to be okay."

Landon sank into the open chair on the other side of me. "I'm allowed to worry about my girlfriend when she's been shot."

"You are," I said. "I'm also allowed to take care of myself because I'm an adult."

"Whatever," Landon grumbled, grabbing a slice of bacon from my plate. "What? You know you're not going to eat it all. I was overreacting."

I squeezed his hand. "It's a good thing you're cute when you're hovering."

"Eat your breakfast."

"Really? You're killing me," Clove said.

"I'm sorry," I said. "I forgot. You want to know what Sam and I talked about."

"Yes."

"We talked about you," I said. "Sam said he didn't break up with you. He said that he suggested you not be seen with him because he didn't want your reputation to take a hit. He was worried people would turn on Hypnotic because of your relationship with him."

"So he broke up with me?"

"That doesn't sound like a breakup to me. That sounds like a man trying to protect his girlfriend."

"She's right," Thistle said, grabbing her own plate of food. "Sam was trying to protect you. Suck it up."

"Then why didn't he come over here last night?" Clove asked.

"Maybe because Bay was shot and he didn't want to intrude," Thistle said. "Maybe because he's been living in the woods for two days and he needed to shower before he came over here and swept you off your feet."

"Do you really think so?"

"I think you've gotten yourself tied up in knots," Thistle said. "Eat your breakfast and take the chill pills Bay is hoarding for Landon."

Landon scowled. "I am not overreacting."

"No one said you were overreacting," I said.

"We were thinking it," Thistle said.

"I think it's nice," Marcus said. "He wants to take care of her. If Thistle was shot, I'd do the same thing."

"Eat your breakfast," Thistle ordered. "Have you heard whether they caught Nick yet, Landon?"

"I haven't checked in with Chief Terry," Landon said. "I'll call him in a little bit."

I was surprised. "You're not going down to the station?"

"I'm not leaving your side."

"That's going to make going to the bathroom interesting," Thistle said, waggling her eyebrows.

"You're not funny," Landon said.

His phone chimed from the counter, and I watched as he checked his texts. "What is it?"

"Chief Terry says that Nick was sighted on the north side of town. He's going there now."

I waited.

Landon was fixated on his phone screen, his face conflicted. I could see it. After a few moments, he put the phone back on the counter and headed in my direction. "So, I was thinking we could spend the day in bed. We can watch some television, maybe find an old movie or something."

"I think you should go."

"You don't want me here?"

"That's not what I meant," I said. "I think you should go on the search with Chief Terry. I know you want to."

"I'm not leaving you," Landon said. "Nick is still out there."

"Marcus is here," I said. "We're not leaving the house. I think you need to see this through. You're not going to relax until Nick is in custody. I need you to relax, because you're going to give me an ulcer if you don't."

Landon sighed, shifting his gaze to Marcus. "Are you willing to stay here?"

"Absolutely," Marcus said. "I think we'll all feel better when Nick is in custody. I'll watch them."

Landon rested his hand on my shoulder, considering. "Okay. Keep them inside, and don't let them drink."

"Why can't we drink?" Thistle asked, incensed.

"Because I want you all clear headed in case something happens."

"Fine," Thistle grumbled. "I'm going to totally tie one on when Nick is in custody, though. Prepare yourself."

"I'll mix the chocolate martinis myself," Landon said. He rubbed my shoulders softly. "Make sure you keep them safe," he instructed Marcus. "I think we've had enough drama for one week."

"**I PROMISE** we'll stay inside."

Landon and I were at the front door twenty minutes later, his hair still damp from the shower. "Make sure you do," he said. He tugged on a strand of my hair. "I love you." He leaned down and gave me a quick kiss, smiling when he pulled away and saw the surprised look on my face. "Did you think I forgot what we said to each other last night?"

"I ... actually, I thought maybe you said it only because you wanted to make me happy," I admitted.

"That's not why I said it," Landon said. "I felt it. I said it. I mean it. I love you."

"I love you, too."

"I know you do. I just wish it didn't take you getting shot for us to say it."

"Did you want it to be special?" I was teasing him. The moment was heavy so I thought it was warranted.

"I always pictured a picnic in my head for some reason," he said. "I definitely didn't think it would come on the heels of you being shot. I just wanted something ... different."

I wanted that, too. Still, I wouldn't trade the warmth rushing through my heart for anything. "Hurry back."

"I'll keep in touch." He kissed me again. "Be good."

I watched from the front window as he pulled out of the driveway, a goofy grin on my face. When I turned, I found Thistle and Clove staring at me. "What?"

"Oh, you guys finally dropped the love bomb on each other," Thistle said, holding a hand to her heart. "It's just so ... cute."

"Shut up."

"I think it's sweet," Clove said. "I guess Aunt Tillie won the pool."

"What pool?"

"We all had a pool betting on when you guys would admit you loved each other," Thistle explained. "I thought it was still months away."

"I hate you guys sometimes." I threw myself down on the couch.

"Bay's in love," Thistle sang.

The front doorknob turned, drawing our attention. Did Landon forget something?

"Cripes. He can't be away from you for five minutes," Thistle said.

The door flew open, revealing Nick's menacing figure in the frame. His chest heaved and his eyes stared wildly as he clutched his gun at his side. He wore the same clothes from the day before, and he looked as though he hadn't slept.

"Or not," Thistle said.

Landon was going to have a fit. I just knew it.

THIRTY-FOUR

"Holy crap!" Clove jumped when she saw Nick. "You framed my boyfriend!"

"And you shot Bay," Thistle said, glaring at Nick.

"That, too," Clove said. "You're a very bad man."

Marcus moved forward, uncertain. "Nick ... ."

"Oh, hey Marcus," Nick said. "I haven't seen you since that baseball league the summer before I left for college. Well ... at dinner ... but we didn't really have time to talk. How have things been?"

"Okay," Marcus said, eyeing the gun in Nick's hand. "How are things with you?"

"They've been better," Nick said.

"So I've heard." Marcus' movements were slow as he slipped around the arm of the couch. "What are you doing here, man?"

Nick glanced at the gun. "Don't worry about this," Nick said. "I have no intention of shooting you."

"That's good," Marcus said. "I think we've had enough shootings for one week."

Nick rolled his eyes. "I barely clipped her." He gestured at me. "See. She's fine."

"I doubt Amy Madison feels the same way," Thistle said.

"That was an accident," Nick said.

"Like yesterday?" I asked.

"That really was an accident," Nick said. "I just got excited. You're the one who jumped in front of the bullet."

"I was protecting my aunt," I said. "You could have killed her."

"Like that would have been some great loss," Nick said, his eyes darting between the four of us. "Oh, come on. You people can't really like that old biddy."

"Of course we don't like her," Thistle said. "She's an awful person who acts up for attention. That doesn't mean we don't love her."

"I want to be just like her when I get old," Clove said.

"Me, too," Thistle said.

They turned to me expectantly. "I need more time to think about it," I said.

"Is now the right time for this conversation?" Marcus asked, agitated.

"It depends on how much you value family unity," Thistle said.

"Not a lot right now," Marcus said, taking another step forward. "So ... um ... what are you hoping to do here, Nick?"

"I need to borrow one of these witches," Nick said. "I don't care which one."

"Not it!" Clove, Thistle and I all answered in unison.

"Why do you need a witch?" Marcus asked. He was trying to maintain control of the conversation, but we weren't offering him much help in that department.

"I need to find my money."

"The money you stole from the bank?"

"And Mrs. Gunderson," I said. "You know, Mrs. Gunderson, right? The elderly woman who was abused by her husband for years."

"Get over it," Nick said. "I barely hit her. If she had stayed in the kitchen instead of being a busybody nothing would have happened to her."

"That's a great way to look at it," Thistle said. "It's almost as if you've managed to completely make none of this your fault."

"It's not my fault," Nick said. "The world keeps conspiring against me."

"Maybe that's karma," Clove suggested.

"Whatever," Nick said. "So which one of you wants to be my witch for the day?"

"We're busy today," Thistle said. "Can you try back tomorrow?"

"That really doesn't work for me," Nick said. "I need to get out of this town, and I need to get out now."

"So go," Thistle said. "We're not stopping you."

"I kind of want to stop him," I said.

Thistle lifted her finger to her lips. "Shh. Not now."

"Listen, I think you guys are kind of funny," Nick said. "You're all hot, too. Your hair is kind of a mess in the morning, but I can live with it. I still need to get away from you."

"We want that, too," Thistle said.

"So find my money."

"I already told you we can't find your money," I said. "We don't have a spell to look for lost money. It doesn't exist."

"Why don't we use the locator spell we used when we were looking for money down by Hollow Creek?" Clove suggested.

Thistle reached over and smacked the back of her head. "Nice."

"What? Oh." Clove realized what she'd said a little too late to reel it back into her open mouth.

"Finally! Someone who is willing to help." Nick gestured to Clove. "Come on. You're the witch I want."

"You're not taking her," I said.

"I'll bring her back," Nick said. "I should have taken her in the first place. She's far less mouthy than you two."

"If you touch her, I'll scratch your eyes out," Thistle warned.

"Nick, I can't let you take Clove," Marcus said, holding his hands up in a soothing manner.

"Why not?"

"Because you've killed someone," Marcus said. "You shot Bay yesterday. I can't let you just walk out of here with Clove."

Nick leveled the gun at Marcus. "Are you sure about that?"

Marcus didn't flinch. "Yes."

"Are you seriously willing to die for Clove? She's not even the one you're sleeping with."

"If I have to die for Clove, then I'll consider it a sacrifice well worth making," Marcus said. "I can't let you take her, though."

"What if I want to take Bay?"

"No."

Nick pressed his lips together as he glanced around the guesthouse. The silence was overwhelming, but none of us broke it. When the door nudged further open behind Nick, my heart jumped. Landon was back. What if he surprised Nick and was accidentally shot? I'd come to the conclusion that Nick didn't know how to use the gun purposefully.

Instead of Landon, though, the figure that moved through the door was a surprise.

"What are you doing?" Lila asked, waving her hands dramatically. "I've been waiting in the car forever."

What the hell? "Lila?"

Lila looked me up and down. "Nice look. I especially like the furry pajama pants and bedhead. How did you ever snag that FBI agent when you look like that in the morning?"

"Why are you here?" I asked.

"I'm waiting for Nick," Lila said. "He's supposed to have a lot of money and he's taking me with him when he leaves to spend it."

Now I was really confused. "You're Nick's partner in all of this?" How did that work?

"Of course not," Lila said. "I had no idea what he was up to until we caught up over lunch the other day. Since I was going to be stuck staying here if I didn't find a new ... benefactor ... I figured leaving town with Nick was as good a plan as anything else."

"I've been visiting her out at the Dragonfly," Nick said. "I've been sneaking in after dark because Lila doesn't want to have to pay an extra fee for having an overnight guest. We're in love again."

Lila rolled her eyes.

"That's why the locator spell hit on the Dragonfly," Thistle said. "Nick must have been out there. We just didn't see him."

"When did you find out about the money?" I asked.

"The other day," Lila replied.

"And you didn't think that calling the police was a viable way to go?" I asked, angry. "He killed a woman."

"It was an accident," Lila said. "And, to be fair, I did consider telling your boyfriend about Nick's little endeavor. I thought he would be so enthralled with my bravery he would fall at my feet. I was going to tell him that day I ran into you at the festival, in fact. But he refused to listen to me."

"That's because you were throwing yourself at him," I said.

"And that made him want to throw up," Thistle interjected.

"Oh, shut up, Thistle," Lila said. "You're bitter. I get it. Your life hasn't turned out as you thought it would. You're dating a stable hand, for crying out loud."

"Hey!" Marcus was affronted.

"Oh, you're yummy to look at," Lila said. "You'll end up happy ... as long as you realize Thistle is going to ruin your life and you move on from her."

"I'm going to beat the crap out of you," Thistle said.

"Whatever." Lila studied her fingernails. "Have they found your money yet?"

"We don't know where his twenty grand is," I said. "I've already told him we didn't take it, and we don't know who did."

Lila stilled. "Twenty grand?"

"Yeah. That's how much he stole from the bank and from Mrs. Gunderson."

"But ... ." Lila swiveled, hands on hips as she faced off with Nick. "You said you owed half a million."

"I do."

"You stole only twenty grand."

"I know. Why do you think I'm so desperate to get out of this town?" Nick asked, oblivious.

"I can't live on twenty grand," Lila said. "Look at me." She ran her hands up and down her body. "This takes a lot of money to maintain."

"Because it's all fake," Thistle said.

Lila ignored her. "How far do you think we're going to get on twenty grand?"

Nick shrugged. "I figured we could go to Canada. People are always saying the cost of living there is cheaper. Twenty grand should last us twenty years."

"Omigod," Lila said. "I can't believe this is happening."

"If it weren't for the gun, I would find it funny," Thistle said.

"Well ... I can't be involved in this," Lila said, shaking her head. "We have to get out of here."

"I can't leave without my money," Nick said. "I don't even have enough to fill my gas tank."

"How were you going to pay your bill at the inn?" Clove asked.

"Aunt Tillie is going to be angry," Thistle said. "She hates people who try to sneak out on their bill more than anything."

"Don't mention that woman," Nick snapped. "She got me struck by lightning."

"You weren't struck by lightning," I said.

"I was so."

"No, you weren't," I said. "If you were struck by lightning you would have an entrance and exit wound. You don't."

"And you'd probably be dead," Thistle added.

"That old woman is evil," Lila said. "I've been shaving my upper lip for two days. It keeps growing back. How long is that going to last?"

"Until she takes the spell off of you," I said, not bothering to lie.

"When will that be?"

"When you stop pissing her off and become a nicer person."

Lila was incensed. "Are you saying I'm going to be like this forever?"

"Yes," Thistle said. "Now get out of our house."

"This isn't a house," Lila said. "It's a closet. How can the three of you live here together?"

"Get out!" Thistle was on her feet. "I've had enough of both of you. You're the worst criminals ever."

"I am an awesome criminal," Nick said. "I haven't been caught yet."

"They're right," Lila said. "You're a terrible criminal. You're also a bad liar. I knew I shouldn't have believed you in high school when you told me everyone was doing it and I knew I shouldn't believe you when you said you were rich. I'm out of here." She turned toward the door.

"You can't leave me," Nick said. "We're in love."

"We're not in love."

"We've been sleeping together for days."

"That was boredom," Lila said. "I really wanted the FBI agent. I think Bay cast a spell on him. That's the only explanation I can come up with for why he would rather be with her than me. Does he know you've done this to him?"

"I think you should both go," I said. "Landon will be back any second. I don't think he's going to be happy to find you guys here." Landon was going to go crazy if he found Nick near me again. He was hanging on by a thread, and that thread was going to snap faster than Lila's bra strap in middle school if Nick didn't get out of here.

"I'm not leaving without my money," Nick said.

"We don't have your money!"

"I can't stay in this … hovel … one more second," Lila said, turning on her heel and flouncing out the door.

"Lila!" Nick started to follow her but seemingly thought better of it because he paused and swiveled back around. "Clove, come with me."

Clove shook her head vehemently. "No way."

Marcus moved closer to her. "You can't take her."

"I have to take one of them," Nick said. "I'm out of options."

"I'll go." The words were out of my mouth before I realized what I was saying.

"No," Marcus said.

"I'll be fine."

"I won't be. Landon is going to kill me."

"One of us has to leave with him," I said. "I started this. I'll finish it."

"Bay ... ." Thistle's face was a mask of emotion, worry and anger warring for supremacy.

"I'll be fine," I said, mostly believing it. "Don't worry about me."

Nick gestured toward the door with the gun. "Ladies first."

Lila was standing by the passenger side of Nick's car when I hit the front porch. "You locked the door," she said, irritated. "I can't get in the car when the door is locked."

"You locked the door," Nick snapped. "I thought you were leaving."

"I'm not walking," Lila said. "You're going to have to drive me back to the Dragonfly. I'll figure out something when I get out there. Hey, Bay, is your father rich?"

I gritted my teeth and refused to answer.

"I can't leave without my money," Nick said. "You're going to have to wait."

"Well, great," Lila said. "Let's find your money then. I can't spend one more second out here in this ... crapfest. It makes me feel dirty."

"I think that's the Chlamydia," I shot back.

"That shows what you know," Lila said. "I got rid of the Chlamydia months ago."

I rubbed the spot between my eyebrows. "Okay. I don't know what to say to that, so I'm just going to ignore it. Nick, let's head back toward the greenhouse."

"My money isn't there."

"I know that," I said. "We still need a place to start."

"Let's start here."

It was like talking to a wall.

"Find his money, Bay," Lila said. "I'm starting to get bored."

That would be a nice problem to tackle right about now. "I ... ."

The air crackled, signifying magic was afoot. I straightened and looked to the sky, expecting another lightning bolt. Instead, Lila jerked forward, leaning over as she gripped her knees in an attempt to keep from hitting the ground. "Not again!"

"What's going on?" Nick asked, taking a step forward. "Are you dancing?"

"Yes. This is exactly how I dance," Lila said, careening forward and slamming into a tree trunk. "Oomph."

"She never did have any rhythm," Nick said.

I knew what was going on. Someone was manipulating the poppet. That meant … . I scanned the bushes on the far side of the driveway, Aunt Tillie's garden hat popping into view as she straightened. She smiled at me, and even though the situation was surreal, I felt better knowing she was there.

She pointed toward the side of the guesthouse, and it took me a moment to realize what she was silently ordering me to do.

"We should get to the greenhouse," I said. "We need to get you your money."

Nick pointed at Lila, who was now rolling around on the ground and flapping her arms like a wounded bird. "Shouldn't we do something about that?"

That would be the kind thing to do. "No." I started moving to the far side of the guesthouse. I had no idea what awaited me there, but I knew Aunt Tillie had a plan. I had to trust her.

I was two feet in front of Nick when I turned the corner, my eyes widening as they landed on Sam. He grabbed my arm and pulled me behind him, stepping forward and cutting off Nick's path as he rounded the corner.

"What the … ?"

Sam slammed his fist into Nick's face. Hard.

"Holy crap!" Nick grabbed his face, dropping the gun on the ground and causing it to go off.

I jumped, checking myself over quickly. "He missed me."

"He got me," Sam said, grimacing as he hopped up and down on one foot.

"He shot you in the foot? There's seriously something wrong with that gun."

"You broke my nose," Nick howled. "You have no idea how much this hurts."

"You just shot me," Sam said, tumbling backward onto the ground. "Sonovabitch!"

The sound of something banging on metal reached my ears and I glanced over my shoulder. Aunt Tillie was using the poppet to have Lila repeatedly slam herself into the car. It was starting to look dangerous. "Aunt Tillie!"

Lila ceased moving and fell to the ground, spent.

Aunt Tillie shuffled out of the bushes and headed in my direction. "That was fun."

"How did you know what was going on?"

"I saw Sam sneaking around," Aunt Tillie said. "I had to investigate."

"I wasn't sneaking," Sam said, grasping his foot and trying to stem the flow of blood. "I saw the idiot with the gun go inside. I was trying to help."

"That's sneaking," Aunt Tillie said. "If you're going to take on jerks, you have to be upfront about it."

"You were hiding in a bush," I pointed out.

"I wasn't hiding. I'm short." She glanced at Nick. "What's his deal?"

"Sam punched him in the face."

"And what's wrong with Sam?"

"Nick dropped the gun and shot him in the foot."

Aunt Tillie scowled. "Have you ever taken a gun safety course? If anyone ever needed one, it's you."

"I'm going to kill you," Nick screamed, lunging for the gun.

Aunt Tillie shook her head, and the gun scooted out of Nick's reach. He tried again, and the gun moved farther. Aunt Tillie was toying with him now.

"You really are a witch," Nick said, giving up and throwing himself on the ground. "Do it. I'm ready. Smite me."

I was impressed he even knew what that meant. "We're not going to smite you," I said.

"Speak for yourself." Landon moved into view and grabbed Nick's shoulder, flipping him over and slamming his shoulders against the ground. When did he get here?

"Hey," Landon said. "How's it going?"

"I'm just waiting for the locusts," Nick said.

"Good, because here they come." Landon slammed his fist into Nick's face.

"Omigod! I've surrendered. You can't do that!"

"That's what you get for shooting the woman I love." Landon pulled me in for a tight hug. "I'm never leaving you alone again."

I couldn't decide what part of that statement I liked better.

THIRTY-FIVE

"How did you know to come back?"

Landon and I snuggled on the couch in The Overlook's library, dinner still an hour away. The afternoon had gotten away from us, multiple arrests and endless questions from law enforcement lasting until late afternoon shadows formed.

After a long bath, a stern lecture from Landon on self-preservation and a thorough brushing of my hair so I didn't have to listen to my mother complain, we'd decided to spend the rest of the evening at the inn.

"Aunt Tillie called the police before she decided to save you all herself," Landon said. "We got out here as soon as we could."

My eyebrows flew up my forehead. "Seriously?"

"I know. I'm baffled myself."

I rested my head against his shoulder. "Are you blaming yourself for leaving?"

"Yes."

"You couldn't possibly have known that was going to happen," I said. "You know that, right?"

"My head knows that," Landon said. "The problem is, if something bad happens in this town, odds are that it's going to happen to you. I should've realized that if Nick was going to make a move, he was going to make it against you."

"Live and learn."

Landon snickered. "You're okay, right?"

"I'm fine. Have you heard how Sam is doing?"

"He was barely clipped," Landon said. "He was treated and released. I saw him on the front porch talking to Clove when I came in."

"I was barely clipped, too. You seemed a little more worked up when I was barely clipped than when Sam was barely clipped."

"Yeah, but you're prettier than Sam is," Landon said, grinning.

"And ... you love me." I was still getting used to it.

"I do," Landon said, leaning over so he could give me a kiss.

"Oh, get a room," Aunt Tillie said, breezing into the library, a wine glass in her hand. "If you don't, I'm going to get the hose."

"I heard you won the pool," I said, changing the subject.

"I did," Aunt Tillie said. "That five hundred bucks is going to come in handy since your mothers are making me turn the money I found in the greenhouse over to Terry."

I froze. What?

"You found the money?" Landon asked. "When?"

"And when were you going to tell us?" I asked.

"I found it the other day," Aunt Tillie said. "It was in one of my pots. I thought the fairies had finally smiled upon me. They know I have some intense shopping in my future."

Speaking of that .... "What are you trying to buy?"

"Do you really want to know?"

Did I?

"No," Landon said. "I don't want to know. Whatever it is, hide it. Hide it well. If I find it, I'm going to take it from you."

"How can you treat me like this after I saved Bay today?"

Landon rolled his eyes. "You did not save Bay today."

"I did so."

"You did not."

"I did so."

"You played with Lila and let her injure herself," Landon said. "It was funny, but it was hardly heroic. Sam saved Bay."

I glanced at him, pursing my lips as I took in his chiseled jaw and serious eyes. "Does this mean you like Sam?"

"Are you asking whether I like the man who saved you from a crazy person with a gun?"

I nodded.

"Yes."

"Are you going to be nice to him?"

"Yes."

"Are you going to give me everything that I want because you're feeling all lovey-dovey right now?"

Landon rubbed his nose against mine. "Yes."

"I'm definitely going to puke," Aunt Tillie said.

Landon shot her a look. "No one says you have to be in here with us."

"This is my house."

I patted Landon's arm. "We can leave right after dinner. I think we could use some alone time."

"We're going to the fireworks tonight."

That was a surprise. "We are?"

"It's a festival," Landon said. "We've barely gotten to enjoy it. We're going to the fireworks."

"I love fireworks," Aunt Tillie said.

"You're not invited."

"I can go to the fireworks if I want," Aunt Tillie sniffed.

"Go nuts," Landon said. "You're not sitting with us."

"Maybe we should invite Thistle, Clove, Marcus and Sam?" I suggested.

"Absolutely not."

"Why not?"

"I love your family," Landon said. "I do. I find them entertaining and I even enjoy spending time with them."

"But?"

"But we're not spending time with them tonight. It's going to be you and me. Period."

"We're still having dinner with them," I reminded him.

"No, we're not." Landon got to his feet when my mother walked into the room, a picnic basket and blanket in her hand.

"Here's your dinner and blanket," Mom said, beaming at Landon. "I think it's very romantic that you want to give Bay a nice night. I think it's even nicer that she decided to brush her hair for you."

I rolled my eyes and scowled.

"Thank you," Landon said, taking the basket in one hand and extending the other in my direction. "Let's go, Trouble."

I was still confused. "You're taking me on a picnic and to see fireworks?"

"Yup."

"That's so ... normal."

"That's why it will be a nice change of pace for us." Landon waved his hand in my direction, silently urging me to take it. "No one is going to shoot at you. No one is going to cast any curses. No one is going to yell and scream. It's going to be ... perfect. Now come on."

I took his hand and followed him out the front door, casting a quick look to the lounge chair where Sam and Clove were making out like teenagers as we passed by. "Have fun," I said.

Clove never moved her mouth from Sam's as she waved me off.

"Don't wait up," Landon called to them, tugging me toward the driveway.

Aunt Tillie stepped out on the porch behind us. "Oh, gross. You two, too? I'm going to have to de-sex this house tomorrow when all of the guests leave. It's like living in a brothel."

Sam shifted his mouth away from Clove's. "Don't you have somewhere else to be? Anywhere else?"

"You're on my list."

I smiled at Landon as he opened the passenger door and ushered me into his Explorer, situating the picnic basket and blanket at my feet before giving me a soft kiss.

Witchy life was good these days. I wondered how long the peace would last.

"You're both on my list!" Aunt Tillie was hopping up and down on the front porch as she faced off with Sam and Clove. "I'm not joking!"

Not very long, apparently.